aquaboogie

PRAISE FOR AQUABOOGIE

"*Aquaboogie's* 14 stories animate the two-inch newspaper blurbs, buried behind obits and white-sale ads: young black men clipped by drive-by bullets, families who are frequent victims of search-and-seizures, communities bereft of options . . . She lends resonant voice to the lives of people often enmeshed in indistinct or ignored margins: day laborers, elementary-school cooks, factory workers whose lives are torn by one tragedy after another and who tell of it in a mixture of humor and pathos."—*LA Weekly*

"[Straight] makes the reader feel like an across-the-street neighbor watching all the action from a front-porch glider while sipping a glass of sun tea . . . These are modern legends."—*San Diego Tribune*

"From the very first story . . . we are drawn into this world . . . The dialogue in these stories flows like a river of talk, pulls you along with its rhythms until you're in it; you're the reader, then the listener, then the speaker."—*St. Louis Post-Dispatch*

"[*Aquaboogie*] is a novel in stories, so you can read it in one gulp or in pieces. However you do it you won't be sorry . . . you will have been transported to hot California, to a black neighborhood, the Westside of Rio Seco (Dry River), outside L.A., and into the kitchens and schoolyards and the minds and emotions of the people who live there."—*Maine Progressive*

"Rarely is a black community so precisely, humanly and searchingly deliniated as in *Aquaboogie* . . . A truly distinctive voice."—*Minneapolis Star Tribune*

"Her collection of stories vividly captures people who know the rhythm of their own lives. They twist and turn to its beats, yet they remain partially submerged, trying not to drown."
—*Washington Post Book World*

"An astute, bracing debut . . . this sings of the brief happy moments and ever-looming tragedies and defeats in the lives of discretely voiced blacks chorusing here in dialect."
—*Publishers Weekly, Critics Choice*

"[Straight] defuses the stereotypes by writing about characters from the inside."—*Vogue*

"These stories are lovingly crafted and as dense to read as poetry. They demand to be read slowly, one at a time."
—*St. Paul Pioneer Press*

"Her truly indomitable characters are among the strongest in recent American fiction."—*USA Today*

aquaboogie

SUSAN STRAIGHT

MILKWEED
EDITIONS

©1990, Text by Susan Straight
All rights reserved. Except for brief quotations in critical articles or reviews, no part of this book may be reproduced in any manner without prior written permission from the publisher: Milkweed Editions, 1011 Washington Avenue South, Suite 300, Minneapolis, Minnesota 55415.
(800) 520-6455
www.milkweed.org
"Aqua Boogie" (Bernie Worrell, William Earl Collins, George Clinton III) © 1978 Marlbiz Music, Rubberband Music & Rightsong Music Inc. All rights on behalf of Malbiz Music. Administered by Rightsong Music Inc. All rights reserved. Used by permission. Also, Used by permission of Bridgeport Music Inc.

Published 2007 by Milkweed Editions
Printed in Canada
Cover design by Christian Fuenfhausen
Interior design by Barbara Jellow
The text of this book is set in ITC Stone Serif.
07 08 09 10 11   5 4 3 2 1

ISBN-13: 978-1-571310-58-3
ISBN-10: 1-57131-058-4

Milkweed Editions, a nonprofit publisher, gratefully acknowledges sustaining support from Emilie and Henry Buchwald; the Bush Foundation; the Patrick and Aimee Butler Family Foundation; CarVal Investors; the Timothy and Tara Clark Family Charitable Fund; the Dougherty Family Foundation; the Ecolab Foundation; the General Mills Foundation; the Claire Giannini Fund; John and Joanne Gordon; William and Jeanne Grandy; the Jerome Foundation; Dorothy Kaplan Light and Ernest Light; Constance B. Kunin; Marshall BankFirst Corp.; Sanders and Tasha Marvin; the May Department Stores Company Foundation; the McKnight Foundation; a grant from the Minnesota State Arts Board, through an appropriation by the Minnesota State Legislature, a grant from the National Endowment for the Arts, and private funders; an award from the National Endowment for the Arts, which believes that a great nation deserves great art; the Navarre Corporation; Debbie Reynolds; the St. Paul Travelers Foundation; Ellen and Sheldon Sturgis; the Target Foundation; the Gertrude Sexton Thompson Charitable Trust (George R. A. Johnson, Trustee); the James R. Thorpe Foundation; the Toro Foundation; Moira and John Turner; United Parcel Service; Joanne and Phil Von Blon; Kathleen and Bill Wanner; Serene and Christopher Warren; the W. M. Foundation; and the Xcel Energy Foundation.

The Library of Congress has catalogued the earlier edition as follows:

Straight, Susan.
    Aquaboogie / by Susan Straight ; foreward by Doris Grumbach.
        p. cm.
      ISBN 0-915943-59-X
      I. Title
    PS3569.T6795A88 1990
    813'.54--dc20   90-41192
                                                              CIP

This book is printed on acid-free paper.

MINNESOTA
STATE ARTS BOARD

NATIONAL
ENDOWMENT
FOR THE ARTS
A great nation
deserves great art.

For DCS, the baddest dude from East to West

And for two teachers who have gone on,
James Baldwin and Bill Bowers

contents

acknowledgments

The author wishes to acknowledge the publication of several of the stories in this collection, some in slightly different forms, in the following: "Buddah" in *TriQuarterly* #71, Winter 1988; "The Box" in *TriQuarterly* #73, Fall 1988; "Back" in *Ploughshares,* Vol. 14/2&3; "Tracks" in *Contact,* Winter 1989; "Off-Season" in *Passages North,* Summer 1990; "Training" and "Esther's" in *Ontario Review,* Fall 1990; "Safe Hooptie" in *North American Review,* Fall 1990, as "Two Days Gone."

Thanks to Jay, Ada, Richard, and Holly.
Special gratitude to the California Arts Council, Poets & Writers, and the Watson Foundation, John and Gail Watson, Directors

aquaboogie

westside stories

With the rhythm it takes to dance to
What we have to live through
You can dance underwater and not get wet.

from "Aqua Boogie"

CHARACTER LIST

FIRST GENERATION	SECOND GENERATION	THIRD GENERATION
L.C. & Pashion Carter		
Grampa Harris		Max / Demone Harris
Rosa King	Floyd & Revia King	Nacho / his cousin Snooter King
	Charles King	Donnie and Rosa King Charles Morris King III
	Carnell & Retha King Lanier & Lee Myrtle Chatham	Trent & Brichée King
	Red Man & Mary Tucker	Darnell & Brenda Tucker
	Roscoe Wiley	Louis (Birdman) Wiley
	Berta Collins	Esther & Joe Hill Karen & Eddie Chandler

aquaboogie

NACHO / APRIL

Nacho usually found the first five or six cans in the English class-rooms at the far end of the hall. He lined them up on the wooden shelf at the front of his cart, where the spray bottles hung from their notches and swayed gently like lanterns. He piled the cans into a pyramid, and all night while he wheeled through the halls, he was careful not to knock them over. He thought of them as hood ornaments: red Coke cans, green 7-Ups, purple and orange Crushes. They gleamed like metal-flake paint in the dim hallway lights, their vivid colors transforming the cart into a lowrider skimming slow over the floor, only inches between the base of the trash can that sat on the wood and the asphalt-gray linoleum.

He had oiled the wheels so that the ride was as smooth as possible. By now, in late spring, the sun set during the early break, at seven, so the first hours of his shift weren't bad. The fading light hung gold, reflecting through the window shades as he closed them. Nacho glided through the classrooms on the west side of the base-ment to get all the sun he could, sliding the dust mop in long arcs to the beat of the music on his headphones. He dropped the next few cans he found into the trash bag hanging with the spray bottles, and when the light grew more intense, the way it did when the sun was on its way down, he headed toward the auditorium.

The building sat on a hill at the edge of the college, and because wall-high windows surrounded the auditorium, Nacho could see all the athletic fields and dorms if he stood near the brick walls encircling the huge room. He parked his cart against the door; he could time it now, without any clock, so he could lean against the bricks when the spring sun had finished warming them, if there had been a sun that day. It was the only moment during the night when he allowed himself to think of home; he squatted with his back to the bricks and felt Rio Seco, the stucco on his father's house like a baking oven against his palms when he leaned there with Snooter and Ray-Ray.

It had been a long winter. When he called his father and Snooter, his father said, "Boy, your nuts gon shrivel up from that cold," and Snooter said, "What you paintin this week, more snow? Individual snowflakes, cuz?" He almost laughed at himself and wanted to leave. Snooter was the one who had come East first, after he joined the Air Force. He was stationed at Westover, and when Nacho took the bus out to Massachusetts to visit, they went out to Amherst to check this girl. Snooter got kicked out of the service for smoking big weed, but Nacho had gone back to Amherst and stayed.

The cassette he was listening to ended abruptly, and he looked at the hall clock. He'd forgotten for a moment that he planned this, timed the songs so that just about now, the right one would come on. He turned the Funkadelic cassette over and listened before he raised the volume; the vibrations of heavy shoes clomping down the stairs to the basement began, and Nacho thought that since Wysocki had been hired two months ago, break time was almost like a routine. It was for the new boy's educational benefit that the shit had started, really started, he thought. He unplugged the headphones to let the music out.

"I am Sir Nose D'Void of Funk
    I can't swim
    I never could swim . . ."

The drums echoed loudly, and Zadnek stopped about five feet away. "He's got the usual jungle music on. Hooga booga booga," he said, but his arms stayed straight, hands jamming the pockets of his pants so that they hung away from his butt. Nacho stared at him. Zadnek was tired.

Donohue, the middle-aged redhead, pulled his thin lips inside out with his fingers, locking them into place so they looked like thin strips of steak. He shuffled around, bending his knees.

"See how he's squatted, Wysocki?" Zadnek said. "There ain't no chairs in the jungle." He paused. "Ask him."

"How's life in the jungle, bunny?" Wysocki said. He was fat, about a year younger than Nacho. Slow, but warming up with these excellent tutors, Nacho thought. He smiled at Wysocki, keeping Zadnek a shadow in his peripheral vision. "Wysocki, man, I ain't in the jungle. This is the ocean, man, and you're in it, too. Can't you hear the music?"

Wysocki looked at him as though a floor tile had spoken. Nacho had never answered him before. The chorus played.

"Never learned to swim
Can't catch the rhythm of the stroke
Why should I hold my breath
Feeling that I might choke?"

A moment hung in the air, and then the music swirled and pounded. "See, he can't even talk like a human," Zadnek said. "They speak a different language. Nigger babble." He walked toward the radio, and Nacho jerked the cart. The cans in the bag rattled, the stack fell, clanking onto the tile. "Playing building blocks instead of working, huh?" Zadnek said.

"Nickel a can," Cotter said.

"Yeah, for fuckin bums that dig in the trash," Donohue smiled.

Nacho opened his mouth, but all four had turned away toward the break room. Zadnek's pants shifted flat over the empty space where his ass should have been, and the khaki slanted back and forth with his steps. Nacho ran his thumbnails hard over the pads of his fingers, wishing again that he could talk instant shit like Snooter. He turned the radio up louder. His cousin would have said something in a flash. Nacho thought hard, listening to Snooter's voice. Something like, "Let the bass line hit ya where the good Lord split ya, motherfucker." Zadnek was supposed to have cancer of the butt. "It'd be therapy, baby," Nacho called toward the closed door.

He walked toward the auditorium entrance, then heard the deep hum of talk grow louder; the break-room door had opened, and Zadnek came out. He didn't look far enough down the hall to see Nacho but walked the few steps to the basement soda machine and bent his neck, looking for something on the floor. Loose change, Nacho thought, always lookin for some money. Damn, he must can't see shit. Zadnek bent quickly and pushed his fingers under the edge of the machine, then stood up and went back to the room. The faint yellow light coming from under the door was nearly the same as the last daylight that had hung near the windows, Nacho thought, hearing the slap of hands on a table, and he went back into the auditorium.

"Here's *my* ducats," he said aloud. There were only a few cans scattered around the room, but next week, when finals began, there would be a lot more, he thought. Students would get nervous about their tests and drink soda. He'd thought it was comedy that he'd ended up in a place where cans, unsquashed, brought five cents each. At home, his father kept huge barrels behind the house, and the boys had to stomp all the cans inside and take them to the junkyard once a month. It was only twenty or thirty cents a pound, barely worth the gas. But here, with all the cans he collected at work and from the lawns of the frat houses he passed on his way home at 2 A.M., he made enough each week to pay for the phone call home. He hated those five minute calls, when you just finished talking preliminary shit about each other and had to hang up. The more cans he found, the longer he could talk.

Shoot, he thought, I'ma save the money for last tonight. Go ahead and do the bathrooms so I can finish early and get in the refrigerator before them Cylons take over again at lunch. Cylon Warriors. He smiled, pulling the cart toward himself. He saw Snooter's surprised face, long ago, when Nacho told him that Cylons weren't the ones all dressed in white with no faces, only helmets; that was the Storm Troopers, in *Star Wars*. Cylons were all in silver, on "Battlestar Galactica." "Damn," Snooter had said. "But Cylon *sound* better, don't it, cuz? *I* know what it is." Snooter was always looking, listening for the sound of the word, the way it turned in his mouth and then in the air when he let it go. And he was right; years later, people in the neighborhood would say, "Man, them Cylons dogged my check this week," or, "Yeah, homey, that Cylon chick was fine for her kind."

Nacho was near the windowless rooms and offices on the other side of the basement, and he propped open the door of the men's restroom. Why I'm thinking so much about Snooter tonight? I know he ain't thinking about me, he's talking some girl into some loving.

Nothing pleased Snooter more than inventing language. He always talked in secret tongues when he and Nacho were cutting some rich man's yard and the man was within earshot, opening the patio door to see what they were doing, getting into his car. "He got a *wine* hooptie, man, and I ain't got but Moe and Joe, but I ain't never gon have to wear no *helmet,* I tell you that right *now."* Mr. Everest had a new BMW, and Nacho and Snooter had feet, but he was wearing a toupee, and Snooter always managed to mention it in his presence.

The bathroom didn't look bad. I never was able to whup anybody with my mouth, Nacho thought, going into the stalls to push out the tangles of toilet paper with his foot. No new writing.

The first night he'd worked in the building, a wet evening that made the air inside the bathroom feel trapped and moist, he'd been in a daze, worried that he wasn't cleaning anything right, and in the second stall, he'd leaned over the toilet to get into the corners. He saw the words, magic-markered in heavy, dark blue on the wall just above the seat.

If Black is Beautiful
I just created a Work of Art

Nacho looked away, at the pictures of genitals, the cusswords, and then he looked back at the words alone over the toilet. Anybody could write Fuck Niggers, but somebody had thought about this one for a while. He found a wire brush and cleanser in the cart and started to strip the ink off the tile, then off the painted metal stalls. He scoured the spider-penned sayings off the sides until the thin layer of paint faded away, thinking about what he and the other guys had always written on surfaces. Their names, where they were from, not as fancy as the Chicanos, but enough. White boys always wrote about fucking some girl or fucking with somebody else. When he stood back and looked, the worn-away patches where the metal showed through were cotton-edged as clouds, full and dark on the pinkish institutional walls.

Now he pulled the mop out of the bathroom and onto the hall floor, standing it up to let it dry. Emptying the trash, he listened to the short clanging of the metal wastebaskets, like dogs barking in the tunnel of the halls. The mop-water shrank into wispy ghost shapes as it evaporated on the grayish floor.

Ten minutes before the lunch break, he opened the door to the room; a cool rush of smoke and coffee air pushed past him from the greasy couch, the long wooden table where the janitors ate and played cards. Nacho opened the refrigerator. He rarely brought anything that needed to be cooler than the building already felt to him, but tonight he'd packed canned pineapple, and he wanted it chilled.

He wondered what Zadnek was eating, looking at the only two bags left in the racks. If Zadnek had cancer of the ass, could he eat?

How did he go to the bathroom? Nacho pushed the door closed and turned to leave.

Zadnek stood by the soda machine again, his neck bent over like a floor lamp, and Nacho thought, What a fool. Ain't but four or five students been through here in the last three hours, this time on a Thursday, and he still looking for money.

Zadnek started when he heard the door shut. "What the hell are you doing?" he said hoarsely.

Nacho held up his lunch bag.

"Still can't speak English, huh?" Zadnek said.

"You really blind, too?" Nacho said, surprising himself.

"What the hell is that supposed to mean?" Zadnek said, his face thin and folded as a rag.

"Too? Too. Means along with whatever else ain't right with you." Nacho went down the hall to the stairwell, and after the door closed behind him and Zadnek couldn't see, he started up the five flights.

A flattened seat cushion sat against the brick wall that ran the length of the roof. Nacho had taken it from one of the student lounges when he began to eat his lunch there. A vent blew warm air toward him, air that smelled like California, dry and static. He could see so many more stars here than in Rio Seco, where the smog and lights blurred the sky. He turned the knobs on the radio to see what he could get. On some nights, stations came in from all over: WWWE in Cleveland, oldies on WGY from Albany, CKLW from Windsor, Ontario. On other nights, nights which looked identical as far as he could tell, there was nothing at those thin lines on the tuner, and he wondered what in the air blocked the waves from reaching him.

He laughed at the voice he could hear faintly. "This is Big Bozo, playin one for Big Stick and Dog Breath and all the other truckers out there. WLW in Cincinnati, the country's country!"

The pineapple juice rushed thick against Nacho's teeth. All winter he'd eaten canned fruit, not up on the roof in the snow, at first, but in the break room. He'd never been so close to so many white guys before, and one night he realized he was doing what he'd always watched his father do, standing in the yard waiting to get paid: he wasn't looking at their faces, into their eyes, because they were looking so hard at him. They seemed to watch him eat, watch every movement. He couldn't see them looking, but they were. They talked about the students, cussed them for their sloppiness, their money, their stupidity. They talked about what electricians were making, fuck yeah, and insurance, all things he knew nothing about. When the Celtics came up, they looked his way pointedly and praised Bird and Ainge. They seemed to look deep into his mouth when he said, "How you doing?" and then one night he heard Cotter and Zadnek after he'd left but still stood outside the door probing his teeth with his tongue. "Did you see what color his gums were? I've seen em black as tar on some."

He didn't want to look into their mouths, or their ears, and soon he felt their eyes on his pants. He began to go up on the roof then, in the fall, and when the snow came, he ate in the auditorium.

He would get his lunch from the refrigerator and leave.

"Somethin stinks," Zadnek said whenever he started to leave.

"Yeah, but my food's been tasting better lately."

"Wait, now, the stink, it's leavin."

An Official Running Nigger Target was taped to the refrigerator door then. HEAD SHOTS DON'T COUNT UNLESS METAL PIERCING CARTRIDGE USED read the words at the bottom. Nacho took out his matches and burned the shape of an icicle through the words.

He rubbed his feet over the gravel on the roof. Sometimes, when there was a full moon, he brought his sketch pad up with him and drew the telephone poles and wires near his father's house, with rows and rows of blackbirds sitting strung out like jewels. He made their tail feathers long and ragged, their backs shiny. The colors of the night seemed easy. When he'd registered for the art class, he'd thought he would draw leaves on Amherst sidewalks, the way they curled and seemed to hold light inside them, like water, for long moments in the evening. Or icicles when he saw them grow, thick and shiny-wide as dozens of buck knives opened and hanging from edges. But what came from his pencils and then the brushes he'd learned to use were tumbleweeds in the fields, wrought-iron fences. He drew them the way he always had, sliding the pencil back and forth, leaving the gleams with empty space in the gray, burnished lead.

The instructor, Mr. Bowers, said, "Try some color. Do the shades you see at home." He saw sides of buildings, gold dates falling from palms to litter the sidewalks, his father's aqua-blue truck. The autumn leaves and bluish snow faded, and he could only recreate home, it seemed, but Bowers said that was the way it went, that strange colors sometimes helped you see the familiar ones more clearly.

Nacho breathed in the dry heat from the vent, like a wind from home. He remembered one night right after he was hired, a night when neither Zadnek or Donohue came in. When Nacho went to the refrigerator, only Cotter sat at the long table. "Hey, are you really from California, no shit?"

Nacho sat at the far end. "Yeah."

"Do they really have girls walkin around on the beach like that? Playin fuckin volleyball with no clothes on and shit?"

"I don't know. I never went to the beach."

"Fuckin A, you said you was from there."

"Rio Seco ain't even close. It's a couple hours from the ocean."

"Shit!" Cotter laughed. "You have to watch it on TV like any asshole from here. That's pretty funny." He kept laughing, and Nacho smiled. But later, when he no longer ate in the room, Cotter danced close to him for the others.

The cans had been crushed from top to bottom like biscuits, left wherever they'd been, wherever Nacho would have found them. In the trash cans, on desks, at the edges of the floor by the brick walls. Not all were smashed right; some sloped awkwardly from off-center stomping. Nacho rolled one of the worthless cans into the auditorium aisle. The shiny green color made him think of insect blood, the liquid green of a severed caterpillar. He felt a pull at his stomach, thinking that he should be with his father, working outside, pushing together piles of cut-smelling leaves and trimmings, steaming grass. This indoor dirt, the used Kleenex, vomit from students with hangovers, dropped gum, was what made Zadnek and the others nastier than they already were. In the yards, you were alone; people might watch you, dog you sometimes, but they didn't fuck with you *daily.*

He sat in one of the seats and turned the cassette back on. Imagining a car, he rested his elbows on the desks and leaned back; that was why he didn't hear Zadnek and the others in the hallway. When they slammed the door against the wall, he jumped up and pulled off the headphones. Because he was so surprised that they'd come again, so soon, he spoke first.

"Your usual one-a-day fuck-with-me vitamin wasn't enough, man?" he said to Zadnek. "You a junkie and a half now, right?"

"Sittin on your ass as usual," Zadnek said. "You never do shit around here. Got a problem? Maybe I should write you up." He didn't smile, but the low cheeks looked higher, lifted up.

Nacho saw him look at Wysocki. "It ain't gonna cure you, these one-a-days," Nacho said to Zadnek, just as Wysocki stepped forward.

"Hey, King," he said, "a nigger and a Puerto Rican both jump off a seven-story building. Which one lands first?"

There was silence, and then Donohue said, "Who gives a fuck?!" He and Wysocki both laughed, and Nacho said, "Wy*sock*i, man, he's gonna die anyway. You can't cure him." He looked at Zadnek. "I got your nigger right here." He touched his fly with his fingers and left them there.

"You black-ass bastard," Donohue said, coming at him. "Lemme cut it off and make you into a real man." Nacho felt the blood jump into the back of his neck and stiffened, ready, but Cotter had his arms behind Donohue, twined through.

Zadnek's face was the gray pink of the bathroom stalls now, and his mouth drew back deep into his cheeks. "There's nothin to cut off. Come on, he can't do nothin, he doesn't have the guts. Look at him." But Nacho saw the fear in Zadnek's eyes.

After he heard them go up the stairs, he looked at the cart. He touched the bag and could feel that the cans inside were ridged, crumpled, too. He left everything and walked to the door.

Walking home, he looked at the maple trees curling their long branches over him, making another tunnel, as if he were still in the hallways. Last week, Mr. Bowers had looked at something he was doing in class and said, "What's that, a fern? Awful big as far as proportion."

"It's a pepper tree," Nacho said. "That's the way they grow. They have pink berries and smell dead like pepper."

He could try to find a job in town. But the art class was only free because he worked at the college. He slapped his key ring across the trunk of one of the maples, chunking into the bark again and again. The smell of water rose from the sidewalk; the cement was always layered with something—he liked that, the leaves, then snow, the uncovered debris and film of water now after winter. He'd tried to explain that to his father, tried to tell him about the colors and their backward-ass ways. "Shit, color ain't payin for nothin unless it's that pale, dirty green. I knew when I seen Snooter's ass get off that bus alone you were doin somethin stupid. How you eatin?"

Nacho unlocked the door and walked into his room. It wasn't even close to two-thirty, when he usually got home. He turned on the radio and sat on his mattress; he couldn't call until about nine. Then it would be six in California, and Daddy and Snooter would be getting ready to leave. It was hotter now, and they had to start earlier and take a break in the middle of the day to rest from the sun.

"What's wrong, cuz, you cold?" Snooter laughed. "Oh. Man, I forgot, it probably up to sixty degrees by now, huh?"

"Shut up, Snooter. Y'all fixing to go?"

"Yeah. So did it snow again, or is that all done? I can't believe you still there. You see I got out before that shit was even *forming* in the clouds."

"It won't snow again. Where you gettin ready to go?"

"I think we doin old Miss Linsey's house first. Hey, man, did you happen to see Fiordaliza?"

"You ask me every week. I told you she went back to Puerto Rico."

"Because of her mama. Cho, I coulda *had* that girl."

"Nah, she was too smart. Shit, she was the one brought me to the school to look around, so you half responsible."

"Why you stayin around so long, cuz? What's the prognosis? It gotta be a female, right?"

"Damn, Snooter, why you keep askin me? I told you about the art class."

"Then you a sorry-ass liar, cause I can hear you pissed about somethin. Why you don't quit fakin and tell me?"

"Yeah, right. It ain't a girl. These Cylons are gettin on my nerves."

"How many of em is it?"

"Too many."

"Well, pick the smallest and get to nubbin. Ain't no other way to stop it."

"Right. Just so I could go to jail. They'd love that shit. I could be in jail at home, at least be arm-wrestling with Ray-Ray and Dokio, get them big I-done-time arms."

"Not with Dokio, man. Blood got stuck yesterday, in the stomach. Don't nobody know who did it yet."

Nacho felt the spit flow from the sides of his mouth. "He gone?"

"Yeah."

"See, man, shit like that make me want to stay away."

"You ain't gotta be in it. We could use you on the truck."

"I want to finish somethin here. My class."

"So do the smallest dude, Cho. Take him out."

He sat on the mattress again, looking at the change he'd spread on the floor. Quarters and nickels from the last bag of cans. Snooter's solution had always been the same, in school, in the street. Take him out. Knock it out the picture. The only thing Snooter was really scared of was dogs. He always carried a stick wherever he walked.

They should be there by now, Snooter and his father, at Miss Linsey's yard. When they were little, his father had taken them to work with him on the weekends and in the summer. On a street named Hillcrest, four of the huge yards were rimmed with dirt trails where Dobermans chased back and forth along the fences. They leaped and snarled continuously until Mrs. Whoever came to lead them into the garage. Snooter was always scared. He dreamed of dog teeth in his shoulder and spit dripping down his neck. Sometimes he'd wake Nacho up in their bed, hitting and fighting. "Why you poppin air?" Nacho would shout, angry.

"Man, I was whuppin Miss Linsey's dog," Snooter would answer, breathing so hard that Nacho knew he hadn't been whupping but losing. When they were older, still riding in the back of the truck on Saturdays, before the bed was full of branches and clippings, Snooter would swing his stick through the air. "I'ma see membrane fly, she let that dog come near me this time." But when she did, one day when she saw Nacho and Snooter picking up over-ripe avocados and oranges and dropping them into a bag (she was the kind that let them fall and rot; they could clean up the black fruit, but taking good ones was stealing), Nacho saw her go back into the house and a few minutes later, the dog came bounding out, sniffing, his shiny coat wavering as he chased Snooter to the fence.

Miss Linsey watched from the doorway, calling him back immediately. "Get back here, Marcus, get *back.*" The dog ran through the doorway in front of her.

Snooter wanted to come back with his .22 that night and shoot the dog. "She'll bust us, man, serious," Nacho said. "That ain't the way." He thought for a while, and the next time she took the dog with her to get him bathed, Nacho stood under the orange trees, dropping lumps of sugar he'd been carrying in his pockets. The ants clustered onto the sugar within half an hour, and he knocked the lumps into a jar. Snooter watched, and Nacho said, "Too bad we can't catch roaches. They woulda been the best."

"I don't know what you think you doin," Snooter said. He followed Nacho to the house; Nacho reached into the kitchen window and undid the screen. He crawled into the house, telling Snooter to watch for Miss Linsey, and dropped the ants and sugar into spaces under the cupboards and in the backs of bottom drawers. When she came home, her lawn had been mowed, the landscaped hill in the back smooth as a whale. "I don't know if it works or not," Nacho told Snooter. "Do you feel better?"

"Shit. I don't know."

When he woke up with thin light near his face, he looked at the money on the floor beside him. He turned over the quarters so that the eagles were facing up. Ducats. The rain outside made the room so dim that the money barely shone against the wood, as hard to see as it must be for Zadnek, he thought. Scuffling and pawing on the linoleum.

He went to the closet and took a small bottle of silver oil from the top. He'd tried to paint chrome bumpers and handles onto a drawing of a cherried '57 T-Bird, but it hadn't looked right. He spread newspaper on the floor, and put books around the edge to keep it hard and flat. He dropped the paint, holding the small brush down straight. The drops were tiny at first, too small, and he'd thought they'd be larger. It took a bigger brush and two dips into the bottle, then quickly he lifted the brush to let the paint run off onto the paper. He scattered the quarters and nickels to test the size.

It took almost the whole morning to do the silver. When he sat down to look, he thought of Donohue and Wysocki.

Blood. He pricked his thumb with the end of his buck knife, but not enough blood squeezed out to make a serious drop. He'd have to use someone else's blood.

An hour before work, he went into the basement. None of them ever came early, and on the Friday before finals, there were no students around. He walked through the halls, half-expecting to see one, because on watery, misty nights like this, a few might shuffle and whisper down the tunnels, trying to avoid the rain, looking like ghosts hugging the walls when they saw him. Their skin was clear and insubstantial, and their eyes white when they looked away from him, scared, embarrassed. If he surprised a guy when he came into the bathroom, the cheeks would flash red instantly, as if they'd been slapped, and the head would remain stiff as a flower.

Zadnek. Nacho stood by the soda machine and put some of the money on the floor, then went upstairs to the main floor and lobby, where Zadnek worked. Two more machines stood in a corner; he arranged the rest of the money around them, placing two quarters with their edges just sticking out from under the Coke machine. Go on and scramble and scuffle, he thought. Get happy. Trip out cause you so lucky—some other fool paid for your soda. Your big dream.

On the third floor, for Wysocki, he dropped large circles of blood from the container of liver he'd bought. This pork liver. Came outta pig feet, pig ears, all that shit you was lookin for in my lunchbag, baby. This is blood, that's what you think you want. He made sure there were several wide pools in the bathrooms, and then he went up one flight to the fourth, to put the red sticky drops onto Donohue's floor, near the warren of teachers' offices. He went to the end of the hall, then walked past again to see the glisten, the height of the thick circles. Mop this shit up, man. You be on them floor, scrubbin like women. But work hard, cause it'll come off.

He went to the break room in the basement to wash his hands, then remembered Cotter. He looked at the clock. What for Cotter? Sweat was on his back and behind his knees, and he went out the side door to the stairwell. It was still raining, and he looked out at the roof before he went back down the stairs to walk home.

At three in the morning, he went back to the side door. He'd stuffed a wad of paper into the lock. He walked up the stairs quickly and sat on the roof, where the mist rose into his neck, swirled around his chin; Zadnek would lock his stairwell door, but Donohue never checked his. Zadnek always complained about it. He closed his eyes and thought of the blood, how Sammy Harris had gotten shot and fallen on their front porch one night. The next morning, the blood was coagulated, and when Nacho tried to wash it off, it left faint outlines, traces on the cement as though it had begun to grow into the surface. The blood would have been easier for Wysocki and Donohue, still fresh, just smeary when they wiped at it.

He heard their voices rise up to the roof; they were walking away to the parking lot quickly in the cold, wet air. After the night was quiet again, he went to the side door and walked down Donohue's hallway. The floor was foamy gray with the scum of new mop-water.

He started in the basement again, watching the silver drops of paint carefully, the circles they made when they fell and flattened, leaving them around the machines on both floors. The silver was dull, awkward and strange, in the air, but when it lay on the gray tile, it was pretty and unexpected, brighter than a slug you might see near a machine. *Now* mop, old man. After you run your hands all over this dirty floor, up under the machine, after I put your ass on the floor, go on. Take a brush to this shit. Make you thirsty enough you need a soda.

On the third and fourth floors, he did the red. He left pools the same size, and drops as small as if they'd been shaken from a cut, and larger circles like a nosebleed. He watched his hand slash, dip. The shapes were right, the color. It ain't gon come off, Wysocki. It's gon grow, every day, under your feet.

For Cotter, black. The paint tapped the floor and spread into a couple of puddles, like a car had been parked there on the floor. A lowrider. Nacho laughed. He walked back to his floor, the basement, and he looked at the miniscule splatters on his shoes and saw red, black, and green, and then he laughed harder. The right colors, he thought. Red, black, and the supreme mean green, in the silver form. He listened to the water drip steadily from the roof, as if he were in a cave. He touched the moist walls, walked to the bathroom to pee. While he stood, he seemed to see the pale student faces, the way the upper lips lifted in confusion when he walked inside, when he bought paper at the student store. He looked at the toilets, the stalls, the thin ballpoint writing, the lush magic-marker words. This is my floor, he thought, it ain't no point in dogging myself. I'll have to come back and scrub, or this the last art class. He went back into the hall, kicking the trash can, hearing it echo down the corridor, muffled, the way it sounded when the mist filled the alley behind his father's house and softened the sound of men going through the garbage, or dogs. Nacho picked up the black paint and pushed open the bathroom door again. He flicked a dark mist onto the mirror, swirled CHO carefully on the wall over the sinks, and then began to put differing sizes of drops on the toilet seats and the stalls, making spatters, abstract patterns and small pictures then, drawing tumbleweeds and blackbirds with his brush.

training

DEMONE / MAY

Max smoke a Super Kool before he did it. He show me the cigarette—it gotta be a Kool, he said. The dude selling it dip the cigarette in the stuff they put on dead people—bombing fluid, Max told me. I remember I seen a guy smoke one at the playground and when he started shooting hoop he died, so I said to Max he shouldn't do no Super Kool, but he said that was all he had. "I been smoked everything else. I can hang. I'ma be gone soon anyway." Then he started walking to the train tracks, and when I went after him, he threw rocks at me. He could pitch good when we use to play baseball, and he was tagging me in the legs so I wouldn't try and see.

"Demone, aren't you able to do those problems?" Miss Jackson all in my face, and I didn't even see her. The book plus and take away, easy for babies, but I only did five because I heard the jet go over and I started thinking about bombs, did it have bombs just in case something happen before it could go back to the Air Force base? Then I think of bombing fluid. Miss Jackson sit down and lean close in my part of the table, so I can see the gold specks in her eyes. She real lightskin and got a short natural. "Do you need some help? Don't be afraid to ask me during the testing." Max wasn't gone from my head yet. I couldn't see the bombing fluid when he show me the Super Kool. He wouldn't let me touch it but the white part look dry. "No questions, sweetheart?" she say. Max told me no go, little bro, you can't smoke none. You too young. Miss Jackson ax me again. If the bombing fluid already in the Kool, do it stay in their bodies when they dead, I want to know, so the undertaker didn't have to put none in for the funeral? Like she gon know that.

"Demone, you know by now that these are just diagnostic tests. Do you remember what diagnostic means?" Shit. My grampa use to work on cars before he got the sugar in his blood. Diagnostic on the motor cost you thirty bucks to find out what's wrong. "They're not tests you can fail, remember?" She lean over here again, but then the dude in the corner call her. Johnny Ayala. "Hey, Miss Lady, I need help, I'm serious." He call her every five minutes, can't do nothing by himself. Everybody in here stupid. They all sleep or reading except me, Johnny Ayala, and that girl name Kim. "I'll be right back, Demone. Keep working."

It ain't even time for the first train yet and I already been thinking about him. The 9:30 train. I don't have to look at the clock to know, I could tell by the light. The sun shine past Miss Jackson desk, go to the wall next to me so I can see all the holes from the pins to hang up papers. She put my birthday up there yesterday, she only know cause it's on the Educational Handicap paper. Everybody in this class have they birthday on the wall and Miss Jackson announce it. Demone Harris—May 19—ten years old. She talking about, "You'll be celebrating it with us next week." Max birthday was May 2. He always five years older than me for seventeen days.

I'm fixing to do these math problems cause the first train ain't even came yet. They so easy it don't take but a couple minutes. Right when I'm finish she come to correct them and start smiling. "I knew those were too easy for you. I'll go get the next level."

Then it was cool for awhile, she watching me do these problems, more plus and take away but bigger numbers. We start on another part where she axing me questions, putting zeroes on the paper, and she say, How much is this, how much is that? Stupid stuff. I told her a hundred, a thousand, ten thousand. A hundred thousand. Then I look at the next one and I know it's coming but I forgot to get ready. I know what the number is but I ain't saying it. Max real name. I try thinking how Grampa watch the Million Dollar Movie all the time after we came to live with him. I keep looking at all the zeroes and don't want to hear it. Max real name Maxmillion. I can't hang with this.

"Come on, Demone, you said you liked math better. Look at how well you've been doing. Don't close up on me again." She waiting. "We have to finish . . ." It ain't even time to be thinking about him again. "You don't want to start the writing, do you?" She say it like she fixing to make me. Math is cool—the numbers don't change what they mean. Just move around when you do a problem. I told her I don't like writing. Got all them rules and change every minute. You suppose to write it this way and then go home and don't nobody talk like that. I forget all the rules. She ain't leaving. "Demone. One thousand, ten thousand . . ." See. It's one grand, ten grand, hundred grand. Million. I can't hang no more, so I go out the door and Miss Jackson talking about, "You can't leave the room until recess, Demone, you know that. Come on back, now. Please." I walk around the playground, but I stay close to the portables where we are, way far at the end so nobody won't see me. Portables like trailers and you could hear coolers drip down the sides. After the portables is the fence, then the tracks. I was walking for awhile and she didn't even call the principal to bust me, but I remember the train fixing to come soon and I don't want to see it, so I go back in the class.

She sitting at the other table with this white paper, don't say nothing to me. I can feel the train coming from way off, close my eyes, but close or open don't help. If they close, I can see anyway. The train shaking the ground all the way past the orange groves, past all the new houses around this school, and he have to blow the horn cause before the school is Third Avenue. He blow at all the streets. The horn sound different on different trains. When you far away, they sound clear, but this one fuzzy like somebody car stereo if he don't have no woofers to bring out the bass right. Now the train shaking the walls hard cause we in the portables, not the real classes. I ain't fixing to cry. I don't never cry.

Everybody quiet cause of the train. I feel the floor shaking, the chair, the wheels bamming on the tracks. I ax Max why he say he gon kiss the train, and he start laughing, hold the Super Kool like it was a lizard and he just catch it. We use to catch lizards and fight them. "Don't you remember them three dudes was looking for me?" I told him yeah, I know, it was Lester and Jimmy and that real tall dude they call Birdman. "You know Lester a serious rock daddy. He don't play. He gave me some shit to sell, talking bout I could start this week." I told him I seen it, little rocks, and they ten dollars each. "I never tried no rock-cane candy before. I tried a couple and then me and Roger smoke the rest." I told him Lester and them forget, he could go to L.A. and stay with Mama til Lester forget. "Lester want his money and I ain't got it." I told him it's only a hour to take the bus to Mama house in L.A., come on, I'll come, too. He start laughing again. "Mama don't want none a me. Or you. She got that baby by Robert and he don't want us in the house. Don't even let your mind trip like that. You so young." He rolling the Super Kool around. "Ain't this a bitch. All that rock candy I had and now I gotta smoke this nasty shit just to get me set up. This shit is for wackheads." I told him don't he remember that dude in the playground and he say, "Lester got a .357. I rather do it myself instead of wait for him do me with that."

I can't never open my eyes, this train still coming, shaking the table, but it Miss Jackson shaking the table when she sit down. "What's wrong, Demone? Are you feeling ill?" I don't want to look at her. All these other dudes sleeping and she ain't ax them are they ill. Everybody sleep in Educational Handicap. When I came last week all they heads look up like them dogs be on the dashboard in lowriders. Mrs. Linders bring me here from my regular class. I could hear the trains and I didn't do my work. I didn't know she was bringing me to the portables and they even closer to the tracks. Miss Jackson be walking around the room and talk to everybody so they won't sleep, but some dudes been smoking weed before school and ain't nothing keep them awake.

She put her hand on my arm, and it feel like when my mama use to wake me up in the morning. Miss Jackson hand soft and her fingernails red. Mama use to call me real soft when I was in first and second grade and then me and Max walk to school in our neighborhood, on the Westside. We have to pass that coyote-dog name Sin next door, and then walk by the tracks to school. The rocks all smell like trains, like smoke and wheels, and sometimes we seen flat pennies that got ran over. But then Mama marry Robert and go to L.A., and the next year I had to come on the bus to this school in Hillgrove. Mostly white kids and some Mexican kids can't speak English, and our bus from the Westside.

Those numbers on the paper still in front of me. Miss Jackson push the paper around and all the zeroes in a row like them flat pennies on the tracks. One grand. Two grand. Lester said he make two grand in a week. He making big cash, serious ducats, Max said. "Do you feel better now?" Miss Jackson ax me. "I've got an idea. We'll stop the math now and do some writing. We can write about anything you want. What were you thinking about so hard, with your eyes closed?"

She put out some line paper and two pencils, put her hand on my arm again. "Anything in your head, sweetheart."

I tell her, "Training."

"Okay, training for a job? What kind of job?"

"Uh-uh. My brother Max went training before. He got on one train and went all the way to L.A." I see them gold freckles way inside her eyes. She start smiling, look at the end of the pencils where they sharp.

"Did you watch trains when you were younger? Do you watch them now? My brother and I used to wave at the engineer where we lived in San Diego. Do you and your brother ever do that?" She fold her arms so her fingernails look like big drops of blood on her skin. "Write all this down, Demone. All about trains, everything you think about them. Anything is a good start." I see them pale blue lines on the paper and then the door open behind me, the hot air blow in from outside. A teacher bringing in this girl so Miss Jackson get up from the table. Everybody head look up at the door. "I think we need to talk about her," the other teacher say, and Miss Jackson tell me, "I'll be back, Demone." She always say that.

It's a lot of paper she brought. Everything about trains. I write 9:30 and 11:00. I put the pencil down cause it slippery in my fingers. After recess the train come at 11:00. Now it's May but every day hot. The only cool place in Grampa house is the bathtub and at night when I sleep in there, I hear the train blow the horn, echoing in the tub all around my ears. Do the engineer blow the horn? I wonder. We never wave at the engineer. We threw lemons at the wheels and they go flying like hand grenades on TV. Me and Max go down to the packing house, where they put the oranges in boxes, and you could find free ones on the ground. Sometimes the train slow down there and that's where Max jumped up on one of the cars when he rode to L.A. He didn't come back for three days. He said wasn't no trains coming back to Rio Seco and he got a ride with a truck. Grampa beat him with the belt.

Miss Jackson still talking to the new girl. She fixing to give her the first diagnostic tests I had last week. She start out axing a lot of questions about what do you eat for breakfast and where do you sleep. She give you papers to take home, but Grampa don't never look at them. They on the table by the TV. I didn't tell her I sleep in the bathtub, not in me and Max bed.

She gon be busy for a long time. Recess be soon and then the 11:00 train. The longest one. It go out of Rio Seco and in the desert, past Arizona, Max told me.

"I'ma kiss the train," he said. "Ain't no other way." I ax him could

I have some Super Kool, too, if he fixing to go, but he smoked it and start picking up rocks to scare me. He can't talk so I understand him. "That Kool be like a pit bull and don't let go," he said, and then his mouth moving around but nothing come out right. But he could still throw. I tried to stay but the rocks hurt my legs. I went behind a big palm tree, and if I came out he hit me again. I heard the horn from way up Third Avenue, the 11:00 train. That palm tree all rough against my hands, something wet on my legs. The horn blowing a long time when the train get close, blow over and over, and I was scared to look even if he didn't throw rocks. I didn't see nothing but I heard something little. I don't know what it was. The train start screeking the brakes, and I ran back to Grampa house. I didn't see nothing. Something soft drop on my neck, a hand touch me, or a bird falling out the palm tree, maybe Max shirt flying in the air, and I knock over the chair. Cause it Miss Jackson again, and every time she touching me it pull me out from where I am. Scare the shit out of me. She looking over my shoulder. "Demone, I'm disappointed. It's time for recess, and this is all you've written? 9:30 and 11:00?"

I'ma go to the door, but she pull my chair back up, talking about, "I think you should write at least one good sentence before you go to the playground."

"I'ma write later," I told her.

"No, I want you to write one now. We have to get you into better habits."

"You gon be busy with the new girl."

"That's not true. Come on, sweetheart." She holding a can of 7-Up. Once I was sick and Max make me tomato soup, thick up with milk, like blood getting lighter and lighter. But then I was so thirsty and he went to the store, bring back a 7-Up. I never taste anything so good in my throat since that soda. "Demone," she say, and sit down next to me again. I write, "I never rode on a train." I go outside to the playground and it's all the other kids near the fence. I keep looking at the tracks and then climb the fence, so I can walk home. All the kids start yelling about they gon tell the yard teacher. I got some rocks, fixing to throw them, but they smell like smoke, so I just keep one and walk down the tracks, land on every next piece of wood so I have to take big steps.

hollow

NACHO / JUNE

For a minute, it looked to Nacho like the city was gone, Rio Seco erased from the valley below and only a dirty smudge left, like when he'd gotten mad at himself and wiped out a drawing instead of just throwing the paper away, rubbing hard with the eraser so that even the trashman couldn't see how bad this one was. The bus started down the long slope. Most of the other riders had been sleeping the hour since L.A., but Nacho was used to night-shift time, and he'd been awake while the sun rose in front of them to tint the smog.

It hung thin-layered as dryer lint, not graying the entire sky like fog or clouds, just a blanket of June haze held together by car exhaust. The bus was still up in the blue, and Nacho knew once they got into Rio Seco, the smog would just be air, but he stared now. He'd been gone, what, a year and a half?

Past the city, the smog misty and reddish in the new sun, mountains rose up to the east, separating it from the desert, each craggy outline lapping the next. If he took a picture of this and asked the white guys, the janitors he'd worked with back in Amherst, they'd never guess where it was. Layers of layers, like mystical lands he'd seen in books at the university library—Nepal, Bolivia, the high mountains of Kenya. California—the only thing the other janitors asked him about was Hollywood and the beach, and they didn't believe him when he said he'd never seen either. Never been out of

28

Rio Seco except twice to Compton, to visit some girls with Snooter. Nacho smiled. The Irish guy had asked him about blondes and bikinis, and the other guys got mad. Nacho wasn't supposed to be looking at that, native Californian or not, being a nigger.

He wouldn't tell his father and Snooter about the harassment, or how he quit the job. He'd just say he got tired of winter, which Snooter was expecting. Snooter—yeah, one of my hundreds of cousins. Zadnek, his boss, had said, "Willie Horton, that's your cousin, right? I thought all niggers were cousins."

The river-bottom was mostly dry but for a ribbon of grayish water near the center. Past the bridge, the downtown offramp curved around, and then Nacho was outside the bus station, heading up Sixth Avenue, passing new office towers with sleek, aqua-mirrored windows rippling in the light. Then a square building with salmon walls and mint-green railings—serious Miami Vice. He wondered if his father had cleaned up any of the construction sites, if he'd had to hire one of the winos from Lincoln Park for day work. Probably still cussing if he had to give the dude lunch.

Under the dank freeway overpass, he shivered, and then smelled the old orange packing-houses, tangy scented ground beside the street. Just past the warehouses was Lincoln Park; he saw the circle of men around a fire, more flopping feet dangling from car doors. It would be warm today, and pretty soon they'd abandon the fire for the shade of the carob trees. "What up?" called someone, and Nacho squinted. Victor Miles, he'd gone to school with Nacho. "Not much, homes," Nacho said.

The Westside. Nacho walked slower, listening to the way haze muffled sound. He would have known it was gray without opening his eyes, just by the softened noise. DaVinci Street, Vincent, Van Gogh, Pablo. Picasso. He was going to have to get on the truck first thing. They'd talk big shit, Snooter and his father. He knew they heard him when he turned the corner. It wasn't but six on a Friday morning, and nobody else would be up; his feet crunched over a shimmer of brown glass. Their voices stopped. His father and Snooter sat on the rusted folding chairs in front of the house, drinking coffee, looking the same as when he'd gone. I'm ready to sleep, he thought, not in the mood to go to work. I'ma tell Pops I need some rest before I start talking. He slung the duffle bag off his shoulder onto the driveway.

They glanced at him, lifted up the coffee cups. Nacho waited. Okay, it's on me. Why am I back? Ask me no questions, I'll tell you no lies. That's what you always say, Snooter. Nacho circled his teeth with his tongue.

Snooter turned to Nacho's father. "Uncle Floyd, you seen Ed? Nigga done lost his whole *grille.*"

"So I heard. Roscoe told me."

Nacho shook, a tiny tremor like a dreaming dog. He'd missed each word and syllable, all those months in Amherst with the Polish and Irish guys whose voices fit together flat and tough as puzzle pieces. All the "niggers" sharp as triggers in his ears. He dropped the bag on the dry grass. "You a lie," he said. "Who hit Ed's truck?"

Snooter looked long at him, but his father watched two dogs troop up the street. "I ain't talkin about his truck, cuz," Snooter said, bending to lace up his workboots, and Nacho felt the fatigue from days on the bus; he wanted to lie down in the grass, curled on his side. Am I supposed to wait until you decide to jam me up? I don't know the code no more.

"Huh," Snooter pushed through his nose. "Truck!" He leaned his chair against the stucco and smiled. "That dude Ed workin with punched him in the mouth, homes."

Rubbing the hair around his forehead, stretching the skin, Nacho couldn't see what he was meant to see. "So?"

"Front four, man. The grille. It's missin when he smile at you."

Nacho shook his head, laughing, when Snooter walked to the truck. Snooter was going to test him. "You comin?" his father said, standing up.

"Where y'all goin?" Nacho asked.

"Where we goin. To work, lazy nigga. Don't matter where we goin, it ain't fun. Where we ever go? We don't take art classes and travel across the country. We just work." He and Snooter had put their coffee cups on the hood of the small Toyota pick-up in the driveway, and Nacho knew his mother would take them inside when she came home from the graveyard shift at the hospital. She'd be in her uniform, hair a perfect cap around her face, gold chains and rings gleaming against her penny-bright skin. The blood came back to his head, where it kept leaving after the hours of flashing-past telephone poles and shifting bus gears. He left his bag in the Toyota's cab and got into the big truck after Snooter.

He could tell—when they headed up Third Avenue toward Hillgrove that they were going to the dump first, and he dipped his head in annoyance. The truck, a 1955 Ford, groaned up the hill because, as usual, his father had piled rubble to the top of the wooden gate—concrete chunks, Sheetrock, plaster. The iron would be gone, given to Leo, who collected scrap metal, and the wood was piled in the backyard for winter. They must have cleaned up another construction site. Nacho smelled his father's coffee breath, Snooter's coconut hairdress, but no one spoke, and he closed his eyes, feeling the painful, scraped tingle in his palms already: his gloves had been gone from behind the seat for a year, and Snooter and Daddy would only laugh if he asked to borrow theirs.

"Rest your artistic ass, man," Snooter called from the window. "We'll be back." Nacho's fingers pulsed from the rough concrete, and his knees felt as though webbing tightened around the caps. Inside, his mother was asleep on the couch, one long earring trailing around her lobe. She heard him, though, and swung up from the cushions.

"My baby's home!" Nacho smiled and hugged her. Angie and Pam were only thirteen and fifteen, but they were her "girls" and he'd always been her baby.

"The girls are at school, and I was just taking a little nap before I start cooking."

"Where's Aint Rosa?" he asked. "I thought she was still cooking for you and for Esther down the street."

His mother paused. "Your daddy didn't tell you?" she said, frowning. Nacho sat on the end of the couch; his back felt like minty liquid was draining from either side of his spine, painfully cool, collecting in his feet.

His mother said, "Ruskin and them are tearing down Green Hollows and putting up office buildings. Your daddy and Snooter supposed to do the cleanup, next week, I think. Aint Rosa moving to that new Seniors' Tower downtown.

"Ruskin? Daddy still working for him?"

"Still doing odd jobs, cleanup and hauling." His mother brought a pile of green beans into the living room and started snapping. "Lord, Aint Rosa drives me crazy, that noise she be making with her lips all the time, and always talking about Tom Cruise's wife or Burt and Loni's baby, some such nonsense. But I'ma miss her taking care of the kitchen. This night shift catching up with me after all these years. Didn't you work nights out there where you was?"

Nacho nodded, closing his eyes. Ruskin. He couldn't believe his father and Snooter still did Ruskin's shit work. He remembered a few months before he and Snooter had gone back East, when Snooter was tired, had been out all night with Juanita, and Daddy was hollering all day. "Back that damn truck up, boy!" he'd shouted at Snooter, and Snooter accidentally grazed a mailbox, one of those big-money cast-iron types. Ruskin came tearing out of his front door. "I just bought that, King!" he yelled at Daddy. "You can damn well pay for a new one if it's damaged."

"I'll check it out right now, Mr. Ruskin," his father said. "My boy here's sick today."

"No, he's too damn lazy to turn the goddamn wheel." Ruskin must have had a bad day, Nacho had thought, standing near the truck. "Goddamn scatterbrained nigger ruined my wife's irises last year digging where he wasn't supposed to," he muttered, and Nacho looked into Snooter's eyes, but saw his father's shadow cross the fading sun. Nacho heard rising cement costs, Mexican laborers who didn't understand English, rain in Ruskin's voice; he saw calculations and remembrances of that mailbox price tag at HomeClub in his father's sloped shoulders and quick stride. Snooter came around the back of the truck and laughed.

"Ruskin just making money left and right," his mother said softly. "He did that new freeway to Coronita, and your daddy said him and his wife just bought them a house down at the beach. Must be nice."

"Aint Rosa can't cook for you then, huh?" Nacho said. Slow—his brain was still concentrating on the fiery-cold in his muscles. "She can't walk to the Westside from downtown."

"Baby, you don't sound right. You better go in the back and lie down. Your daddy and Snooter be home to eat soon."

Nacho pushed himself up from the couch. He didn't want to be home when they came in and talked about his softened hands. "She probably need some help moving her stuff, huh? Who's packing it up?"

His mother raised her brows. "Ain't nobody that crazy, Nacho. She got forty years worth of junk down there."

"Well, I need to take a walk. Been sitting on the bus too long."

"If you really going down there, bring me some a her greens. They grow sweeter in the hollow."

The grass in vacant lots was brittle yellow, but when he crossed the arroyo and neared Green Hollows, he could smell the wet. Under the trees, in that deep dent, the earth was always moist, kept a film of water. He saw only four of the long, thin shotgun shacks left, their olive-green sides peeling. The greens that grew around each house, the always thick, tender grass, the springy tumbleweeds at the edges of the hollow, that was what he'd thought Green Hollows was named for when he was a child, he realized, but it was for the paint, uniform on all the houses that had once been quarters for the orange-grove workers. The big farmhouse, white and three-story with scalloped shingles near the roof, was gone. A block wall ran along the edge of the hollow, and gray-stucco office buildings butted up against the cement.

Aint Rosa had never worked in the groves; she had been a cook for one of the elementary schools since she came to California, and she still wore her white nylon uniform every day. He saw her ghostly form in the doorway, waving.

"Nacho! I got a cobbler, oh, yes, I knew somebody was coming!" He stepped onto the tiny porch, stacked with *National Enquirers* and *People* magazines. "You know, Fergie's fixing to have her baby any minute, and it's gon be another girl."

"Yeah?" he said, following her into the kitchen. The cobbler's sweet steam hung around her gray braids for a moment and went out the window. A pile of greens, trimmed but not washed, sat on the table.

"These are for your mama, when we go back," she said. "My greens is always more tender."

"You planning to walk over there today, Aint? I thought you were packing up to move over to the Tower."

She jerked her head impatiently. "Don't nobody want this land—your daddy's just talking to hear his own self. I got too much stuff to fit into one a them little tiny rooms. I seen them, your mama took me over there once. A bitty closet and a hot plate—uh uh."

"Mama said you were moving next week." Nacho saw that she wouldn't listen; she put a piece of too-hot cobbler in front of him and started to wash the greens, putting them into a grocery sack. The oilcloth was slick and cool against his forearms, but the air was summer-warm, and he pushed the plate away.

"Blow on it a little," she said. "You got time, cause I needs to wash these dishes before we go to your mama's."

He stood in the yard, watching her lock the door, remembering all the summer days he and Snooter had come to the hollow to climb the pepper trees, lie behind Aint's house in the shade of the huge peach tree, beg her for teacakes. She took her time, and then they walked up the slope to the street. On Picasso, she stopped at Esther's. Esther did hair and sold lunches, and Aint Rosa leaned in the doorway to call, "I'm coming back soon." To Nacho she said, "Your mama keep insisting she want to cook for herself. I won't be long over there, I bet. I don't know why she going on about this. She need her rest. You see where Liz Taylor went to the hospital for exhaustion? Women got to have they rest."

He woke up at 5 a.m. and couldn't go back to sleep, staring at the shadow of shifting palm fronds against the wall of the bedroom he'd shared with Snooter since they were children. Snooter's parents had died in a bus crash on the way to Vegas when he was only six. Nacho looked at the empty twin bed—Snooter never slept here anymore, he could tell; he had four or five women calling all the time, and he rotated, depending on who had the best cooking skills if he was really hungry that night, and who had the best bedroom skills if he wasn't.

Saturday morning, Nacho thought. I'm in this narrow-ass bed; I slept on a bus seat for days, and a mattress on the floor back in Amherst. I ain't got shit to my name. He went into the kitchen, padding softly across the carpet, and took a piece of Aint Rosa's fried chicken out to the front yard with him. He sat on the folding chair, the early morning air warm and dry, wondering if Snooter still bothered to sneak in. He'd been a master creeper all through high school, entering the girls' houses and this one without a sound.

He didn't want to go to work with them. Saturday morning—the yards all up and down Arroyo Grande, those huge lawns and hedges that always needed trimming. And he'd argued with his father about Green Hollows last night; about working for Ruskin, and helping to make Aint Rosa move.

Back in Amherst, he'd dreamed about the hollow, imagined it always when he cleaned the dark, winter-wet hallways and mopped the linoleum, smelling that same clinging, sharp water. He didn't want to think about the earth there compacted by bulldozers, sectioned off for parking and block walls. His father would be up soon, Snooter would cruise in and wait for Daddy to bring out the coffee, and they'd say, "Them sissy hands ready to work today? Ain't done nothing useful in a year." Nacho threw the chicken bone into the trash can at the curb and headed for Sixth Avenue.

The sun began to rise when he stood in front of Quick Pick Liquor, drinking a cream soda, and a truck pulled up next to him, loaded with mowers, shovels, and rakes. Trent got out. His father had been Daddy's cousin, had died while Nacho was in Amherst, he remembered. "What up, cuz?" Trent said, exaggerating the greeting like they used to in high school. Nacho thought of Amherst again—"When none of em knows the daddy, they can all be cousins . . ."

"Just kickin it," Nacho said. "You gotta work this early?"

"It gets hot quick, man, you know that, and I don't do too many yards anymore. Mostly setting up the landscaping for the new houses, the irrigation and stuff. I got a big job today, and I don't feel like frying around noon. Why you up?"

"Avoiding them damn mowers you parked in my face," Nacho said, and he waited until Trent bought a six-pack of Pepsi and came back outside.

"You just back in town and your pops already working your ass? Bad as mine was."

Nacho said, "Sorry to hear about your dad."

"Thanks, man. I don't plan to work that hard and die that young," Trent said with a strange bubble in his voice, almost a gargle. "You want a ride, check out my new crib?"

He was surprised when Trent passed through the Westside and headed for the sloping hills where orange groves had been. Row after row of two-story houses terraced the hills now, so close together people could shake hands out their windows. So new he couldn't see any trees. "Snooter said people were moving out here from L.A.," Nacho said. "Daddy must got big-time work with these new yards, too."

"Cheaper here than L.A. or Orange County," Trent said. "But the people are cheap, too. I bet your dad doesn't have any yards up here—all Mexican, cause they work for less." He turned into a tract with a high block wall screening it from the street. "So you working with your dad again, huh? Snooter, too?" He sounded comfortable all of a sudden, Nacho thought, and he didn't like the smile in Trent's question.

"I'm just killing time until summer session at the college, man," he said. "It's all about school."

"I heard you were going to college back in Amherst," Trent said. "Why'd you come home?"

"I was just taking some art classes, drawing and painting," Nacho said, looking out the window at the perfect, fresh sod in the yards. "Got tired of winter, man, snow will kick your natural ass." He spoke quickly, hearing how stupid the words sounded even as he said them.

"So what you plan to do with your art? I mean, how do you make a living? You planning to be a graphic artist or something?"

Nacho was hot in the forehead. "I don't know, man, I just do it, I like it."

"Sounds good," Trent said, the same way Nacho said it to a guy in Lincoln Park who said he was going to stop drinking. "Here's the latest homestead."

"Damn, Trent," he said, looking at the two-story house, with an oak and stained-glass door, three-car garage, and a mailbox like the one Snooter had hit at Ruskin's. "Latest?"

"I buy and sell them. Sure cash," Trent said. "That's number three." He stopped, said, "You want a tour? It'll have to be quick."

"No, I better get back," Nacho said. "I'll come check you out one night when we both got more time." Nacho watched the houses slide past, the immaculate cement driveways. Three Mexican guys were building a block wall to separate two houses, and another crew was weeding the bank outside the entrance to the tract.

"Your dad should have gotten his contractor's license," Trent said suddenly. "These dudes are making big money." Nacho looked at him, and Trent said, "My dad and yours used to do cement back in Mississippi. My dad told me they could have made big cash out here, but they ended up doing yards and hauling."

Nacho remembered his father doing odd cement jobs around the Westside, curbs or planter boxes. He always criticized other cement work, showing Nacho the uneven slant or rough edges on a job, but that was when Nacho was small.

"He's getting ready to clean up Green Hollows," Nacho said loudly. "He got all kinda work now." He saw the block walls surrounding the office buildings.

"Yeah, it flooded a bunch of times when we were kids, remember?" Trent said. "It's a health hazard, I read in the paper."

They drove in silence. When the car slowed to turn onto Picasso, Trent said, "So, Snooter still have a bunch of ladies?"

"More than he can handle," Nacho said, his hand on the door.

"Some things never change," Trent said. "Easy, man." He pulled away slowly, looking at the back of the big aqua truck.

The high snore of the mowers, the weed-whacker almost sparkly-sounding when he ran it around the edges of the lawns—he'd forgotten that the noise could be lulling even as the sun grew stronger.

They drove to a deli for lunch, and Nacho knew that was a big concession for his father, who liked to work straight through noon. Sitting on the curb by the store while they waited for Snooter to bring the sandwiches, Nacho looked at the layers of green stain, craggy as the mountains, on his father's boots. "I saw Trent this morning," he said.

"He show you his house?" his father said. "Don't tell me."

Nacho felt the heat from passing cars drift around his ankles. "He was talking about you and his dad used to do cement work. I forgot you did that. Why you didn't get your license?"

"Cause I was busy." His father lit a cigarette. "Busier than you ever been."

"Serious, you coulda made your own jobs instead of waiting for somebody like Ruskin to call you all the time. Trent said yards are getting harder to come by."

"He ain't lying. Every fool with a Japanese truck buy a mower and start driving around looking for work." His father stood up, kicked the boot heels against the curb, restless to get back.

"So why didn't you?" Nacho pressed.

"Shit, boy, who the hell are you? I was tryin to feed your ass, Snooter's, buy you shoes for school. We had a ice box in 1952, nigger, me and your mama living over there off Second Avenue in a cracker-box. Wasn't about no career and shit. You and your classes. We been here from Grenada two years, just got out the service, and some white man seen me walking near Lincoln Park, asked me did I want a couple day's work. It was September, and Snooter was cryin for some kinda shoes he seen at the store. I didn't have time to sit around on my artistic ass and think about life like you do."

Snooter stood behind them with the paper-wrapped sandwiches, translucent from the salad oil. "And I was stylin in them shoes, Unc." He smiled and said, "I been tryin to pay you back ever since."

In the truck, Nacho winced at the sting of jalapenos in the sandwich. His mouth had forgotten. The green heat stayed at his lips all afternoon, and when they were home, sitting in the yard, he kept licking them to feel the momentary coolness. Lanier and Red Man, his father's friends, came by soon, and they argued about Green Hollows.

"You a hot lie, Floyd," Red Man said. "That woman was Indian, all that long black hair down to her knees and straight as rope."

"I remember who you talkin about, Lucy was her name," Lanier said. "I always heard she was white, too. Had about five kids runnin around in the yard every time I went down there."

His father said, "She was French, came over here lookin for some nigger she met in the service during the war. I don't care what y'all remember."

Nacho held the beer can to his lips. Esther, across the street, came out onto her porch and walked down the steps slowly; she hung a wet cloth on the chainlink side fence, and Nacho's father and Lanier shouted at her to wait. They walked into her yard, hands in their pockets, and Nacho was puzzled, watching them give her money. A dollar—that was what each handed to her, Daddy's big bent fingers around her wrist for a second, him smiling with his face down. Nacho couldn't hear what they said, but then he remembered that she'd just brought home a new baby, and he realized suddenly that his father and Lanier, all of them were the old men of the Westside now, the ones he and Snooter used to be scared of when they rode bikes across a lawn or made too much noise close to the fish at the city lake. Aint Rosa's husband Johnny used to always give his mother a dollar, press it into her palm and whisper something, when she brought home the girls.

When his father sat down again, he looked at Nacho. "You gon take the Toyota over Aint's in the morning and move her dresser and bed."

Nacho shook his head. "She says she ain't moving. The Towers only one room, a studio, and she says no way."

"Don't start now, boy. She know the truth, and we gotta start tearing them things down Monday." He took a long swallow of beer. "Go over there early, before it get hot. Aint don't do good in the heat anymore."

"Yeah, and it's always cool in the hollow."

His father turned away, to Red Man. "He think Green Hollows is a valuable piece of architecture like it is. It got artistic qualities, he fixin to tell us next." He said to Nacho, "Try that on the city. It'll go over about as well as a fart in a crowded room on a hot summer night." Red Man and Lanier laughed.

"Man, it's better than offices," Nacho said, standing up. "You know what I'm saying."

"You're trying to make it sound better than it is," his father said. "Just like you do with them paintings. You see trees and look right past them big old rats down there, whup a pit bull if they please. Electrical always goin out cause the wires from 1910. Aint couldn't turn on the TV and the porch light at the same time."

"Boy getting sentimental, huh?" Red Man said, and they all laughed again. Nacho went inside, to the back room. Snooter was ironing his clothes.

"Who you going out with?" Nacho said, sitting on the bed.

"Me and Beverly headin out to Club Seven." He sprayed starch on the pants. "What you trippin on, with your long face?"

"Monday."

"It's just a job, man."

"It's the whole thing, Snooter. Ruskin's gon make the big cash, Aint Rosa be crowded into the Towers, and we just comin behind to do the shit work."

"We comin before." Snooter pressed hard on the crease.

"You don't *want* to hear. Cool, Snooter, keep thinking with your other head." Nacho bent behind the bed to get his bag. He hadn't even unpacked it.

"Well, cuz, *thinkin* would be some heavy action for yours. Mine's busier than that. So you think you too good for the truck. Your ass ain't gon get rusty and dusty. What—you find a new janitor slave? Oh, you was livin large in Amherst, huh?"

"I was studying, doing something I wanted to."

"Well, I'll just keep studyin my favorite works of art—Juanita's ass, Teresa's lips, and Beverly's neck. I dig sculpture, okay?"

Nacho took the duffle with him and went out the back door, climbing the fence into the alley. His lips tingled, his chest was tight, not with anger but jealousy. He'd felt the usual foolish warmth in his belly when Snooter said the girls' names, the same as all the years when Snooter went out, when he described what they did, when Nacho saw them and could only look, not speak. He went to the McDonald's on Sixth and sat in the back, eating fries. From the bag, he pulled out the hard folder with his sketches, careful to wipe his fingers. He found all the Westside pictures, the tumbleweeds with their tiny pink flowers that bloomed in October. One of the other students in his class had said, "It's an interesting idea to juxtapose tumbleweeds and flowers, but isn't the idea artificial? Like those cactus in the store that people glue straw flowers to." He couldn't explain it right, that the rosy blooms nestled between thorns for a few weeks, a faint mauve mist in the fields.

The next one would be Green Hollows; he pulled it closer to him, slowly, remembering how he'd pecked and dipped with the pencil, sharpening it over and over; he'd filled in the ferny leaves of the pepper trees, the notched thick bark of the trunk, and the gnarled empty bulges where bees lived. His teacher, Mr. Bowers, had found two Rembrandt prints and brought them to class for Nacho—they were almost the same, the dense black loops and lines, the dark trees and a farmer. Nacho had been shocked when he saw the way the tree branches, in Holland, bent and curved against the sky like his.

He stared at the drawing now. The black and gray against the cream paper made the hollow look misty-dark and shaded, the dust cool enough to cling to the earth and not rise around his feet when he walked. Aint Rosa was a wraith, hanging in the doorway of her house, not in her cafeteria uniform but in a long, white cotton skirt, her headrag above her eyes.

When he got to her porch, it was late, the lights all off, and in the half-moon light, low spiderwebs thick as fog hugged the ivy around the base of the house. He was quiet, listening to the crickets, lying on the long seat his father had taken from the cab of an old truck.

Wings flapped overhead twice, and he remembered Birdman, who lived down the street from his father, telling him about a hawk that lived in the tallest eucalyptus tree there. The night was warm, and he slept with a shirt around his neck to keep off spiders.

But as the morning light heated his eyelids where he lay with his head near the edge, and as Aint's whispering feet scuffed against the floor inside the house, he felt panic; he had nothing good to tell Aint Rosa, nothing to tell her at all, and he pushed the bag softly under the card table near the seat. Stepping off the porch silently, the dust soft around his shoes, he walked past the boarded-up houses; in one of them, he saw a light, smelled match smoke. Someone was getting high in the house where plywood had been pried off the windows. Nacho walked faster, toward the end of the hollow where a ditch led into the arroyo.

The arroyo cut all the way through Rio Seco, and he ducked into the huge flood-control pipe near downtown; the pipe was dry and chalky. His father had said there hadn't been any rain since December. Nacho remembered hiding in the pipe when they were small, he and Snooter and Darnell and Birdman, their backs curved to fit the clay. He came out and passed through the edge of downtown, watching the winos look frightened when he neared them.

He kept thinking he heard a car behind him, going too slow, but he was afraid to look around and see if it was a cop; he looked bad, carrying nothing and rumpled from sleeping. He knew he was heading for the Methodist Church.

On the last few times they'd all walked down the arroyo, Nacho had left the others to keep on toward the river-bottom, and he'd stopped at this church, peering into the arched doorway at the dank, cool wood inside, the stained glass and faint colored light on the floor. He'd been glad that Snooter and the others laughed and didn't want to come with him, because they'd only get loud and cause trouble. It was always Sunday afternoon when they came, and the church people were gone, but the doors open.

Sitting on the cement bench at the edge of the lawn, looking at the arched, recessed doorway, not open yet for the people in suits and nylons, he imagined how he would draw the sculpted blossoms, the delicate intertwined rope. The most beautiful church in Rio Seco—a dome with a cross on top, blue and gold tile edging it, and the magnificent doorway. Six rounds of carving, each edge just behind the other to draw in the eye, and the massive curves were each a differing pattern. Seashells linked with a curly vine, the point-petaled flowers, heavy braided rope, diamonds, rounded daisies, and a chain of squares.

He heard tires crushing the sand in the asphalt behind him, slowly, and he was afraid to turn around. Johnny Law, he thought, and definitely wanting to know why I'm sitting here. He heard the door slam, and waited with shoulders straight.

"What you studyin?" his father said.

Nacho took his thumbnails out of the pads of his ring fingers and didn't answer.

"Lookin suspicious as all hell, police be by here in a minute to wonder which old lady you plannin to rob." His father sat on the other bench. "Or you get in the Methodist habit, too, when you was in Massachusetts?"

"I'm looking at the doorway, okay?" Nacho said. "Art, all right? I was wondering how long it took somebody to carve all those flowers and designs. They're all perfect."

His father laughed and threw back his shoulders in a stretch, got up and walked to the arch. "Shit," he said.

Nacho jerked his knee up and down. "Yeah, like I expected you to see what I'm talking about? You never saw cathedrals in France, not even in books."

His father was still laughing. "Boy, you don't know shit. Ain't you never looked at that?" Nacho followed his father's finger to the far end of the facade. Etched into the bottom square, the cornerstone, was "First Methodist Church—Erected 1955 A.D."

"You use a mold on these. I made one for Esther's mama when she moved into the new house. Made her three benches for her yard, with flowers on the edges." He was quiet, and Nacho could hear pigeons stirring inside the bell tower. "Only time I did that," his father said, turning back toward Nacho. "You been sitting there on that bench, sitting back there all google-eyed, thinking about some dude with a chisel, sweatin on each flower. Sweat turning to dew drops on the petals and shit." He lit a cigarette and flicked the match toward Nacho. "We got a full day's work." He walked toward the truck.

"So?" Nacho said, pressing his thighs against the cool bench. "You can go to Lincoln Park. You don't need me. I'm too ignorant for you, and you too ignorant for me."

"Boy, stop talking that shit before I whup your back-East ass." He started up the engine and backed the truck into the street, and Nacho turned back to face the church. He heard the truck move away. When it was quiet again, he walked up to the doorway and ran his hand over the seashells, the braided rope. Tiny holes, like pores, speckled the flowers and shells, and he could see the hair-thin lines where blocks of each pattern had been cemented together. The artist had placed them perfectly, each scallop and leaf fitted together as one. The cement was rough against his palm. He turned, and the big wooden doors swung in, a draft of dark air pushing out. The startled face of a small, old woman, pale skin and hair and pink-framed glasses, floated like a tiny moon in the black doorway. Nacho walked quickly toward the street.

When he turned the corner, the truck was there, idling, and he could see two big pots sitting in the bed, close to the cab. They were greens trees, in the black-plastic containers Red Man raised them in. He knew his father had gotten them for Aint Rosa. Hesitating, he saw the iridescent oil spots at the bottom of the door, where the swirls of color clung to the rust, and he pulled it open.

safe hooptie

BRENDA / JULY

Darnell and me were driving to his house like always, but *nobody* out on they lawn, not even the Thibodeaux boys and they *live* on the grass. This supposed to be a Friday night, it's summer, and people should be washing cars, breathing some air, getting ready to go out. When we got to Picasso Street, I saw the record player wasn't out on the front porch at Darnell's. Mr. Tucker, Darnell's father, play records on Friday evening, put the old beige stereo facing out to the street so you can hear it for a couple of houses. He play Billie Holiday, sad Billie, and some scratchy records by Earl Grant. I wanted to hear them, the organ real husky and low swinging in the background, because nobody play music on my street, but I knew tonight me and Darnell wouldn't be sitting on his car in the driveway. No Tiny or K.C. coming by to say, "What up, homes?" Darnell always say, "The Lakers, man, they up by ten games." Tiny answer, "I heard *that,*" and always looking down the street to see who at Jackson Park. He usually start singing, "In the Westside, the cool cool Westside, where the people gon party all night."

Tonight it wouldn't be kids walking by to yell, "Take that old stuff off the stereo, man. Play some Ice T, some Eazy-E. Bust a rhyme out them ancient speakers." None of Mr. Tucker's friends, Roscoe Wiley and Floyd, standing around to laugh at the kids. "Red Man ain't hardly playin none a that rap mess. Listen. These people *singin,* not hollerin. World a difference, boy." Darnell's arms wouldn't be around me at my waist, and his father working on a old battery or motor. The street was empty all the way down to the park. Nobody out in they yard or in the street because the cops looking for Ricky Ronrico, and they been searching one night and one day. Longer than it sound.

Everybody in the front room, near the swamp cooler. Darnell's little sisters, Sophia and Paula, making those string bracelets all the kids are wearing. Darnell tell his father, "I heard it on the radio comin back."

"Where was y'all working this week?" his mother ask. Darnell with the firefighter crew they run in the summer, out in the dry mountains all over the county, from the desert to near L.A. I only see him on the weekends, and he pick me up straight from work.

"We was over by Chino Hills. Rattlesnakes everywhere. I heard the two cops got shot on the south end, over on Eddy Avenue past the mall. That ain't no black neighborhood."

"So? Ricky Ronrico shot them and he black for a fact. Bout as no good as that sickly stuff he name after," his father say.

Mr. Lanier standing there with a big shopping bag full of plums. "And you know they figure he somewhere on the Westside." He live on the next street, always musty because he got a bunch of pigs out somewhere. My mother use to buy chitlins and pig knuckles from him every New Year's, before we moved away from the Westside.

Mr. Lanier say, "That why I *walk* over here, ain't taking no chances with my brake lights. Rio Seco finest in the streets tonight, lookin hard."

It's only the TV talking then, and I know everybody's thinking about 1973. I was eight, and the only thing I remember was all the red lights flashing on my bedroom walls cause the cops came and took Mr. Wiley from next door. He was gone all weekend. Somebody had ambushed two white cops at Jackson Park, but I just knew the lights looked like Hawaiian Punch spilling over my bed, and I thought they were so pretty then.

"What they lookin for this time?" Mr. Lanier say.

"It was white sneakers back in '73," Mr. Tucker say. "That's what they said the fellas did it was wearin. What was them two cops name?"

"I don't rightly remember," Mr. Lanier say.

"Please and Christensen." Darnell talks real quiet. He never forget anything. "Kelvin and every other Westside brother between sixteen and thirty went down to the station, all weekend."

His mother looking at her catalogs, don't say anything. Her oldest son, Kelvin, live in L.A. now. Darnell's father light another cigarette. "White tennis shoes," he say. "But they got Roscoe Wiley and that other poet, the one use to teach in your school, Brenda."

"Brother Lobo," I say.

"Kept his ass for a week." For a second between the commercials, we could hear the drip of water from the cooler, the fan going around over our heads. Mrs. Tucker put in a beautiful one, with wood and lamps, this summer.

"So who they want this time?" Mr. Lanier say again, getting up to go.

"They want Ricky Ronrico," Mr. Tucker say. "And they talkin about somebody hidin him, wantin to harbor him. Huh." His face pull itself together while I watch, like his eyebrows and that big nose and mouth get in a line straight up and down as a totem pole, piled on top of each other. Like he's Indian all the way through. That's why they call him Red Man. "Damn sure wouldn't hide him if he came to me."

Nobody on Picasso Street liked Ricky because he always raced his van up and down by the park. But that wasn't what Mr. Tucker was thinking about, I know. Hearing that name remind him of the time Darnell spent two nights in jail, in the same cell with Ricky. Thinking about that still make Mr. Tucker hot.

"Go on and take Brenda home, now," he say, real loud, to Darnell. "This ain't no time to be out. And bring your ass right back."

"Huh," Darnell start to say, but then his father cut him off.

"You know you gotta drive her up to the Ville, and I ain't playin."

When we close the front door, I hear Mrs. Tucker say, "He twenty, he ain't a boy no more," and Darnell's father quick to stop her, too.

"That's the point."

At first, I think he's mad about the way his father talk to him. He don't say anything going down Picasso, waiting a long time at every stop sign. "Good enough?" he whisper real strange at the last two, looking out his window. I look out of mine, and I see the chainlink fences around yards like they lit up, electric, because the sun just now going down. The folding chairs on somebody's lawn seem like they on fire, glowing metal. I can smell the cooking meat, the way it drift through the streets when we get closer to Canales Frozen Foods.

Only railroad tracks to pass now, on Third Avenue, and then Canales and The Pit. After you leave the Westside, you smell nothing but orange groves for a few miles. My cousins from L.A. always laugh at me when they come out to visit Rio Seco. "Man, y'all niggers *country*. Only a hour away and might as well be in Mi-sippi. Y'all ain't got no clubs, no disco, nothin live. You got Jackson Park and The Pit."

Nobody's even parked down there at The Pit now, that dirt lot bare as the desert. My mother use to work at Canales—they cook the meat for Mexican food, frozen burritos and tamales, and when the shift is going, the whole Westside full of a smell so rich, so warm and spicy, it's nothing better. Mama said the meat itself was real poor, but when I was small, I'd walk down there to meet her getting off work, sit in the heat by the fence and breathe that smell, sometimes mixed with the barbecue smoke coming from the roof of The Pit. I couldn't go nowhere near even the parking lot of that place—it was where people drank and played cards and ate ribs, and beat each other up.

Darnell look over there, laugh a little now. "Them old-timey kind that hang out at The Pit know better than to come out tonight. They scared of they own shadow cause *it's* got a Mi-sippi accent."

I've known Darnell since we were five, when I lived on Picasso. He's been like this three times: when his friend Roger got shot at our graduation party, when he got out of jail that time last summer, and now. It feels strange not knowing what to say to him, and we're almost all the way up Third to the Ville already.

Everybody from the Westside call it the Ville because it was only white people lived up here, on this slope, back then. Honkyville. We left the Westside and moved up here when I was nine. Some Japanese people, three or four Mexican families around by then, and after we came, the Orlandos and Tyners move here from DaVinci Street. But everybody on the Westside still call it the Ville and laugh at my father, say does our grass grow greener and our mail come earlier? When the Santa Ana wind blow the power out, do the city come and fix it a hell of a lot faster than they do on Picasso?

All the orange groves thin out now, and we pass by the little park just off Third. About five cars there, stoner white boys drinking beer, smoking at the picnic tables. Darnell say, "Can I get a swig, *homes? Can we chill in the park with you?*"

"Getting mad ain't likely to change the situation, Darnell," I say. "Don't you go driving crazy on the way back to the Westside."

"What do you suggest I do?" He finally look at me, and the scar push out mad and jagged on his forehead, just heading into his hair. Even when he got that, it turned into something else. He and his father were looking for a radiator at the junkyard, and he ran into a pole, split his head open. I took him to the emergency and they made us wait. Blood all in his hair, his pants got mud at the hems, and I was trying to clean him up when the doctor take him into a room. Darnell came busting out a few minutes later, said, "We *gone.* Now." He told me the doctor didn't believe the pole, kept laughing,

"Your woman must have hit you over the head with something awfully heavy. What did you do to deserve this?"

While I laugh about stuff like that, Darnell get blind mad. I say, "I suggest you come inside when we get to my house. Cool you down."

"I gotta be up at six to help Daddy fix the big truck. He's supposed to pick up a load of brush somebody cleared off for fire season." When we stop at the last four-way before my street, a boy pull up beside us, gunning his engine like firecrackers. Darnell looks over and wait til he drive off. "I suggest white boy racin his hooptie around fast as he want. Probably got a open container of Jack Daniels on the seat and shit. Hair *streamin* in the wind." He don't even bring his lips close to mine when he pull into the driveway. I thought he would walk me to the porch so I could stand on the steps above him, like always, and look into his eyes, touch his eyebrows, straighten them with my fingers.

Pop come up behind me when I look through the window to see Darnell's car go down the street. "What the hell were you doin? You never even came after work to eat."

"John, she never come home on Fridays, I been told you that." Mama's sitting at the dining room table picking through a bowl of beans, sorting out the rocks. "Darnell always pick her up since he workin for the Forest Service."

"You didn't have any business bein on the Westside tonight, Brenda," Pop go on. "When this Conservation Crap over?"

"At the end of summer," I answer. "Was it on the news, even in L.A.?" Rio Seco's close enough to get on TV sometimes, but not usually.

Pop sit back on the couch. "City gettin bigger, and bad stuff always play on the news." He turn to the nine o'clock early broadcast. "It was on the TV back in '73," he say.

The blonde lady doesn't smile. "Police are following several leads in Rio Seco tonight in their search for murder suspect Ricardo Ronrico, who is believed to have shot and killed two police officers late last night. Officers Terry Kimball and Gregory LaDonna were attempting to serve Ronrico with a warrant to appear in court for sentencing on a parole violation when he allegedly shot them in this residence on Eddy Avenue." They show the house, the neighbors standing around, cop cars everywhere.

"Bastard get us all in trouble," Pop say. "How in the hell he get a name like that? He your age, Brenda?"

"He's older than us, about twenty-five. Darnell say his brother name Falstaff after some beer and his sister Virginia Dare."

"Oh, and how in the hell Darnell know him if this fool older?"

Mama say, "John, why you always assume the worst about Darnell?"

"Cause she don't need to be drivin around with him and him only. His car looks like hell. He musta done somethin to get in all that trouble last summer," Pop say, and I'm tired of hearing this.

"He was just sitting in the driver's seat, playing the radio, I *been* told you," I yell. "Him and Londale were taking down the election posters for Mack Ellison. Someone you didn't vote for cause you said a brother couldn't win for county supervisor."

"Then why the cops take him in? Cause he didn't have no driver's license and no business bein there in that rich neighborhood." Pop's voice echoing.

"At least they was taking *down* the signs," Mama say. "You always complainin about them bein up for months after an election."

"Darnell don't have a license because of that insurance shit, cause that white dude hit him and Darnell didn't have insurance. Yeah, they had warned him, gave him tickets, offa *that.* You know how high insurance is on the Westside. You were laughing when you bought it last time, too, because of your *address.*" I feel that water pushing behind my eyes, starting to come up my throat, so I go in my bedroom and shut the door.

Mama come in a while later. "Did you eat at Darnell's house?"

"I wasn't hungry. I had a big lunch at work."

"You sit outside in that nice plaza they got in front of the county building?" Mama lean against the edge of the bed. "I always think about you sittin out there with all the other secretaries, and them cute little cafes and boutiques they got now. Look like L.A." Every time she even mention the county building, I hear how proud she is about my job. I had to stop telling her not to call me a secretary, I'm only a clerk, because she won't listen.

"Yeah, Mama, I sat in the sun. I'm going to sleep now." After she close the door, I look outside my window, listen for the helicopter. It takes off from the top of the county building, where they got a helipad. Sometimes when I'm at Darnell's, in the front yard in the dark, the police shine the spotlight from it and cut over us jagged as lightning. Circling loud and angry as a wasp, make the whole street silver. Mama always asking me what new flowers they planted in the county plaza this month. I sat out there today, next to the fountain pale blue like glass. People popping open their soda cans loud, little rifle shots. I can't stop thinking about Ricky Ronrico, about what those red flashing lights in my bedroom would look like now, me in Darnell's blankets on the couch. I lay in the bed for a long time, hearing the helicopter then, humming distance, hoping Darnell went straight home and didn't run into Tiny or someone else who loved to instigate, just stand on the corner and talk smack.

When I wake up, I know they still haven't caught him. I could feel it somehow, almost see Ricky Ronrico's face, and I call Darnell right away. He say the Westside still steppin light and drivin slow, but not *too* slow, and I can hear a smile in his voice, know he's thinking about last night.

"You suggesting you still pick me up at the usual time?" I say, and he laughs. He always come about two o'clock, so we can go by the park. I clean house for Mama; Pop already at work, doing an extra shift. He already talking about property taxes due pretty soon, even though it's not till December. Me and Mama make a peach cobbler since we had all these peaches from my Aintie Mae out in Perris. Mama sew up a hole in Pop's other work pants, and I fix the rip in my white blouse. When Darnell come over, Mama's done. "How are things on Picasso?"

"Quiet. People doing a lot of talking, but mostly it's nothin but a long wait."

We tell her we'll just stay at Darnell's and play cards, and won't go cruising or looking for parties.

"Well, why you don't stay here and play cards then?" She turn her head at me like she does when I know she know why we don't stay here. We sit around at Darnell's, and people come over to watch the basketball game or wrestling, and everybody's laughing and talking about everybody else. Nobody come up here. Nobody borrow an egg or bring over some extra greens, and the phone might ring, but the doorbell doesn't. "I won't be late," I say, and she shake her head.

But when we on the Westside, it's not Saturday any more than the day before was Friday. Nothing seem natural at all. The sky was tinged all brown, like usual, but even the smog seem angry, and the palm trees hanging dusty, sorry-looking. The streets gray and glittery, rising in the heat almost, and everything faded, like the color been drained out. The houses and cars pale, people's lawns sand-color; we in one of those old-time photos Mr. Tucker has from Oklahoma, from where he grew up.

The heavy chains are up blocking the parking lot by Jackson Park, and not a brother in sight. "Daddy didn't want me to come and get you," Darnell is saying, but he put his hand on my arm. "I'm tellin you, I had to think twice about it." He smile at me careful, touch a knuckle to my neck. "Good enough?" he whisper.

His father's inside watching TV, talking on the phone. Darnell and me play dominoes in the back, and Tiny comes in after a while.

"Man, it's definitely cooler back here than in the front room with your old man, homes. He so pissed, put you in a *world* of hurt you say the wrong thing."

"I know. And everything wrong. You in the streets, hot as it is?"

"Just kickin it." Tiny anything but tiny. Six-two, got a big natural even though nobody wearing naturals anymore. He just love his own hair, and everything else about himself. "Man, when Johnny Law pull your hooptie over," he say, "you put your hands like *this*." Spread his fingers out wide. "You put them hands on top of the wheel and pray with em apart." He was driving his mother's car an hour ago, got stopped on the way from the liquor store on Third.

"The wheel ain't good enough for me," Darnell say. "Remember when I was at that gas station last year, six in the morning and the cashier trip that silent alarm by accident? Shoot, seven black and whites and I hadn't even picked my pump. I had my hands outside the window, man." He slam down a domino. "Least you wasn't wearin that nasty John Shaft leather piece you call a coat. Lucky it's summer. You usually look so bad cops stop you on G.P."

"My middle name, homey. General Principle."

"You ain't marked down my fifteen, baby. Oh, I know it hurts." He look up at me. "We ain't goin nowhere today, I can see that." I give him the points, and Tiny go into the kitchen for some Kool-Aid. No air is moving at all.

Miss Ralphine from across the street is sitting at the table with Darnell's mama when we come out the bedroom to walk Tiny to the front yard. Her face is small like a baby's under her wig, and even though she must be seventy, the only wrinkles are on her forehead where she raise her eyebrows all the time. I know what she's fixing to say. "Brenda! How you and this boy? When y'all gettin married? I needs to go to a weddin soon."

She been asking for two years now, since we graduated together. I smile and tell her I don't know, while Darnell and Tiny pass under the fan and look up for some air.

"Where you think you goin?" Mr. Tucker say. Him and Mr. Lanier just outside the front door, looking at a battery recharger.

"Damn, give me a break," Darnell say, and then he lift up his hands. "Sorry. The feet stops here." I see Jane Jones walking down the sidewalk, wearing her uniform. She works at Church's Fried Chicken on Sixth Avenue. "Tiny, Darnell. And Bren-da," she call out, saying my name all slow. She still won't forgive me.

We went to work experience at school together, for a year. Bank of America took us for clerk/tellers, and we figured out how to talk different, talk white, dress right. Like I do at work now.

But Jane was twice my size, her shoulders big as Darnell's, and dark. Brother Lobo, the poet, used to call her "the real thing." Ebony. I was always jealous of her face and skin when we were little; her jaw was so smooth, her neck so long, and she never had marks on her skin like I did. Mine light enough to show nicks and scratches for months. When it came time for the county and the banks to call us for jobs, though, I saw how they checked Jane out. We were both talking right at the interviews, but her hair, her shoulders. She could relax her hair every day, and it would still be African; she wear a short fade, and it make her neck even longer.

She never asked me about the job at the county. I didn't see her for a long time, and Darnell told me her mother had gotten sprung, started smoking that rock cocaine. Jane had to take care of her, so she got a job at Church's.

"You gon walk with me, Tiny," she say over her shoulder, "or Brenda gotta have a harem?"

"Don't be opening your mouth tonight just to see if your tongue work, boy," Mr. Tucker holler at Tiny's back.

We stay in the back room then, and Darnell mess with my hair, tease me about my neck. "What if I give you a most embarrassing souvenir of my love?" He try to pinch my neck, and then he's kissing me, but

Sophia and Paula keep running in and out to get something. We give up and go in the front to help Darnell's mama cook, because everybody who barely knows the Tuckers could come by and eat on a Saturday. We make chicken, fry up with pepper and onions, string beans, macaroni and cheese, neckbones and blackeye peas for Mr. Tucker. Yellow cake with chocolate icing. That's how she cook every Saturday.

All the kids eat, and Mr. Tucker, Mr. Lanier, and then Roscoe Wiley comes from down the street. They all sit in the living room and watch TV, Sophia and Paula and they friend Takima go singing out the back door, and Darnell take me out to the side steps by the kitchen. The night got hotter instead of cooling off, it seems, and we can smell the greens tree tangled up the chainlink like it's cooking in the air. Pop told me about a storm he sat through once in Tulsa, time going fast but in circles.

Nobody walk by, and then we hear the helicopter again for a long time, over near Seventh Avenue where all the hotels and restaurants are. Miss Ralphine come over to say they got a SWAT team at the Holiday Inn; they plan to find Ricky Ronrico tonight, and that's headquarters, she heard on her police radio. They must think he's in the Westside for sure.

Only Mr. Tucker left in the living room now, and Darnell and me watch "Invasion of the Body Snatchers" with him. "Not a dark face on the screen," Darnell say, and he keep getting up to drink something, sit down careful so he don't touch my leg. "This shit getting old," he say, "and we out of soda." The helicopter circles around like a race car on a track in the sky. When I wake up, the phone ringing and the movie's been off. The police just raided Mr. Wiley's house on the corner, and he talked big trouble when they tried to take his son for questioning. Said they heard he had evidence in the house, and went through all the rooms. Darnell's mama tap her foot on the linoleum fast as a cricket, and when Tiny come in the screen door everybody jump. "Boy, what in hell you doin out?" Mr. Tucker say, his whole face pomegranate red. Red Man. "Get your ass on the couch where it belong on a night like this."

"Man, this ain't Alabama," Tiny say, but then he smile. "I couldn't miss the food, now." He don't even eat, though, just sit on the floor far away from Mr. Tucker. "Lester and Jimmy and Birdman say blood cool and they hope he get away with it. He probably in L.A. anyway. Ain't no place to hang in this country-ass . . ."

"Shut up, boy, fore I shut you up," Mr. Tucker holler; I feel tight in the chest. If we say Ricky Ronrico's name, they'll come busting in for us.

"You call your mother, Brenda. You won't be home for awhile."

On the phone, Mama sound mad, but she say he's right. Anther TV show is gone, and I think Darnell asleep, but he staring at the wall. The old beige stereo sits quiet next to the fireplace, under the picture of the African queen. She's even darker from all the years of smoke settled on her.

Mr. Tucker asleep in his big leather chair, and Mrs. Tucker go into their bedroom. Tiny still on the floor, and me and Darnell the only ones awake. He doesn't have a bedroom; he's slept on the couch since I've known him. He put his arm around my neck for a minute, and I rest my chin on that soft part by his elbow, but then he shift away again. "Too hot," he say. Huh.

On the eleven o'clock news, the blonde lady starts out with, "Rio Seco police have captured murder suspect Ricardo Ronrico, the object of an intense manhunt since Friday." He was in a house on Gate Street, way back on the south side where he shot the two police. On the screen, his hair is all nappy, his eyes flat and red, lips with a gray ring around them. "My man sprung, seriously sprung. Rock daddy," Tiny say, and I didn't even know he was awake.

"Clues as to his whereabouts were found in a raid of a house earlier in the evening," she go on, and Darnell say, "Yeah, *tell* me. Treasure hunt time. How many stolen TVs and shit you think they found?"

"Blood knew better than to hang out on the Westside," Tiny say. "Nothin but a anthill. Stompin easy." He look at me. "Unless you want to move to the Ville like Brenda."

"Shut up, Tiny," I say. "Don't start on me."

"Wasn't nobody bangin on your daddy's door, huh?" he keep on, and the blonde lady smiles. "In our next story, children learn about the great outdoors in some of the Southland's many summer camps." The little white kids race around, building fires, hiking in the woods, and Darnell say, "Please."

He pull me up from the couch. "I be back soon, Tiny. Brenda's daddy gon be breathin fire, so it ain't like I'll be lingerin." I'm about to say something, and I hear Mr. Tucker's chair creak.

"They got him," Tiny say to Darnell's father, and I'm pushed out the door.

The car seat warm as the couch was. I kiss Darnell's neck, give him problems driving. I won't see him again for another week. I look out at the streets, see Lester and Jimmy walking, and Darnell honks, but he doesn't slow down. It feels strange driving, like we still in a bottle even though the car windows are open. I unbutton Darnell's shirt, and when we're getting ready to pass the canning plant, I pull on the wheel. "Stop for a minute," I tell him, and he let me turn into the parking lot.

I feel like things should be all messed up, tumbleweeds and palm fronds and boxes thrown around like after the winds come in winter. I want to tell him I'm afraid for him every day, but he won't listen, I know. "Go close to the building," I whisper, and it's the weekend, so I can't smell the spicy breeze I want. I pull Darnell down onto the seat, and he say, soft, "You know I don't have no protection. I didn't think about it."

"I know," I say, and kiss his eyelids, put my hands like fans on his back. I think if the helicopter flew over now, shone the floodlight on us, they'd see my arms covering the back of Darnell's neck, where the skin so soft and blind.

cellophane and feathers

ROSCOE / FEBRUARY

Mockingbirds must have been fighting over the territory at the edge of the prison, because Roscoe had heard them singing frantically, at their best, some time after three that morning. He lay there until daylight and couldn't go back to sleep, listening to the birds twitter, call, warble, each song more anxious and perfect than the last.

He knew what they were doing only because his son Louis had come home years ago from the junior-high library to tell him that the mockingbird who sat on the telephone wire above their fig tree wasn't singing for joy all day and night that spring, but fighting to keep other birds away. By the time the road crew got on the bus, Roscoe's head banged against the glass when he fell asleep; he sat next to the window, trying not to think about Louis, and shook his cheeks to the left and right to wake himself up. But Jesus Trevino's hair was black and iridescent, feathered as a crow's wing, in front of him. Damn, he thought, birds all night, birds all I'm likely to see today. Crow time right now, when at home on the Westside the only people who would be up were Red Man, Floyd and him, the ones who worked outside and started early. Roscoe let himself wonder what Louis was doing this early, where he was sleeping. Louis was the one who called it crow time, had his father thinking of it that way ever since. The huge black birds thought they *owned* the streets this time of morning, stalking up and down the asphalt and into the yards, diving and calling to each other. Louis used to come into Roscoe's bedroom, wake him up and ask, "Daddy, what are they saying to each other? They talking about *something,* huh? But I don't know what it is."

Roscoe saw desert outside the windows, not the landscaping that meant they were headed to work the city freeways, and he rubbed his eyes, the skin in front of his ears. If he'd been one of the old-timey, suspicious women from Mississippi, the ones who always sat talking in squinty whispers when he was small, he would think of magic, that someone was working a strange power on him. Yesterday had been exactly a month done of his three-month time, and the road crew had worked in Rio Seco, along the main freeway that ran through the city. He'd found a matchbook with an elegant, every-colored parrot glossy on the cover. One match left. The bird sat inside a fancy letter P, and on the back "Palms Resort Hotel and Country Club" curled across the shiny white. He stared at the parrot, saw his son's face rapt at the pet store, the vivid reds and yellows, blues and greens of the perfect feathers, and he'd put the matchbook in his pocket. Only two hours later, during the afternoon when the traffic from L.A. back to Rio Seco got heavy and slow, he'd seen Louis.

The Sixth Street exit, main offramp to the Westside, the last place he wanted to be in his bright orange county uniform, matching plastic bag in his fist, the outhouse bobbing along on the truck next to him and Jesus. He'd just dropped another nasty disposable diaper into the bag, and then he heard a thundering drum from a car stereo, jumping against his skin it was so deep and loud. When he turned, Louis' face was just sliding back around, away from him. Louis said something to Jimmy, who was driving the Suzuki Samurai. What all the boys called the dope man's vehicle of choice. Roscoe knew Louis wasn't dealing, but he hung around with Jimmy, partied with him and Lester. The Suzuki was caught on the offramp just ahead of him, and the bass thump went through Roscoe's ribs to his heart, it felt like; Louis didn't turn around, kept his shoulders tight until the music began to fade up the ramp to the green light.

Hell, what had he wanted the boy to do? Wave? Pass him a swig of soda? Holler out, "Thanks for going to jail for me, Pops?" Roscoe listened to the grumpy voices scattered through the bus. Damn, he thought, I'm too old for this shit. He pulled out the matchbook from his pocket, looked at the parrot. Birdman—that was Louis' nickname.

Shit, and whoever was working that evil on him had stirred something into something for the last two days, because when he looked up the desert was butting up against Palm Springs; he flipped the matchbook over to read the script again, shook his head. He'd been born in Palm Springs, hadn't been out this way for years. *Damn,* he was too old for this. Jesus started up again about his wife, the child support he couldn't pay, which was why he got picked up. He was getting out in two weeks, he whined, how was he gonna pay it now that he'd done time for three months? "Man, shut the fuck up," Williams said from across the aisle. "I'm so tired a hearin about your wife I'm ready to kill you so the bitch can get Social Security." The men laughed, and the bus tires crunched on the gritty sand at the edge of the highway just outside Palm Springs, pulling off to let the first ones out.

They didn't double up out here. The trash was scattered by the wind that swept through the desert every day, the wind he remembered from his childhood when it tossed and rubbed sand against the walls of their tiny house on Indian land. Not as much garbage stayed beside the road in the desert, not like the city freeways that they usually worked. All the Rio Seco County system, that stretched to the edge of Los Angeles County and came the other way almost to San Diego. Near the cities, the clothes and cans, shoes and icechests were thick in the oleander and ice plant along the banks, and he was always teamed with Jesus. He'd thought it would be better to work alone, instead of hearing Jesus complain all day, but now he thought that Jesus and his laments about wife and money were almost song-like. Yeah, a boring, repetitive song, but background music, where you could listen if you didn't want to let your brain work. And Jesus was a couple of miles ahead, probably talking to himself.

The wind blew the bag against Roscoe's legs and he stood, looking down from the roadside at the shifting grains of dust. The sun was winter-bright, and he felt his cheeks rise close to his eyes. He still looked young, not many lines around his eyes because he'd always worn a hat when he worked, he thought; no lines around his mouth because he didn't smile. All those years of trimming trees, hauling brush and branches to the dump with Red Man, but his skin was still smooth. Yeah, and so? So the judge hadn't believed he was almost forty-two when he sentenced him to road camp. Usually the younger guys got camp.

Red Man was only a few years older than Roscoe, but he looked sixty from all his squinting and frowning and laughing in the sun. If my brain could have wrinkles, though, Roscoe thought, from too much frowning and squinting and shit, it would damn sure be cracked and lined as the mud down there. The ditch that cut between the railroad track and the highway was dry patchwork. Like a quilt, he thought, mud in little patches, the edges curled up because no one had sewn them down. He stood very still, didn't feel the twisting bag slick against his arm, and saw the image, all colors and the rims of the mud squares, and then a car passed, tore a seam through the air. How poetic. He bent to the ground. Yeah, put another Coors can in the bag. You're not a poet anymore. Pick up the trash and leave the metaphors in the ditch.

But they kept coming, made everything look like what it wasn't. The brittle bush with stiff gray branches, bare clumps in winter, caught Kleenex and baggies and wrappers; some of the plants had so much shredded tissue hanging from the stems that they looked like cotton, ready to pick.

"Niggers and Mexicans picking cotton," he said into the wind. A Cadillac rushed past, going at least eighty, and he shouted, "Your tax dollars hard at work." Only February and hot as hell, sweat already between my shoulders, but don't worry about us in the heat. That's why we were imported from Africa in the first place, remember? We could stand it better than those paleface settler types. And Mexicans, they *beg* to work in the fields, right?

He pulled at the tissue. Where had he seen cotton? He walked, saw the long stretches of fields, the huge bales of picked cotton and the snowlike traces in the ditches by the road. The Golden State Freeway, Interstate 5, from L.A. all the way to up near Oakland, and he'd been riding with Claude Collins, keeping him company on his trucking route. Claude had stopped the truck for Roscoe, smiled when Roscoe got out and said, "Man, I've only seen this stuff in pictures! Look at it. King Cotton!"

"I seen enough of that in Mi-sippi to last me till I die, man. Get back in here, we got time to make," Claude said, shaking his head.

Everyone on the Westside—Red Man, Claude, Lanier, Floyd, their wives—they were all from Mississippi, Louisiana, Oklahoma. They laughed at Roscoe when he talked about being born in Palm Springs. He watched the cars flying past. "With me you got the best of both worlds today! How would you know that?" he shouted, asking them. "A nigger born in the desert, got some Mexican blood, some Agua Caliente Indian somewhere in here." He saw the hills purple behind the cars. "No, you say, you didn't know niggers *lived* in Palm Springs! Don't let that stop you—you gotta get to Palm Canyon Drive, to the shopping." He thought of bumper stickers he'd seen—Born to Shop, and Shop Til You Drop—and laughed.

"Those Indians owned all that land you heading to," he said to a dark blue Mercedes, taking out his matchbook again. Section 14, the only place colored people could settle when his father came from Mississippi, and since the Indians owned it, the few white people that he saw when he was small were selling something or collecting money. But it was all underneath hotels now. When he was eighteen, in what—'66?—the resorts wanted Section 14, so all the houses were condemned. No one would sell them land, except on the Northside of the city, another square, and Roscoe told his father he was leaving. "Ain't nobody telling me where I can live," he said, and his father shouted, "All them hotels goin up, you know you gon get a good job. Where the hell you think you goin?"

"To L.A. I'm a poet," Roscoe said, and his father laughed, threw balled-up sheets of notebook paper at him.

"You gon write poems to the bank?" he yelled. "You fixin to eat them goddamn poems?"

Roscoe touched the brittle bushes now, stroked the spiny branches, the spires. Blowing air out through his nose, he shrugged his shoulders. The first poem he'd ever written was for a bush. He walked through the desert, going home from high school, and close to the road he saw a big, pointed bush; someone must have emptied out an ashtray there, because butterscotch wrappers, deep clear gold, and foil from chocolate kisses studded the branches. In the desert sunlight, it was a Christmas tree, glittered and reflecting against his arms, and he wrote a poem for the bush. His English teacher said it was very good, but not what she'd expected from him. "Aren't there things you want to write about from your experience, your race?" she said.

The flatbed with the guards came toward him slowly, and he saw the outhouse rocking in the wind. He turned away. Nobody ever used it—there were plenty of bushes, gullies, where you could pee. And you held the other till you got back to "the facility."

Frayed steel belts, black and flattened like dead snakes, lay along the asphalt. He kept walking. They didn't keep an eye on you as close out here; where you gonna run? Long way to anything. And you definitely weren't getting a ride from somebody passing by—nothing but Cadillacs, BMWs, Mercedes filled with one kind of people, and the four-by-four trucks carrying off-road vehicles and the other kind that came out here. Less than likely to pick up a brother.

They were driving like maniacs, too, and the traffic was getting heavier. Why were there so many cars today? He paused to pull a piece of white plastic from a stretch of barbed wire; the wind puffed it tight as a pillow between the strands. OK, it was Friday, and Monday was a holiday. Presidents' Day, uh-huh, people starting their patriotism early.

The trucks weaved around the older people who cruised stately in their big tanks. A few trucks even passed on the shoulder, raising swirls of dust down the road from Roscoe. Shit, if he did that once he'd get a ticket so fast the dirt wouldn't have time to settle. He wondered whether the Rio Seco cops would be giving him tickets for the rest of his life, to pay him back, or if the three months he was doing would be enough to turn him into a good nigger. Three months time for tickets.

After the two white policemen had been shot on the Westside in 1973, he'd been taken down to the station along with every other black male wearing white shoes. That was what the suspects wore. How old had he been? He tied the plastic bag closed and left it on the edge of the road. He'd come to Rio Seco from L.A.; he was twenty-two. Spent a weekend in jail with all the other Westsiders, getting yelled at, threatened. "Who shot them?" over and over.

Then last summer, an addict named Ricky Ronrico shot two cops coming for him on a parole violation. Shot them on the other end of the city, but of course they came looking for Ronrico on the Westside. And they'd been about to take Louis by the second night, because he and Lester and Jimmy were fool enough to stand on the corner and talk shit on that long weekend when cops were everywhere and angry. Rio Seco's finest cruised past again and again, and when Louis came in the house, Roscoe said, "go in the back room and shut up," even though he hadn't seen Louis for a couple of weeks. The two officers were in the process of tearing up the living room, talking about evidence and getting ready to work their way to the back, and Roscoe stood there and hollered that he'd sue till he was blue. The call came over their radio that Ricky Ronrico was found, in a house on the south end next door to where the shooting took place, but the next week, Roscoe started to get tickets.

The officers did it practiced and perfect as he and Red Man clearing out the trees and brush from a vacant lot. Red Man with the chainsaw, then Roscoe with the stumper, chewing the wood to chips. The motorcycle cop, stationed around the corner from Roscoe's house, then his buddy, pulling Roscoe over about a mile away to tell him he'd been weaving or making illegal lane changes. Fix-it ticket for the broken windshield on the truck. No seat belt, no insurance— that was a hundred bucks. Another seat-belter, and then no car seat for his baby granddaughter, Louis' girl. "And how you gon tell me what I have to do by law to save my life, or hers?" he said to the motorcycle cop, and the man's sunglasses slid closer to his moustache. Warrants were out by then, and when Roscoe's arms wouldn't meet behind his back because of their shortness and muscle, it was obvious that he was resisting arrest.

The Westside was cleaned out—some went for receiving stolen property just after two white guys came by selling tools and gardening equipment, and some went for old warrants. Make us all good niggers for another ten years.

And Louis was still in the streets, Red Man wrote in his letters. Nobody was at Roscoe's house; his granddaughter, whose mother had dropped her off with Louis, a three-month-old baby, and never come back, was with Big Ma. Around the corner from Red Man's house. Maybe they'd come to visit this weekend.

He heard droning from up ahead, a constant whining like giant wasps or mosquitoes, and he walked faster until he reached the bridge over a dry wash. A long line of four-by-four trucks was parked in the dusty streambed, in the shade of the bridge, and women sat in the truckbeds sipping drinks and watching the men and boys ride up and down the hills in their three-wheelers. The tracks crisscrossed the hills like ribbons, like the land was giftwrapped. Roscoe stared at the precise trails, but then he felt the riders begin to watch him, and heads turned to look. He walked off the bridge, away from the high buzzing and the smiles.

A forest of wind machines stood still and idle past the bridge. The wind scoured his ears, hot and insistent, but the blades didn't turn, and he remembered that some doctor Red Man cut yards for told him that the machines were tax shelters. It didn't matter if they worked. To Roscoe, they looked like trees, trees a maniac had pruned.

When he first began trimming trees, after he'd come to Rio Seco and gotten a gardening job at the university, he'd been afraid to cut too many branches. The supervisor yelled at him until he got ruthless, pruned them right. When Roscoe met Red Man, while they took their breaks and watched the students, he'd shown Red Man the poems about palm trees, about cars and women. But he'd never gotten any of them published; people he sent them to wrote back to say that a black poet had an obligation to write about his race, or that they didn't understand how his imagery fit with power and revolution.

He and Red Man quit the university to start their own gardening and tree-trimming business. Louis was three, Roscoe's wife Joyce was mad, and she left, went back to L.A., saying any fool who quit a job with benefits for a beat-up truck and climbing trees was too foolish to support *her* right. Roscoe told her to go to Palm Springs, visit his father's grave, and tell his father all about it. When she was killed in a car accident, her sister brought Louis back to Rio Seco, to live with Roscoe. Louis was six then, tall and thin, with fingers long as these brittle stems. He was quiet for months, walking around the yard, looking at the trees and birds, at Roscoe; he'd seemed soft, too quiet, but then he began to play with Red Man's sons, shooting baskets in their driveway.

Roscoe looked back at the wind machines, then ahead to the long stretch until the hill where he was supposed to stop for lunch.

Nothing now but barbed-wire fence and telephone poles straddling the gully. He went partway down into the ditch and peed in a long crack that rainwater had worn into the bank. A red hawk bore down suddenly and landed on one of the telephone poles near him, settling to look out over the desert for rabbits. Roscoe stayed still for a moment after he'd zipped up his pants, but the hawk didn't even turn.

The red hawks still hunted the fields near the Westside; he wondered if Louis ever watched them now, hurt his neck looking up for so long, the way he had when he was small.

His son had always been in a trance when the flocks of crows passed over the house in winter, at five-thirty every night, Louis told Roscoe. It took them an hour to cross the sky, crowds of them and then a few stragglers, more pecking and fighting in a stream of black. They nested near the river-bottom, Louis said. He had books with pictures of every bird in North America, and he waited for robins, scrub jays, any of the birds with color. Once he came running inside to tell Roscoe he'd seen a cedar waxwing in the fig tree. Roscoe had said, "Okay, and now he's probably gone. And?"

The kids called Louis "Birdman" one summer when colored feathers were all he looked for in the streets; they laughed at him, pulled him away to the gym to play basketball. And the name got confused when he was in high school, when he was six-five and his hands as big as fig leaves, when the coach pressed him to play harder, to jump, and everyone thought he'd been called Birdman because he could leap. He had a vertical of forty-two inches, but the coaches said he was lazy, that his mind was always somewhere else. Roscoe hollered at him, told him if he didn't start playing better, he'd never get to college, and Louis began then to keep his face as distant and new as when he'd been six.

Roscoe came up out of the gully; he couldn't be disappearing like that for too long. The hawk swept down from the pole, but not because of him, he saw; it curved toward a spot far into the desert, and snatched something off the ground.

Roscoe faced the traffic coming toward him, and now the cars were moving so slowly faces were visible in the windows. A winter holiday in Palm Springs. Snowbirds—what the older tourists from Canada and the colder states were called, the ones who crowded the desert every winter. He saw them stare at him, saw small dogs in the windows sometimes. The kind that were either wrinkled or shaved, pressing their noses to the glass to see him. Some of the cars had kids in the back seats, and he watched all the mouths in those cars moving. "I'm on the chain gang," he said into the wind they made, and he knew all the windows were rolled up anyway. The parents were telling their kids, "Those men in orange are bad men. They committed crimes, and now they have to pick up trash."

Yeah, I *am* a bad man, he thought. I did lots of bad things. He couldn't stop seeing Louis' face kept turned away from him, the Suzuki pumping out music, and these faces all turned to watch him in silence, the purr of expensive motors lost in the racing air.

He'd done bad things. He'd taken Louis up that same highway where cotton laced the barbed-wire fences, up I-5. A small state college in Northern California had offered Louis a basketball scholarship, a free ride, and Roscoe drove him there in the truck, motor rattling loud in the cab. Louis had never been past L.A., and Roscoe hadn't gone anywhere since riding with Claude years before. Hawks sat on fenceposts along the road, and Louis' head swiveled to look at each one. His voice grew higher, excited, while he ignored Roscoe's talk about basketball and the team. "Look," Louis said, "the hawks guarding those fields. Like each one is saying, okay, this is my thirty-nine posts, and don't none a you come near them. I wonder if it's thirty-nine . . ."

He chanted words to Roscoe, to the window, all the way north. "Egrets," he shouted, and Roscoe hadn't heard him so loud, sitting so close to him, ever before. "I can't believe it, a crane, look, standing in that water by the field!"

Mud nests were mounded on the cement overpasses, made by

swallows, Louis said, and once they saw a shimmering tornado of blackbirds rise from a plowed section of land, bodies turning and twisting in perfect unison, swirling and riding to fall and curve back against the sky. Louis was silent for a long time. And when they came closer to the college, Roscoe told him to forget about the bird foolishness and start thinking about practice. It would be harder than high school, and he didn't want anyone telling him his son was lazy and absentminded.

Like his own father had told him, all day, every day, in Palm Springs. Roscoe couldn't stop himself, though, his voice deep and harsh, saying, "You want to see some birds, buy a canary. Put him in your dorm room, and he can sing to you after you win."

On the way back down, after he'd seen the coach, shaken hands a couple hundred times and left Louis in the gym office, thick fog had settled near the college, and all the way down the interstate. Tule fog, he remembered Claude calling it. He could barely see the fences, the hawks hunched down into their thick necks, feathers puffed ragged against the cold wind. They were too close together on the posts, he found himself thinking, watching, and quickly he was angry. Who gave a damn about how close the birds were to each other? But when he passed the exits for Bakersfield, the sun came back, and he stopped to stretch. One of the big white birds that had made Louis' voice jump high in the cab stalked near a pool of irrigation runoff. Was that an egret? It was clean, stark white as the new socks he'd bought for Louis, and with a long, curved neck held high, the bird looked tall as a child.

Roscoe dropped another orange bag. People were still staring at him, he knew, but then he saw a circle of clear, blue-green water ahead, sparkling, wavering in the heat. He almost ran to be closer, and came to a mound of broken windshield glass in a small turnout, aqua chunks that were so greenish moss could be under their surfaces. He didn't even look at the strips of tire nearby, the burned car seats. He laid the new plastic bag down and sat on a rock near the glass, imagined it water. Not much water in Rio Seco; dry river, that was what the city had been named for. But Louis went to the man-made lake with the other boys, and they told Roscoe that while they fished and caught crawdads to boil for dinner, Louis watched the ducks, the geese. They laughed at him, said to Roscoe, "We told him he can't eat no duck, but homeboy wanna feed them ducks. Don't come home with nothin, either."

Louis lasted only a year at the college. He came back to the Westside loud and telling everyone he didn't get enough playing time, in a hick town anyway. No soul, nothing to do. Shit, Roscoe thought, listening to the plastic bag ripple near him, what would he have done learning about birds? Be a professor of birds? What was that word—he'd known when he worked at the university. It came to him after a few minutes—ornithology. Yeah, and what was Louis going to do with that? Look through some binoculars?

He could have been a dope dealer anyway, taught trained pigeons to deliver bags of rock cocaine that Lester and Jimmy sold. Hell, I don't know.

Roscoe heard a low noise, knew the flatbed, the outhouse, the guards were coming up the shoulder of the road, passing the stalled traffic. I don't give a shit, I ain't getting up. Crow time was long over, it was almost lunchtime. But cat time would be the hardest—when the afternoon turned purple and he was back at the facility, when the evening was coming fast and Louis used to say, "Why do the cats come out now? How come they all sit on the porches at the same time? How do they know what time it is?"

Roscoe pulled at his eyebrows, listened to the flatbed with his eyes trained on the glass. The mockingbirds would have a songfight again tonight. He closed his eyes to keep the heat inside them. He'd never known what to answer when Louis asked, when he sat at the edge of his father's bed. "Why's the mockingbird singing *now?* It's three in the morning."

"He's drunk."

"No, Daddy, he ain't singing like he's drunk. Like he's sending a message."

"Message is go to sleep."

When he woke again, Louis's eyes were shining, reflected in the streetlight. An hour had passed, and he was still listening, trying to decipher the song.

esther's

Esther flicked salt into the pie dough and gathered up the sticky ball to roll out crusts for the two quiches. Fitting them into the pretty crimp-edged dishes, crumbling bacon onto the bottom of each, she didn't even have to look at her hands. From the kitchen window, she saw the baby's wet clothes hanging on the drying rack she used specially for them—the tiny squares were all fit together like a quilt, pale in the sun. She sprinkled onions onto the bacon. Quiche Lorraine. She couldn't even remember where she'd first seen the recipe, or why she'd made it, but now everyone on the Westside expected it when they came to the house. Dense, creamy stuff with flaky crust, something no one else she knew ever made.

Quiche Esther. With greens folded in thick, soft strips through the eggs and cheese. She pulled the collards from their pot to press the water out; chicken spattered in the frying pan next to her. Cole slaw already chilling in the refrigerator. Rich green water trailed from under the wooden spoon when she pushed at the greens, and then she saw a square of red blur past the window. A slow blur. Yeah, there she went again—the woman driving the sportscar. What was it? A Triumph, Joe had told her. Esther's husband Joe loved him some cars. And this woman driving past loved her some Joe.

"She's out there again," Esther called toward the living room, where Regina was keeping Arlene company, but they must not have heard, because they would have run into the kitchen in a minute to see what she looked like.

She cruised by slow enough that Esther met her eyes. Cinnamon skin, straightened hair in a bob, and Esther could tell just by the way she held her head that her nails were long and perfect, her eyelashes curled and thickened to fans. Esther smiled into the glass. And the woman's hand came out the car window, graceful as a nodding flower, to rest on the edge of the door; wrist smooth, thin, no strong pushing-out veins and long blunt fingers like Esther's. The car crept away slow as a pillbug, Esther still smiling, but when it was gone she felt nervous warmth in her chest.

"This girl wants my husband bad," she said out loud, pressing the greens one last time and laying them over the bacon. She paused at the sink, staring at the lime tint from the greens water—was that the baby crying? No. But she heard Regina and Arlene from the living room. Now how in the world did they get started talking about that?

"Uh-uh, she had extensions. That girl's hair was real thin, you could tell. Them pale, pale blondes don't have no thick hair, not enough for all the braids she had in that movie."

"I don't know, Regina. I saw her on TV later, and her hair was pretty long."

"I didn't say it wasn't *long*. I said if she didn't have nobody else's hair put in we wouldn'ta seen nothing but ten braids and a whole lotta scalp."

"And after the movie came out, all the white girls started wearing cornrows. Talking about Bo Derek created the look."

Regina snorted. "Shit. Esther was doing some bad braids years before Slow Bo ever showed up."

Esther walked into the living room, laughing at Regina bent over a magazine. She'd figured—Regina read every magazine Esther kept for customers, and thought it was her job to tell them what was important. "Arlene, you come all the way from L.A. just to listen to this crazy woman, or you want me to do your hair?" Esther laid the hair she'd bought for Arlene on the table.

Arlene pressed a forefinger into Regina's soft shoulder. "She *is* the news," she said. "No, Esther, you know I've been waiting for two months for you to do me. I forgot you always take off with each baby."

Esther bent to the bassinet, where the baby slept with her face crushed to the pad, fat cheek twitching. "Look, she's smiling those fake smiles," Esther said, and the women came to see. "Those little jerky ones in her sleep, where she doesn't even know what's making her happy." The grins flashed and left the baby lips quick as sparks.

"Sweet dreams," Regina said. "Dream 'em now."

"Where you want to sit?" Esther asked Arlene. It would take all day and some of the evening to do what Arlene wanted—rows curving around her perfect forehead, all to the right side except three braids woven with gold thread around her left ear, those tiny tails hanging alone to sparkle.

"Start on the floor, I guess," she said. "You comfortable on the couch?"

"I better be comfortable anywhere," Esther said, "we only got an hour before the baby want to eat again." She held up some of the bought hair to Arlene's. The same brown, lit with copper way inside. She smiled. That was why women always came back to her, because she matched the hair perfectly, braided it so that their faces came first. Nobody left her house with hair looking like it belonged on somebody else.

"She keeps driving by," Esther said, parting and pushing Arlene's hair.

"Uh-uh. While you was in the kitchen?" Regina said, eyebrows jumping.

"I don't know what she wants me to do," Esther said.

"Who's this?" Arlene asked.

"Woman from Oakland," Esther said, knowing Regina's eyes were on her.

"Yeah, she got a *fatal* attraction for Joe Killer," Regina said.

"I never knew how he got that name," Arlene said.

"You know that song, 'Killer Joe . . . ' " Regina hummed. "When we was in school, Joe was so pretty somebody called him that, and he said, 'not me, I'm Joe Killer." She looked at Esther, checking, and Esther smiled.

"Everybody had big naturals then, remember?" Esther said. "And Joe's was so big he couldn't fit through the classroom doors sometimes."

"Y'all telling some lies now." Arlene laughed.

"No, now, serious. He was real light, had that hair—the girls use to fall out for him." Regina touched the bassinet and sat down at the kitchen table, where the napkins and paper plates were arranged. "Joe Killer." She looked at the TV. "Esther, Frank came by the other day and said that woman done bought her a condo up there in Hillgrove. She got a job at Rohr—some kinda executive secretary."

"How Frank know?"

"His cousin works out there. I guess she talks a lot, this woman, I mean."

Esther could feel by the strain in Arlene's neck that she wanted to know more, so she said what she always did when she wanted to think. "I have to do this—lemme get it right, now."

Arlene's head tilted very slightly toward the TV, and Esther watched her own fingers splay out, pinch back again and again in the hair. The fingers were ashy up by the knuckles, from doing the baby's wash, and glistening black at the tips from the light hairdress. You so black you sweat coffee. She and Regina and the other girls had been standing around the steps in high school, years ago, and when she'd tried to loudtalk Alvin James, "Shut up, Esther, you so black you sweat coffee" rang against the brick walls.

"Yeah, brother, and I'm so light I sweat cream." Joe Killer said it with a warning in his gray eyes. The first time he'd ever acknowledged the time he spent with her—Alvin jumped back dramatically and said, "Joe Killer, is that *you,* man?"

"That's *me,* brother." Esther thought now that she hadn't heard anyone say that in years. The boys told each other who they were attached to, in those words, who they had *become.* Joe was her.

They always waited for her to speak again first. "Arlene, you wouldn't believe this woman," she said. "Now Joe been had his flings, it's a part of him, and I told myself I couldn't mind. Tell me I'm crazy, but George Green, used to be the history teacher at the high school, remember him, Regina? He would talk about how in Africa, men had several wives because they had to—men got killed in war, hunting, and women needed a break between babies."

"Yeah, easy to say and hard to do," Arlene said.

"But I had the first three babies all in a row, so quick, and I was always tired. I told Joe, serious, he was on the road driving the truck, and I told him go on and have some fun. I won't lie, it hurt the first couple of times he told me he did something. Cause he always told me." She swept loose hairs into her hand. "When he came home, I wasn't *waiting* for it. I waited for him, but not the bed."

"Come on, everybody's love come down," Regina said. "Shoot, Victor too damn tired to do anything when he come home."

"Regina, I'm not trying to prove Joe's a stud." She shook her head. "Forget it."

"No, come on with it." Arlene's head pulled against Esther's fingers.

"That's just the way things work. Except this woman from Oakland thinks she's taking him away."

Regina said, "The baby's wakin up. I'ma get her. What you think Miss Oaktown plannin to do?"

Esther stopped and looked at the baby's bobbing head. "I don't know. Come in here and whup me? Drive by till I move? Huh."

Stroking the baby's shoulder, Esther felt those long pauses when the sucking slowed, the eyes flickered, and then the lips pulled again hurriedly like the baby thought she'd never eat again. She looked at Arlene, watching the first of the soaps with Regina, and thought that the braids were coming along nice. Esther felt tiredness fan out across her back, and she wished Green Hollows hadn't been demolished. All the old people had lived there, and Miss Rosa used to walk up from her house in the hollow every day, to cook the chicken and do the salads, until she'd had to move. Now Esther had to start cooking before 7:00, and then do the wash and clean before people came. The baby dug her bare toes into Esther's leg, and shoes walked across her brain. She'd had to buy new ones for the four older kids last week; Colette, the baby, no, not the baby anymore, Colette was in kindergarten now and wanted a backpack like the others.

Why was she up here thinking about money? She always made plenty between the braiding and the food; chicken was bulk at the warehouse; she bought cheap bacon because it was just the trace of flavor the quiches needed, and the greens were free. Her greens tree, the one Red Man had given her years ago, gnarled strong and thick up the fence in the back.

Two dollars a plate. Money wasn't doing this to her scalp, itching and pulling worry tight around her ears. She could have gotten a job years ago, when she took clerical courses at the city college, but she liked staying home with the babies. Spending a whole hour staring at them: the tiny arms were so straight, only two deep wrinkles and a dimple for an elbow, the knuckles just dots where the fingers began. She felt this baby's head heavy against her arm now, the thick folds of neck stretching when she lolled back. Joe brought home enough money. But he hadn't called today, and lunchtime was coming. She drew her fingers backwards against her eyebrows, down her nose.

"I'ma put Porscha in the back room to sleep, so she'll take a long nap," Esther said.

Arlene walked over to touch the baby's soft curls. "Look at that hair. She was sleeping so good in here, let her stay." Esther dipped her head in a question. "She smells like baby so strong I get it all across the room," Arlene said, embarrassed. "I always loved that smell."

But Esther walked down the hallway. She knew the baby would sleep fine in the bassinet, but she wanted five more minutes with her. Sliding her onto the crib sheet belly-first, she laid a hand on the skin so perfect, so light. All the children were gold, with Joe's neat small eyebrows and nose. What had they gotten from her? Only her hands, she thought, big and square. And the half she'd given to the gold, the darkness added to Joe's light. Perfect skin—she loved to stare at them when they were too small to know she was looking— no scars on their cheeks, no lines around their mouths. Glossy eyes and unmarked as girls in the magazines on the coffee table, there for customers. I'm standing here thinking this way because of her, she thought. Because I know each baby comes home and people say, "Lucky it ain't black as Esther. Blueblood kids got it hard." And the women, all these years, talking about, "Why Joe Killer want to stay with old black Esther? Don't know how he find her in the dark to make all them babies." She put the heels of her hands to her neck and went back to the front room.

"Why you name her Porscha?" Arlene asked when Esther picked up another section of hair.

"I didn't, I let Joe name her. He named the first one, and he want- ed a Lil Joe. He said he would name this last one. 'I ain't never gon be able to buy what I really want, so I'ma call her Porscha, closest I'll get to having me one in my name.' "

Regina said, "All your kids got pretty names. Lil Joe the only com- mon one."

Esther said, "Yeah, I always wanted them to know right off when somebody was calling them. Nobody's likely to say 'Danique who?'"

"How old is Danique now?" Arlene said.

"Huh. Lil Joe's eleven, Danique just turned nine, Anaïs is . . . seven. Colette's six. The names—I found them at French class. That's where I met Joe."

"You a lie," Regina said. "I don't remember that."

"You weren't there," Esther laughed. "Serious. His mama's Creole from Louisiana, and she had some idea Joe should be speaking French. I was taking it for college, and we were the only soul in there, I mean nothing *but* prep-track white kids."

"And you named your kids after some gray boys?"

"Can Joe speak French?" Arlene said.

"Ha! Copied offa me every day. Barely says *quiche* right." Esther tilted Arlene's head. "So in the French book I read about these two women, Anais Nin and Colette. I knew Anaïs was a woman's name, but when he was born, he was so pale, didn't get any color for a year. Light as that French woman's picture, and all this black hair straight in points over his forehead. Fringing down like a girl. The name looked like him."

"That hair got nappy soon enough," Regina said.

"Anaïs and Colette. What about Danique?" Arlene asked.

"I made that up." Esther smiled.

"Ooh, look at what that boy up to now!" Regina called, standing by the TV, and Arlene listened to "All My Children." Esther never paid much attention to the soaps, even though they were on all day for Regina. She felt something connect, something she'd been puzzling out earlier . . . the quiche recipe. It was in that French textbook, too. Essays about food, wine, Edith Piaf. But Edith was just too ugly to name a child, she smiled to herself. That was what she'd thought. And Lil Joe came the next year, after she'd graduated and was going to Rio Seco City College. She'd been braiding hair already, for friends, then, experimenting, and somebody offered her twenty-five dollars to do braids for her wedding.

A man's voice crashed though the screen door, making everyone jump. "Esther, get out here and see if you want this old ugly thang." She saw Floyd, who lived across the street; he and his nephew Snooter had backed their truck into her driveway, and a long couch poked out the end of the truckbed.

"I ain't never seen a couch *that* long," Regina said. "Who gon give you a couch?"

"Your mama called me into Miss Lindstrom's house," Floyd said. "She said Miss Linsey getting rid of this, got all new furniture. I told your mama it need to go to the dump, it's so ugly, but she said bring it to you."

The fabric was faded brocade, dull and gold, but the couch could fit six people easily, Esther thought. "Tina can cover it for me."

Floyd and Snooter carried it to the edge of the front steps. "How old is Miss Linsey now?" Esther asked, giving Floyd some sun tea.

"Eighty somethin," Snooter said.

"Your mama been workin for her long as I been cutting grass," Floyd said, wiping his forehead with his hat. "All the other domestics I see now are Mexican. Berta the only one left to talk to. You make that pie this week? You done taken enough time off with that baby?"

Esther brought them each a plate, and they sat on the steps. "Where Joe Killer this week?" Snooter asked.

"He had to take some furniture to Nashville. He said he'd be home to barbecue this weekend." But he still hadn't called, and it was way past noon.

Snooter bit into the chicken and said, "Oh, shit." Esther looked back quickly, but it was because Marcella and Gail had pulled up.

"You never came by to see me, fool man," Gail said, lip poked out at Snooter. "You was gon bring by a video."

"Y'all got lunch break already?" Esther said. "Let me go inside and get back to Arlene." But Marcella pulled her arm.

"Somebody want you, Esther," she said, nodding toward the street.

"Where she gon park?" Floyd said. "You want me to move the truck?"

"I don't think she's fixing to stop," Esther said, and the red Triumph went past, a little faster this time.

"This is Arlene, ladies. She came in from L.A., and today's her only day off, so I need to stop messing around."

Marcella nodded. "Ain't you Tina's cousin?"

"Uh-huh, that's how she came to me," Esther said.

"And who is this? I've never seen her," Marcella said at the table, where Regina sat.

"Shut up, girl," Regina frowned. She always waited for someone else to start eating before she broke down.

"What the news?" Gail asked. Regina looked at Esther.

"Somebody named Miss Oaktown," Esther said.

"She trying to maneuver," Regina said, cutting into the quiche.

"That girl in the red car looking fire at you?" Marcella said, and Esther nodded. She could tell by the way Arlene's head swayed slightly that she was sleepy, and she remembered her mother's warm fingers in her own hair. Only a few times had she sat and braided Esther's hair—usually she was too tired when she came home from somebody else's dinner. And she pushed Esther away when Esther tried to soothe her, to touch her stiff curls. "Just let me get some rest, now," she always said. "Go on."

And here she was, waiting for Porscha to wake up again, to make those little snuffling sounds that Esther could hear all the way in the front yard; none of her babies ever had to cry before she knew they wanted her.

This was the last baby. Every time Esther fed her, held a foot in her hand while the cheek pressed into her breast, she thought that the helplessness, the stare into her eyes, would be over too quickly. She had measured and compared everything by baby standards for so long, by baby feel—the plump curve of Arlene's chin when Esther cupped her hand underneath to lift the head: that was soft and padded as baby knees. Regina's lips were full and lush as a nursing mouth. Esther listened, but she didn't hear any soft sounds underneath the laughter and talking, the television and the cars passing in the street.

When they started to pull against her hands, to sit up, she loved that, too. Teaching them to hold things, to walk, to read . . . somebody had said to her once, "They like kittens, and then they just cats and nobody want em," and Esther got angry. Lil Joe's wrists turned bony as his arms grew, his two extra chins disappeared, and she watched breathlessly when his eyes got harder as he figured things out for himself.

It was one o'clock. Maybe Joe had found another woman in Nashville, serious this time. No, come on. But maybe he'd gone to Oaktown's condo first, maybe he was back in Rio Seco already.

"Esther, what these kids doing home so early?" Regina hollered, and Esther frowned, blinked. Lil Joe, Danique, all of them were trooping in the kitchen door with their backpacks trailing.

"Teachers got some kind of meeting today," Lil Joe said. "Half day of school is all."

"They never had that when we were in school," Marcella said.

"Where's baby Porscha, Mama?" Colette alternated between kissing her sister's hands and refusing to touch her. Esther thought, she's been the baby for so long. "Go see," she said to Colette.

Lil Joe went back with her and came out holding Porscha. "She was rooting around like that pig we seen in the movie," he said, pushing his nose against her stomach. "Beat box belly on the baby," he blew against her skin.

"Arlene, I'ma feed her. Lay down and take a nap," Esther said.

"No, I want to see the end of General Hospital."

Just as she opened her blouse, the phone rang, and Esther picked it up from the floor. "Hey," Joe said. "What up?"

"Feeding the baby." Esther felt the heat rise in her throat, rather than fall away. He sounded long distance. Am I going to think about that damn condo every morning. . .

"She still don't want nobody holding her unless they got groceries, huh?" he said. "That's my baby. I'ma be home tomorrow—I'm in Amarillo."

"You still planning to barbecue?" Esther asked. The baby pulled hard, and the sharp tingle of milk rushed down.

"Yeah. Why?"

"Thought maybe you had ideas about being busy."

"What you want, Esther? What you trying to talk about?"

"Your friend from up north got a condo. I heard."

"Shit, Esther. I told her about you. I told her find somebody else, that's why she's doing this. Man, you know. . ."

"I know she thinks different."

"I told her you my wife, Rio Seco my city, and she got mad. I'ma send Snooter over there—he'll make her forget about me real quick." Joe laughed, but low so he could hear what she did, as always. Esther imagined what the woman had said to Joe, how she'd laughed when she saw Esther through the window, in the yard. *This* wife with Joe Killer? she probably said to herself. She so . . .

"Don't even think about it," he said.

"Yeah," Esther said. "So easy for you to say."

"It's on you as much as on me," he said. "You want it this way. You told me after the baby. . ."

"I know. I just thought maybe you decided to have two in the same city."

"Don't even trip like that. She just thinks she's hard. I'll take care of it."

Esther laughed. "You sound so puffed up with yourself. Just get home because your kids want ribs and I ain't hardly cooking all that."

Marcella and Gail were washing their hands in the kitchen. And Regina was watching her. "Look at this mess on TV," Regina said. "You get in a accident, these lawyers are sure to get you some cash."

"Like hitting the lotto, girl," Gail said.

"Yeah, but your money would be gone so fast." Arlene shook her head. "People never hold onto a big lump of money like that."

"Let me hold her," Marcella said. "Me and Gail on split shift today."

"I wondered why you weren't in a hurry to get back," Esther said, while Porscha's eyes followed her all the way back to the couch. She pulled another section of hair from the long bolt.

"You always use good hair," Marcella said. "Where they get all that real stuff? They be making that cheap fiber hair, look fake, too."

"The lady at the supply store said it comes from Italy." Esther picked at the strands. "I always think of what they must look like, the ones that cut their hair. They don't make hardly any money for it."

Anaïs ran into the living room. "Mama, a white man standing in the yard writing."

"What? You got a policy man, Esther?" Gail asked.

"No, probably want to sell me a vacuum cleaner. Go tell him I don't want anything."

Lil Joe came in behind Anaïs. "His car got a picture on the door. City of Rio Seco."

Esther's heart beat fast. "Somebody from the city?" Joe had already called. But who came to tell you if somebody died? Her mother was at Miss Linsey's. Was something wrong with Joe's truck? He always parked it in the vacant lot at the end of the street. Illegal for sure.

The man waited at the door. "Good afternoon, ma'am. I'm from the city's licensing arm. Do you have a license to run this business?"

"What are you talking about?" Esther said.

"May I come in?" He followed her, stood looking at everyone. "Are you doing day care?"

"Huh? These kids are all mine."

He raised one brow fast as a roach, and dropped it. "Well, some- one called to say that. . ."

"To say we only allowed one kid now?" Esther stared. "Who called?"

"We had a complaint about the amount of traffic, the number of cars for a residence. It appears that you're operating some kind of business, and I'm just trying to ascertain for the city whether you're licensed."

"A license to have kids?"

"Is this a beauty and hair-care operation?" He stared at the hair from Italy as if it were a snake.

"I'm doing hair for my cousins."

"You have a lot of cousins." He smiled.

"We only allowed one cousin, too? Another new law?"

"Look, as I said, someone complained that cars were blocking the street."

"Don't make me ask about the limit on cars, too, now," Esther said, smiling. The street. "I think I know what the problem is, and it's not me." She looked at Regina. "Oaktown."

"No. How she do that?"

"She's a secretary." Esther pulled her lips up again, grinning fake as a dreaming Porscha. "We have a big family," she said to the man, and he looked at the basket on the table, filled with one dollar bills, surrounded by crumbs from the quiche crust.

"I'm sorry to barge in." He let Esther lead him out, and she watched him stare at the couch, make notes about the cars, Floyd's trucks.

"Poor Floyd," she called back into the living room. "They proba- bly gon get him for that expired tag now."

"And all because somebody jealous," Regina said.

"You think Joe knows?" Arlene asked. Esther stroked the Italian hair, watched Porscha's eyes squint with happiness when her mama's face come into view.

"No, he'd laugh silly. Pretty strange idea, to call the city."

"Where she get that?" Regina said.

"So that was it," Esther said. "That was her best shot." She stood up to catch Anaïs by the ears, steer him toward the table. He never wanted to eat in front of people, and her hand pushed steady at the back of his neck.

sweet thang

KAREN / OCTOBER

Victor Miles outlined the fly of his Levis with rhinestone studs back then. He wasn't fine, not pretty with a Jermaine Jackson face, and he had hard short hair, not a round natural to slide a comb or pencil in over his ear. He was stone-hard, but girls went for that, too. Never smiled, Karen thought, but his teeth showed when his lips were resting; strong bones under the skin, she knew, they made his mouth like that. He had pimp-walked around Rio Seco High when she was a freshman, talking yang to anyone—teachers, coaches, girls he didn't know. Come up behind a girl in the cafeteria line and grab her butt, not pat it on top but push his hand underneath, and Karen would see his teeth. "You want some, take some. You bad enough, get some." The guys would laugh.

He walked toward the convalescent home where she worked, coming from the church parking lot, pushing that leg down hard, stalking—it was him. And everything shone: his pants were double-knit, like ten years ago, and glossy with wear; his forehead and shoulders flashed with sweat—hot Halloween wind warmed the window where she stood in the day room—and his teeth glistened. Still showing through a not-smile, those hard lips. No Nikes or work boots like everyone else wore, but thin-soled black leather shoes, old like church deacons wore.

Nothing past Oleander Manor but bushes squaring the asphalt

strip by the kitchen, then the huge parking lot and the Methodist church that owned the home. Karen never saw people walking here at the bottom of the arroyo. Even the women plump as pigeons in the nubbly suits, the ones who came from the church on Sundays to visit people in beds, they drove across the parking lot to the Manor. On the other side of the street, fields stretched to the river-bottom. Where had Victor come from? Up the block was a Safeway, Flash Video, and a liquor store. Cool as ever, he swung past, and she slid her face against the glass to see.

After the lunch trays were washed and stacked, she began to open the huge cans of mixed fruit, looking at the muddy, thicked-up gravy she had left over. Damn. Lunch, dishes, trays, dinner, dishes, floors, trays, go home and cook something for Eddie and the kids. Wash up after them. She pulled out a Tareyton, felt the paper like baby skin against her fingers; her hands were rough as toast. Pushing open the kitchen door, she stood outside and faced the river-bottom. Smoke from the fire there had risen in fat rolls yesterday, but the wind flattened out the bruise-brown now, mixing it with the smog to stretch across the rim of horizon filmy and long. One of those nasty scarves the patients wrapped around their hair, or their necks, when somebody came to visit. She had hated the scarves when her mother brought them home from her ladies, who didn't want them anymore. Acting like Karen and her sister, Esther, might wear them. See-through things, sticky as spiderwebs.

Go and get a damn chair, she thought, leaning against the wall. Don't nobody ever sit in them chairs, so dirty orderlies have to hose them off every month or that white plastic blend in with the brown wall. The chairs were at the other side of the building, facing the corner and the stores. She tapped her cigarette against her wrist. Fool. Every night you wish it was something out here to sit on. Every night you stand here, chicken to move a chair. Scary, just like Nucoa and them always said in school. Scary to go to the bathroom because

somebody might kick your ass in there. Hold it all day. Scared a
you.

Nucoa was fixing to get fired. She must don't want this job, Karen
thought. She had seen Mrs. Baker's arm when she took an extra plate
of lemon slices to her room. Black and blue, same as last time Nucoa
started pinching. Old people got a different kind of bruise, skin like
paper and pale. The marks weren't the same as when her kids fell or
bumped. Sharp finger-purple bruises.

She lit a match just to see the wind blow it out, and from the high
humped roll of oleander bushes, leaves cracked and split. Karen held
herself still, the match smoke stinging past her nostrils, and the
sticks and stems rustled again, stopped. Lizards twitched around in
there during the summer and ran in all the fields, but it was fall now,
and that pressing down on dry stuff was too heavy for a lizard.
Maybe skunk or possum, she listened, but no snuffling or settling-
down sounds. I hate winter, she thought quickly, I hate when it gets
dark so fast, not even six o'clock and I can see the moon. Get home
and the house would be hot and close, stale as morning breath. Kids
already inside, hungry, nothing in the refrigerator. Echo with her
permanent snuffles, Eddie Jr. with a new scrape.

She moved inside the doorway, but she could still smell the food
from lunch, the air hanging at the jamb, belonging to the job.
The bushes were quiet. Nobody had eaten much today, and usually
they liked mashed potatoes and gravy. Winter wasn't coming right,
though, the wind hot as June, and holidays always put the old
people through changes. I needs me a day off, she thought, and I'ma
have to make turkey in three weeks—so they can all complain about
how it's not as good as theirs always was.

Nucoa pushed into the swinging door like she could smell smoke
all the way down the hall, talking about, "Give me a cigarette, Karen.
I don't got none today."

As if she ever do. "Nucoa, you don't need this paycheck, huh? You
think these old people won't tell?"

She knew what Karen was talking about. "Shit, you in the kitchen all day, you ain't gotta hear it."

"I hear it sometimes. So? They just old, they ain't got nobody to take it out on." She stepped inside to give Nucoa a cigarette, putting out her own. Leaning against the racks holding the trays, Nucoa tried to get gravy off her uniform.

"Nasty Mrs. Cottrell want to splat gravy at me. You ain't had to deal with it, girl. I'm tired a this shit."

Karen turned back to the doorway and looked across the asphalt, the gray rising to meet blurry night. "What you staring at?" Nucoa asked. "Waiting for a shooting star?" She laughed. "A UFO?"

"I hate winter. Dark in a second."

"Nighttime is the right time."

"Yeah, for you." She listened. "It's something rustling around in the bushes."

"I seen some wild dogs down in the river-bottom one time, when me and Marcella came down here after school. With Wendell and them driving around in the sand, acting a fool. German shepherds, mutts."

"Best not be no wild dogs, cause they'll get in the trash." Karen started filling up the bucket. When she bent to pour ammonia into the water, she saw Nucoa's long dark fingers scratch the white stocking at her ankle, and she remembered the pinch-marks. "You trying to lose the job, though, I'm serious," she said, and Nucoa sucked her teeth.

"Yeah, you could hang, Karen, but my mama always did say I had a temper." She sounded proud, and Karen felt anger pulling into her nose with the ammonia. Yeah, Karen don't get mad. She too scary. Scared a you. She stepped away from the rising sharp steam and said, "You ain't no better than Eddie Junior trying to get his little bit a power on Echo, push her when I'm not looking." Then the lighter flashed. "Nucoa, don't . . ." Mrs. Carpio came in. Damn, Karen thought. It better not be on me.

"Vicky, you will be violate your probation. Smoking not permit in the kitchen, you do know this." Her voice was click-click as forks in the sink. All the Filipino ladies sounded like that, and even the two orderlies. Nucoa dropped the cigarette, white slipping on white, into her pocket.

Mrs. Carpio looked into the sink. Every day for two years she had checked to see if it was clean enough. I might get tired one night, Karen thought. Shit. But Mrs. Carpio was just like Mama—everything's a job, if it's a person, a vacuum, a sink. All the same, and you have to keep a eye on it. "Why do you call her Nu-coa?" Mrs. Carpio said suddenly, tipping her head forward. "Her name is Vicky, huh?"

Mop-water swung in the bucket, and Karen wanted to bust out laughing. Nucoa didn't even smile; she looked confused, like she had forgotten why herself. Oh, I can see me telling her all about that, how in school the guys used to watch girls walk by and talk about if they had enough butter, how far it stuck out, how tight the jeans were. Nucoa used to give it up to anybody on the basketball team, and when she got near the gym they would holler, "That's the cheap stuff. Low-fat. Yeah, it ain't butter, it's Nucoa."

The kitchen lights flashed in Mrs. Carpio's glasses when she looked up, but Nucoa didn't even wait for Karen to say something. She just walked down the hall to the day room.

When the water was gray as the asphalt, Karen tipped the bucket over and let the stream flow down toward the bushes. Grass and sunflowers grew there, at the edge of the dry where her water soaked in every night. I better say something nice to Nucoa. Some-timey as she is, she won't give me a ride home. Damn Eddie, he need to get off his ass and fix my car. Can't even sit out there to hear the radio while I smoke. She turned back to the door and stopped—was that white rising from the oleanders? Wisps of fog? She listened again, no sound, but shaky smoke reached through the long leaves; she saw the wind snatch and raise it to the streetlight. She walked to the only other brightness, to the warm-soup air, and hurried to close the door.

"Why we gotta come to this muffler shop? I hate coming downtown," she said to Eddie.

"Cause it's cheaper than the one on the Westside. And don't start about you don't even want to drive near the Manor. I know. You ain't gotta go in today, you don't want to see it. I don't need to hear it."

"You need to hear me tell you I'm tired of riding with Nucoa."

"Yeah, yeah. She used to wait in the bathroom at school. You seen her pull Charlene's earrings out. She don't even remember that shit." He wrapped his arms around the steering wheel like he was holding a woman, dancing, and stretched his back. Echo sat between them, leaning against Karen. She was not quite two. Eddie Junior sat in the back by himself, which he loved. He swung from window to window, singing, "Lions and tigers and bears, oh my!"

"We heard that enough when the show was on last night, huh, bro?" Eddie called, pulling into the parking lot. He didn't look at Karen before he walked into the muffler shop. Eddie Junior ran behind him, and Karen watched the sidewalk, hand on Echo's sleeping arched neck, waiting for them. Wackheads and crackheads and hypes, oh my. She refused to drive this way anymore.

Because Freddy and Chris, and Ray-Ray, those were the faces that looked into the car window at a stoplight, eyes blank and hard as cement, not knowing who she was. "You got a dollar to spare?" She had danced with Freddy in the gym, walked past Ray-Ray when he said, "I want that cutie, the one with the African bootie. You, baby." Ray-Ray started smoking that wack, angel-dusted joints, when they were seniors. She heard Freddy went on the pipe, and Chris, too. Sprung dudes, that's what Eddie and his brothers called the guys who smoked rock. And they were, all wound up so tight their eyes bugged, their adam's apples stuck out—no meat under their skin, no legs in their pants. "Anton, he's sprung, too, man," Eddie had said to someone on the phone last week.

Echo sealed her cheek to Karen's thigh with her warm baby-sleep sweat, and when she looked up, Eddie came toward the car, crossing a shadow on the cement. He lifted the point of his chin an inch, cool recognition, but Victor Miles looked straight past him.

She could walk it, had walked it back when she was small and her cousins took them all the way down the arroyo, from the Westside. They lived in Green Hollows then, where her mother had a tiny house. Karen used to lie under the cool, dusty bushes every day, trying to hide from the peeling and washing, from shelling peas. From her mother's voice. Then her mother had bought a house on the edge of the Westside, on Leonardo Street, a house larger but still so stuffed with brocaded furniture and chandeliers that her ladies were tired of, with glass figurines missing an arm or the lace of a skirt, rooms so silent and forbidden to breathe in that Karen found bushes there, too, in the backyard, and she pretended they still lived in the shotgun shack. The arroyo ran from Green Hollows, which had been razed now, down under the freeway and then alongside a white neighborhood, near downtown; then it went through a flood-control channel of cement, by an elementary school, and ended at the church and the river-bottom. She could walk it, she didn't want to ride with Eddie and fight about the house and everything else. She stood in the kitchen, back to the clock.

"Come on over," he said into the phone. "My old lady can burn. She make some serious beans and rice." Then he called, "What we got to eat?"

"You ain't got shit. I took the kids to Mickey D's last night," she said. "I'm tired of cooking every morning before I go, cooking all day, and when I get home, too."

"I say I'll cook, and you don't eat it."

"Yeah, if I want toast and gravy. That's all you ever make, like it's some big treat."

He slammed his work boots onto the floor. "Well, shit, that's all we had for breakfast at my house. I didn't have no little sandwiches with the crusts cut off and shit."

"Why you want to bring up Mama?"

"Cause she made you think you better than you are."

Karen threw the coffee cup at the wall, and the heavy plastic dented the paint. "That ain't what we talking about! I want something to eat, I gotta make it! That's the point! I want clean clothes for the kids, I gotta wash."

"Hell, I wash . . ."

"Yeah, if I want it wrinkled, stains set in for life . . . "

But he was quiet in the car. When they went into the shadow of the freeway underpass, he said, "Blood thought he was so hard. He coulda graduated—shit, he was in my math class when we were sophomores, talked big yang to Mr. Nichols. He knew everything, even them word problems used to kick my ass."

Oh, they'd been together so long, Karen thought, even before she let herself think of who he was talking about. Victor Miles. She'd been with Eddie half her life, it felt like, and they talked in short-hand. She knew.

"I can't say nothing," he went on. "He thought he was hard, gangster down. It's on him."

Victor was old-time wino, she thought, like the men that hung out in Lincoln Park. Wackheads looked normal in the body—their faces told you what they smoked. And sprung guys were bony as death, ash like pencil lead under their eyes. But Victor wasn't either of those. He had muscles in his pants, thighs filling the brown-shined knit, and red eyes. Olde English 800, King Cobra, Night Train.

"Fire's out. Darnell Tucker said it was people living in the river-bottom started it," Eddie said. "Third one in a month."

She didn't want to think about Victor, and it was easy to go back to what she'd expected. "You had time to be over there talking to Darnell and the Tuckers? Where was the kids?"

"You know where they were. Tuckers only two doors from Mama's."

"Must be nice to hang out."

"Yeah, I'm just a partying fool. Talk to some neighbors for half an hour."

She looked out the window. "I ain't even got time to wash my hair and you can be at your mama's watching football." He swerved around the corner by the Safeway, and she was relieved. She closed the car door without saying goodbye.

Nucoa had "NUCOA" in red sparkling rhinestones down her left thigh, back then. Arlene Thibodeaux had "PAYBACK." Marcella had "PEACHES." And Karen had wanted Sweet Thang, the song she loved—she traced it on paper during class, how she'd write it with a marker, push the pale-blue rhinestone studs through the thick denim. But mama had a comb she loved to whap against the back of Karen and Esther's necks, teeth reaching into skin so fast they couldn't move.

Victor didn't write anything. He had Marcella do his fly, outline it in the pure white flashes. The teachers made him go to the principal, the principal said take off the studs or go home, and he never came back except for lunchtimes, when he'd lean close to small white boys and say, "Lemme borrow a dime, homey. You can spare it." The security officer escorted him out, to make sure he passed the fence around the school.

"You want some a this chicken?" she asked Nucoa after lunch.

"Girl, we done had fried chicken four times this week at my house. We got wings up under these clothes."

Karen breathed in and started. Why was she still afraid of Nucoa? "I heard Mrs. Carpio talking to Cottrell. She'll bust you Nucoa. You got her bad this time. I ain't playing, you need to stop."

"Shut up, Karen. You so scary, worry about being Miss Perfect all the time. You and your mama." She stroked her eyebrows. "If Mrs. Carpio talk to you, you got my back, right?"

High school—you got my back? I got it, people said . . . I'll watch out behind you. Karen stirred the cooking carrots. "You gon lose your job."

"Ain't no money! Lester front me some rock sugar cane to sell, I'm gone."

Karen stared at her. "You hanging around him? I heard he was in jail."

"Not no more. He setting people up. But you wouldn't know."

When Nucoa left the kitchen, Karen went to the day room to collect the cups visitors always left. It was Sunday. A boy screeched up the drive in a Toyota truck, combing his hair hurriedly as he walked to the front door. Plump women carrying bags—Karen knew they were trimmings for Thanksgiving.

She hated working Sundays. Eddie didn't care. He took the kids to his mother's, and he and his brothers watched football, basketball, goddamn golf, probably, if they had to.

Fingers sticking to the squares of frozen food she unwrapped, she thought about the bathroom suddenly, the bathroom at home. They were out of toilet paper, that's what she'd forgotten to tell Eddie. And he'd never notice. Damn, she'd have to walk to Safeway in a few minutes, when she took her break.

The door swung open, and Nucoa breathed into her ear. "Thanks for nothing, cause I don't need you." She slammed her sole against the outer door and walked to her car, Karen watching her from the cement that showed splashes of soap scum.

Crows were thick as pepper in the sky when she made them rise from the fields she walked past, and they circled until she was far enough gone. They dropped walnuts onto the street, pecked hard at the shells until cars came, carried them off in their beaks. Why didn't they attack her? Karen wondered. She was alone, and they covered the eucalyptus and pepper trees while she passed underneath. They shifted nervously above her.

At the checkout, she stood with the toilet paper, juice, and crackers, thinking that Eddie would have to take the kids to his mother's and come to pick her up every night now. She hooked her wrist through the plastic Safeway bag and saw Victor Miles arguing with a boxboy. She couldn't hear what he said, just saw his arm cradling a six-pack of Miller, his eyes rosy with anger. She walked past slowly, looking at the plants by the door, the chrysanthemums like her mother used to buy for Thanksgiving dinner, for the table. He walked through the parking lot, past all the cars, and she looked at her watch. Fifteen more minutes on her break. Touching the flowers, she waited, and realized she was afraid of him.

Beer bottles had always been strewn in the fields, near the oleanders. The kids liked to get drunk in the church parking lot. She couldn't see labels on any of the bottles near her feet now, and she thought, it doesn't have to be him leaving them. But listening for a moment at the oleanders, the leaves sharp as knife blades, she imagined his teeth reflecting the light from the street, and the earring he'd always worn sparkling next to them like a star close to the sliver of moon.

She lay between them on her side. Echo clutching a fistball of Karen's T-shirt, Eddie's hand dead weight on her hip. Breathing hissed up over her shoulders, hovered over her face. Victor Miles with only a sheet of smoke at his hair, the dead flowers and leaves filling in the spaces behind his knees—he lay on his back, she thought, and the wind flew up over the bushes and away from him.

She put out fish sticks and peas, mashed potatoes and gravy. The sky-blue tray looked small by the door. She knew he saw her. Should she call out his name? Stepping back inside, she took a napkin and wrote Sweet Thang, then crumpled it up. The door she left open like she'd just washed the floor, and she stood by the refrigerator, feeling the hum bounce against her skin.

Did the weeds crackle? Hard shoes crushed the gritty asphalt. "Somebody feeding a damn cat?" he said to the doorway. She moved toward him; he'd seen her.

His toe, the pointy tip of the shoe, pushed the tray until the peas rolled off the plate. "You gon have wild animals if you leave garbage outside. I don't know who else this shit is for." He took a paper bag out of his coat pocket. His green Army jacket, the brown pants flaring at the ankle. Golden Arches on the bag—he threw it on the tray. "More trash for you. Ain't that your job?" He looked at her uniform, not her face. She covered up her nametag—Karen: Staff. Sweet Thang. But he walked, fist down like high school.

Hot between her shoulders, she put down her pack of cigarettes where the tray had been, and closed the door.

When the canned peaches had slithered into their dessert cups and swam nestled together, she opened the door, and the cigarettes were gone. She knew he had taken them, because nobody had walked in off the street; between peaches, she'd gone to the day-room window again and again.

When she waited for Eddie, though, in the parking lot where visitors came, she saw the fat pack of Tareytons caught in the cactus by the front door, where the wind must have pushed it along the cleaned cement. She put it in her bag and ran her shoe over the peas and pepper berries and gravel blowing across the empty parking spaces.

toe up and smoke dreaming

DARNELL / NOVEMBER

Spindly little grass and wild oats, that's all there was to catch and crackle. No. This ain't acceptable. This doesn't qualify, Darnell thought. The fire flew with the breeze and barely touched down, hanging like orange cobwebs on the stems, never burning hard but skittering across the field. Darnell clambered up the hill behind Fricke, watching the flames jump across the highway. This roadside went up every year, Fricke had said, and Darnell remembered it from last year, when he'd been here with the Conservation Corps and most of the big stuff had burned off. The cars idling up the highway thrummed in the air, exhaust shaking above them. The blaze disappeared instantly under the water, but little patches of the silence that flame made, the quiet of sucked-up oxygen and reaching heat, landed like rags for a few more minutes. Then they were gone. Disappointment washed hot below his throat. No, this doesn't qualify, hell no. We're just half-stepping, and this is the last one. Not acceptable. Lester always says that, but he's talking about women. Not fires. He'd laugh silly if he heard me.

On the way to the tumbleweeds, he leaned back and dreamed of napalming feed trails in the spring. The heliotorch dropping liquid fire in loops that fell on dense patches of hundred-year-old chaparral, thick and tangled mats of vegetation, making scar-trails, singeing in precise lines for the deer and other animals that couldn't force through the brush. He smelled it, the smoke almost wet with the moist rain still clinging to the leaves.

"When do we torch trails?" he asked Fricke, who sat a few rows away.

"No way," Corcoran said, before Fricke could answer. "Rio Seco County's only gotten three inches of rain for the whole damn year. Fricke said you gotta have five to torch."

"Big-time drought," Fricke said.

"Shit, we been here since what—April?" Scott said. "Season don't usually even start till May."

Darnell kept looking at Fricke, who was one of the permanent Forest Service crew, the supervisor. "Not enough rain's gonna fall while you seasonals are laid off," Fricke said in his slow, twangy voice.

"That's the wet months, though," Darnell said.

"Not this year, homeboy."

"Your home ain't my home," Darnell said. "But we torch first thing when we get back, if it rains, right?"

Fricke laughed. "You better wait and see who gets called back." Darnell stared at him. "Hey, I heard the funding might get cut, might have fewer seasonals up here."

"No way," Corcoran said again.

"Yeah, a second ago you're talking drought and now fewer guys— what kind of voodoo is that?" Darnell said, watching Fricke's eyes, even bluer with the smudges of black underneath from rubbing his dirty sleeve against his face. His Marlboro Man moustache.

"No bullshit, man—I feel a greenhouse effect coming," Fricke said, raising those bushy eyebrows, and Darnell knew he would play dumb cowboy and change the subject. "Hotter and hotter," Fricke said, turning to Perez.

It was Friday. That meant yesterday's puny twenty-acre job near Poppet Flats really might have been the last one, because seasonals could get sent home for good tonight. Panic shifted from side to side in Darnell's stomach, swayed with the shoulders in front of him, rows of dirty collars and heads that wobbled loosely with the bus lurches. Used to the rhythm after the long season, the same mountain curves.

"Friday. Tumbleweeds," Perez said, pinching the skin between his eyebrows.

"Season's gotta be over, man, it's past Thanksgiving," Sutton said.

"I'm going out every night," Scott said, smiling. "Find me some beach babes cause I'm staying with Doyle in Newport."

"Not me, dude. I'm finding sleep, forty-eight hours of sleep," Sutton said. "I don't want no chick snoring, no nobody snoring. No goddamn fire." He pushed Darnell's shoulder. "You don't look thrilled about the weekend. Or you still hate tumbleweeds that much?"

Darnell didn't answer. What, tell everybody I want to stay? No sleep, nasty food no woman would cook, white-boy rock in my ears all the time—say that's cool with me.

"You asking about the helitorch cause you got somebody to fry at home in Rio Seco?" Perez asked, and they laughed.

"I need to fire up that nasty shirt Fricke's been wearing four days straight," Darnell said.

"Ah, but nobody smells it except me, until I go down the mountain. Then I catch women with the firefighter smoke, because I'm not a kept man. Kept on a leash like you, awhoooh." His lips barely showed under the moustache.

"I'ma see her soon enough, okay?" Darnell said. "Bow wow wow." He didn't want them talking about Brenda. They were off the mountain now, on the freeway toward Beaumont. I shouldn't have told them anything. I'ma be in touching range every minute I'm home. Every weekend, Brenda got angrier about how long the season lasted; every Sunday, she kept her fingers on his shirt, his belt, delicate and persistent as the racoons that came to camp for food. My only crime? She's five months pregnant and sometimes I'm out the house for an hour. The mass of fear stayed in his stomach, hard as bad biscuits. Different from fire scared, he thought—that was like liquid smoke his father added to barbecue sauce, warmth that made his muscles slide against bones, his joints swing with the shovel. Fumes turned to the feel of Yukon Jack, the stuff Fricke and Corcoran had given him once or twice.

But this panic, that yesterday's fire was the last . . . stepping off the bus, he raised his arms to smell the ash in his sleeves, while everyone groaned at the tumbleweeds, huge and humped as Volkswagens covering the vacant fields.

Orange vests were scattered against the dead-brown bushes. "Road-camp guys?" Doyle said. "I thought they only did fire roads."

"Don't matter to me." Perez smiled. "I don't care who does em, long as I don't."

"You *do*," Fricke said. "They fork em, you guys supervise the burn."

Darnell looked quickly at the prisoners to see who he knew. None of the other guys ever had to do that; they were all Orange County boys except Scott, who was from San Bernardino. College types, doing their training so they could get hired on regular. I'll have to put in four years of seasonal before they even look at me, he thought, watching the road-camp faces. This is the only time I see a brother all week. Nobody from the Westside today, not like last month when he'd recognized Victor Miles and Ray-Ray. They were doing time for dinky shit: tickets, drunk in public, child support. He remembered when Roscoe, his father's partner, did three months, last winter.

The road-camp guys piled the bushes into the roadside ditch. "I heard these guys are doing a lot now," Corcoran said, leaning against the bus. "This stuff, the fire roads, and somebody said they got a prison crew doing the Highway 74 fires. One every week, just about."

Darnell walked closer to Fricke. "So that's how we save money on seasonals, huh? Get all the brothers and Chicanos for free."

"People would ask what the problem is," Fricke said, and Darnell drummed his heel, waiting through the well, pardner pause. "The jail's overcrowded. Get guys outside all day, and they don't want to fight as much."

"Save that shit," Darnell said. "I know all that fresh-air shit by heart. I spent a year in the Conservation Corps, remember? 'Low-income youths, between the ages of eighteen and twenty-three . . . We promote spirit, instill discipline.' You're talking free labor. And I get a promoted spirit. Uh-uh, save that shit for somebody else." He walked partway into the field, listening to the rattling tumbleweeds and then the muffled tremble of the flames. Perez laughed.

Darnell was whore of the day. He looked again at the calendar—December 1st: Tucker. Moving cans in the dark pantry, he found several jars of Ragu. The camp was still full staff, high alert, and he wasn't making something he had to cook one by one. He fried some hamburger and poured the Ragu into the huge cast-iron pot. When he heard glopping bubbles, he turned down the heat and went to check the bathroom. Leaving the door open, he crouched in the shower to pick up rogue pieces of soap.

Pine needles scraped against the screen; the wind had been high for two more weeks, and the crew was out almost every day. Brush went up from an exhaust spark, or a train wheel striking the track. The air was so dry he felt it deep in his throat even with his mouth closed, rushing down to steal his spit. Smoke in his crotch, his armpit hair. Since the Santa Anas had started, the creosote and manzanita seemed to crackle, waiting, ready.

Thrownaway ovals of Dial were cemented to the floor. Perez and Scott were slobs. Everybody was in a bad mood now, throwing clothes and dishes around because they wanted to go home, everybody but him and Corcoran. Corcoran always talked about his grandfather was a fireman in New York, his dad was in L.A., yeah, yeah. Darnell rubbed the chips like chalk in his palm. They were all waiting for Thompson, the big boss, this morning, thinking he'd say the word. But he'd laughed, said, "Breathe, huh? Two more weeks, minimum."

Brenda would love to wash the smoke out of his clothes one last time, in the washer below their apartment. In the carport. They'd moved downtown, away from the Westside a few miles. Now he'd be stuck trying to get a slave, pay the rent until he could come back to camp in the spring.

Voices came from the kitchen door. Scott and Fricke. The pot lid clanked, and Scott said, "I thought Tucker was whore of the day."

"He is," Fricke said.

"Man, I thought he'd make fried chicken or something. One of his specialties," Scott said. "It's Friday, and we gotta eat spaghetti again."

Darnell moved toward the door. Fricke said, "Specialties?"

"Yeah, you know, fried chicken, watermelon." Scott laughed.

Darnell stood in his face. "Ho, ho, *ho.* When you gon learn to say it right? *Ho* of the day. Speak so *I* can understand you, boy. Cause on the serious tip, your attitude is to the curb." He pushed Scott against the counter, and Fricke's forearms slid up his sides and pulled.

"Man, what's your problem?" Scott said, his upper lip rising square, incredulous, the way Darnell hated. "It was a joke, man."

"I'ma kick your ass all the way to the Colonel, buckethead," Darnell said. "Buy you some Original Recipe." He jerked his shoulder away from Fricke.

Scott was out the door. "It doesn't make a difference," Fricke said. "It didn't apply to you anyway. Fried chicken is a southern dish, and you're a native Californian. Scott's a little ignorant." Darnell shook his head. Fricke always tried so hard; under the Willie Nelson voice, something was there, sharper, or laughing, when he talked to Darnell. Fricke touched the ends of his moustache, not twirling the tips like guys did to call attention to the hair. He just liked the feel.

"You want me around," Darnell said. "You want me next to you when we're on the line, and you're always trying to tell me something."

"You're a demon on the line," Fricke said, "and you're the best at chopping rattlers. I don't know where you get that."

Darnell saw the snakes rushing ahead of the flames, and he smiled, thinking of how he loved to slice the shovel at them, but he knew what Fricke was trying to do.

"We're not talking about my talent. I'm not getting called back, I know it. I'ma tell you something, I hear Thompson when he talks about me, I listened once when you guys were outside. Every time he says my name, it's a hesitation." He stopped, not knowing how to explain. Like when your transmission isn't working right, and the car doesn't want to shift into overdrive, just hanging there at the edge of the gear, and he'd had to think about it—his name, that's what Thompson didn't like.

"That's not it," Fricke said, but Darnell went back into the bathroom. He'd heard Thompson say, "Darnell, Carnell, Martell. You watch the NBA, and half the names are ridiculous. Colored give their kids a burden in them names."

"If you don't get called back, and I'm saying *if,*" Fricke said, following him, and Darnell sucked his teeth. "It's nothing like that. You and Scott are the only ones here on that training grant from the government. That's all it is, just funding. *If* it happens."

Darnell turned. "Save that shit, too," he said. "I'm going down the mountain early."

"I can't bleed the brakes here, we have to go to my dad's." He watched her on the couch, her belly a round mixing bowl, a dome, under the T-shirt. "The Fiat's having trouble getting down from camp."

"You said the season was over."

"Yeah, but I'll have to go up and get my stuff," he lied.

"Only home one day and we gotta go to your father's," she said.

"Everybody on the Westside is gonna tell me how big or small or high or low this baby is, and I ain't in the mood." She kept the side of her neck to him all the way there.

At his parents' house, he followed her into the back room, where he had pressed himself against her on Friday nights all during high school. Everyone used to be asleep, and the gray TV light would flash in her earrings when he pulled back to look at her. He put his lips under her ear and said, "Come on, don't be evil. I'll only take an hour. Ain't nothing to eat at home anyway, go out and help Mama, let her ask you about the baby. She can't wait to be a grandma."

She opened her eyes a little wider, not the slits she'd kept them all day, and pushed him out ahead of her.

In the front yard, his father's shouts floated from the side of the house. "What's today—Saturday? Y'all bring that thing back Tuesday."

Nacho and Snooter, who lived down the street, wheeled out the battery recharger. "Shoot, Red Man, we'll take care of it," Snooter said.

"You the ones let somebody steal my best dolly last month. I brought that sucker in the kitchen every night, and you left it in the yard. *Gave* it away."

Roscoe, his father's friend, said, "They stealing hoses, trashcans, anything. Need to get enough for a smoke of that shit."

Darnell crouched beside the Fiat. "You bleeding them brakes again?" Snooter asked. "You home for good now?"

Darnell shook his head. Snooter pointed toward L.A., to the Sugarloaf Hills near the freeway. Except for a few weeks in winter, they were always wheat-brown, with dirty cream rocks scattered thickly on the ridges. "Somebody done burned the toast and put strawberry jam on it. Y'all help out?"

The brush was blackened, and red phoscheck coated the boulders. He laughed at Snooter. "That's city land, man, not Forest Service territory."

Brenda glared out of the wrought-iron screen door. "You ain't even started yet. Uh-huh," she said, arms crossed high. Darnell slid under the car; he could tell when she was gone because Nacho said, "What's wrong with her?"

"Bellyache," Darnell's father said. "And it ain't hardly gon get better." Folding chairs scraped across the driveway and beer cans popped open. "You best stop hiding up there in the mountains and get you a real job," his father said to Darnell's feet. Darnell jerked his knee, and his father said, "And you need to quit hiding over here, too. I ain't playing."

"So damn dry the eucalyptus are falling like sticks in the wind," Roscoe said. Roscoe and his father trimmed and took out trees, hauled junk and brush.

Darnell knew exactly how Roscoe's face would look, dreamy blurred, his eyes stuck on something not moving. Roscoe was a poet, and he drove people crazy with his arguments about precise words and meanings.

"Winter's supposed to be a different light," Roscoe said. "Silver, I guess, paler, and summer's heavy, hot gold. This winter ain't acting right."

"Give me a break, just for today," Darnell's father shouted.

"Oystershell," Nacho said, surprising everyone. Darnell rested his hands on his chest for a moment. "That's the color. Supposed to be."

Darnell was still under the car when he smelled the burning, acrid and faraway. Pulling himself out, he walked to the street to look at the sky. From the way the smoke rose and roiled, hung there till the afternoon turned plum-dark as sunset, he knew the fire was in the river-bottom again. Homeless people living down there, cooking, and didn't know the wind. This was thick cane and bamboo, black smoke, blazing ten-fifteen feet down into the stand where water and retardant couldn't reach. West of the city, he thought, the sun soon so completely gone that Esther, two doors down, came out looking sleepy, like she'd napped with her new baby, and called to her kids. "How it get dark so fast?" she said to Darnell.

"It's not evening yet," Roscoe said. "Fire." They squinted at the ashes falling like snow, the flakes of gray rocking back and forth until they settled on car hoods.

"Look at that," Roscoe said, head thrown back. Streams of crows flapped over, quiet and straight instead of jostling each other. "They got fooled, heading to the river-bottom because they think it's time to bed down for the night."

"Girl," Esther called, "look at you!" Brenda put her arms around Darnell's waist and bumped the baby against him. Damn, he thought, watching the red-tinged sidewalks, the palm fronds lifting like hair in the wind. No way she'd come with him. And this wind might turn cool tomorrow, pick up some rain. This could be it, the last one.

"What y'all staring at? Helicopter?" she said into his back.

"Bring that belly over here," Esther said. "We looking at the smoke."

"Not another one," Brenda said, swinging around to face Darnell, forehead lowered.

"You better hold that baby," he said, taking Esther's girl gently. "You need the practice." He cradled the head in his arm for a moment, made himself stare at the tiny lips, shiny-wet. And her breath smelled clear and citrus, like 7-Up. He leaned closer, shocked, and Esther laughed.

"Smell good?" she said. "That's why baby's breath is a pretty little puff of flowers." He couldn't look at Brenda; he'd only wanted to distract her. The baby felt heavier than he'd expected, and he passed her to Brenda.

Turning back to the car, he called to Roscoe, "Come help me finish up."

An hour later, the sun lowered itself from the smoke, hanging in the band of sky between the pall and the line of hills. No progress for the crew, he could tell by the smoke, rising just as dark and no white puffs to signal success. The way the whole day had changed, the darkness, called to him like always, like when he was ten, eleven, riding his bike for miles to find the fire, in the orange-packing houses by the railroad tracks, in the fields near the freeway, on the Sugarloaf Hills. He kept his face away from the west, waiting for Brenda to come back from Esther's.

But when she padded across the street, Esther behind her, he said, "You want a milkshake? We can go for a test drive, see if the brakes are okay." She smiled, mollified, and then she must have seen the excitement in his face.

"Nigga, please," she said. "Why the hell would I want to look at a damn fire? Cause that's where you'll end up. All these years, that's all you want to do, sit and watch flames. Every damn summer, Darnell."

"Wasn't nothing else to do. Go shopping at the mall with my Gold Card?"

"No. Uh-uh, don't try and put it on me. You got some death wish, like you want to try hell out before you get there. Popping and burning, and you in a trance. All week I gotta think about you getting hurt, and you got the nerve to want me looking at fire now."

"That's just the baby talking," Esther said. "Y'all ain't gotta holler and argue."

"If that's how the baby talks now, I'm in serious shit when it gets here," Darnell said, getting into the Fiat. He was glad his father had gone inside. "Come on, Bren, I'll take you home." He knew better.

"Take me to the movies, somewhere so I don't have to sit at home and wait for you again. We going out now." Her feet angled outward, like she was off-balance, and Darnell wanted to get out and put his hand behind her back, to straighten it, help her to the car. But he couldn't. His shoulders, heavy as sandbags, held him against the seat.

"I'm gone," he said softly, starting up the car, and he didn't watch their eyebrows.

---

toe up and smoke dreaming   111

The sun slid away, a dull nickel, while he tried to remember which of the small roads led closest to that part of the river-bottom. Red glowed near the Jurupa Bridge: he saw the flames bend forward, slanted by the wind before they climbed the sky again. He drove to the end of the road, around a swath of cleared land, and found the taillights he knew would be gathered there.

The older white men with baseball caps and binoculars, the ones he'd always imagined were ex-firemen, they leaned against their cars and pressed at the barbed-wire fence sagging in the sand. A lone palm tree caught and the top burned wildly, a sparkler held still to the sky. Darnell stood far from the others, hearing kids on bikes behind him, voices high and threading through the dark. The flames were maybe seventy-five feet, but they were far away, shimmering in the bamboo. He wasn't close enough for the shaking silence he wanted, and he paced back and forth, snapping twigs under his feet in time with the cracks of the fire. Brenda used to sit in the open doorway of the car, last summer, two summers ago, and she'd fall asleep, lean back with her feet still on the ground. Her knees were round and pale as faces, watching him. The panic fisted inside him again—his father would have taken Brenda home by now. Her father hadn't even spoken to her since she told him about the baby. Darnell heard the murmurs of the men and went back to the car. He watched the fire pulse until the others were gone; the flames shifted away, and cold ashes stung inside his nose. Trying a few more of the rutted narrow roads, he drove and swerved at the dead ends; none came closer to the glow.

The dashboard swam in front of him. The apartment was dark when he passed by slowly, not even TV light in the curtains.

"None of your buddies here? No Jack Daniels, Yukon Jack?"

Fricke shrugged. "High alert. I have to be sharp." He smiled and poured Darnell some coffee. "I knew you'd be back early."

"Yeah, I watched the sky," Darnell drawled, sitting at the table. "I sniffed the wind like a good rangehand." The windows began to turn purple and lighten. "Why you up?"

He raised his brows. "Why are you?"

"At least eighty-five yesterday, and the wind's still up," Darnell said. "You tell the boss man I left?" He raised both hands. "No—wait, it doesn't matter anyway, doesn't really matter what I do, right?"

Fricke looked at him. "You ever want to toss a match? When you were a kid, waiting for one, you ever throw a match just to see?"

Darnell stared at his eyes, blue like Levis, old ones. "No."

"I did. I was thirteen. Got caught, ended up in Juvie."

Darnell stood up and put his cup in the sink. He heard muttering from the hall—Perez and Doyle were awake. "So?" he said, but then he held his lip with his teeth.

"It's December third." Darnell didn't know what to say. The sun edged out and the sky was immediately bright as noon. No moisture wavered anywhere.

"Scott's to' up again, huh?" he said.

"Does that mean he's playing dead?"

"What?"

"Toe up, playing dead." Fricke raised his foot stiffly.

"Shit, man, you guys and your r's. Whore of the day. *Ho.* Tore up. *To'* up—he's drunk." He went outside to dump the trash.

By the time they got the call, before lunch, the fire had been going since early morning, just about the time he and Fricke had been drinking coffee and looking out the windows. On the truck, Fricke said, "It was way deep in the canyon and the lookouts didn't even see it till now. Big time. Zero humidity, and the fuel's right. Up there behind Ortega Camp."

"What kinda asshole's building a campfire now?" Scott said.

"Uh-uh," Fricke said. "Target shooter sparked it. That brush hasn't gone up in fifty, sixty years. Crews are coming from Ventura and San Diego. We got the west flank, cause there's a bunch of new houses out there past Seven Canyons. I'm sure the residents aren't home, since they drove their Beamers to L.A. to work this morning."

"What are you talking about?" Perez said.

"Nothing. Hope you guys slept good last night."

They passed the houses, behind a wall and wrought-iron gate that said "Canyon Estates." Farther up the highway, they dipped over the ridge and Fricke said, "Your date, gentlemen. She's gonna take you through the night."

They started the line, leaning into the wind, and Darnell felt the prickle above his hipbones, stronger even than when Brenda pulled her fingers up his thighs. His shoulders stretched wider, skin melting away. "Goddamn this wind!" Scott shouted.

"Goddamn a target shooter!" Corcoran shouted back, and smoke flew into their mouths.

Fricke ran down the line, back to the truck, and Darnell saw the smile. The wooden handle was slippery-slick in his hands, the creosote flying in chips. He couldn't hear the others, only the roar he knew was coming toward them. He could never tell what time it was, but they were facing the sun when the tankers dropped water and phoscheck. The liquid hung thick in the air for a moment before it dropped.

In the early darkness, they could see the south flank racing up one of the canyons; they went over the ridge and down into the next descent, and Perez went out with a bad ankle. Fricke muttered beside Darnell, closer in the dark, and the roar was like a blanket over them, high above the harsh breathing and cusswords, the skittering of animals against leaves and branches.

The wind lifted the smoke and then brought it back around, gusting even harder toward midnight. The metallic taste of what he'd eaten still ringing in his throat, he lay down with the others. "If the wind shifts, it'll be here in fifteen minutes," Fricke said. "Just catnap."

Darnell felt the decomposed granite, crumbly against him. Seven Canyons—he remembered Fricke telling him about the firestorm that swirled through there, so many years ago. Like a bomb, a tornado, he'd said, picking up speed, running down the chutes and charring a crew of seven. Each of the canyons was named for them. Darnell thought hard—Miller, that was one of them, and Schmidt. The next gust was so hard it threw pebbles against Fricke's gear, next to him. Darnell stood up. He imagined bears running from the fire, toward him, coyotes low and tails streaming, racoons humping along. The fire ate at the chaparral in waves, rolling fast as a tumbleweed. He thought of the heliotorch—the narrow flames men would drop in the spring. The police helicopter he'd see every night on the Westside, at home. He gripped the shovel and walked away from the others. Fricke was wandering around, on lookout, he knew.

Up the canyon, toward the ridge where the fire would crown. Fricke would see it and yell, "Crowning!" The others would stagger to their feet, clumsy as bears in all their gear. He began to run toward the shaking silence, the air being pulled by the flames, pushed by the wind. If you dug a hole six feet deep, you'd have enough to breathe when the firestorm raced over, sucking the oxygen from your breath, your mouth, reaching all the way inside to pull it from your lungs. He stopped to touch a tree, felt it shaking, and closed his eyes—the roar was close, strong. And then it was a deer, bursting from around the tree, a doe leaping into the canyon and past him. He remembered them, their bellies tight in the spring, walking slowly up the napalmed feed trails, their round pale awkwardness the same color as Brenda's bellyskin, which was lighter, thinner, every time he went home. He turned, the wind-smoke swirling around his ears, crowning now. Fricke? Was that Fricke calling "Tucker!" or one of the others cussing in his sleep? He lay next to a white boulder, a dome beside his arm, the trembling in his face, his coat an envelope he could breathe inside. He saw the veins inside his eyelids, the veins

along Brenda's hips, traced and crossing on a map. His boots pointed to the sky. Toes up. They were heavy, and he flapped them against
the ground, letting them fall to the outside and then pulling them
back inward, up, pounding the toes together so hard he felt his shins
quiver. He had to keep up the pounding until Fricke came.

back

Every night I use to think, I have to get up, because it always like this. Wait, listen, hold my own breathing till I hear him. I would breathe in his rhythm, try and take in the air he done let out his mouth, back then when it was still sweet and warm, like years ago. Most of the time now it smell sick, and there not enough of it for him, so how can it be any left for me to pull in? Now it stink like sores cover up too long, like the mess inside his lungs, but then when I turn away, the wind blow through the cracks in the window, pushing past my shoulders so cold, and at least L. C. air warm on my face.

His breathing use to be strong and deep, so loud I wonder how big them ribs must be. They curve up like a huge turtle shell, then his belly cave in below. I would have my face hard by his chest when we first marry, and the fold in his shirt rub my cheekbone real soft, fall and rub again, put me to sleep even if I were worried about something. I would start to sleep on his bones, be so tired after washing for all them people, and later in the night, I always wake up to find my head done slid down to his stomach, resting there. Now his coughing shake the whole bed, shake loose dreams I don't want in my head. Everything just tremble for a minute when he stop, and I wait. I don't sleep at all, the whole night. Sometimes I be tired, sometimes no. But I lay here all night with my head up in L. C. back, be afraid to dream, afraid to let him breathe without me. I know each breath count.

117

It was a time when I would just get up with the shaking, stay out in the kitchen till the sun come up. When I first know he was sick, I would wait every minute out there at the table, wait for him to leave this world, his breath sound so bad. The air catch in his chest like a fingernail drag down a screen. I hear him cough and wonder did he still see them tiny sparkles behind his eyes like I do when I cough real deep? Them little showers of light I used to watch when I were a baby girl, red and falling I use to see, and then I would cough even more. L.C. must don't see them after all these months of coughing. They must be use up.

Back then, when I realize he were coughing all through the night, into each morning and don't stop, not worse and not better, I couldn't stay in the bed and listen. When the sky start to get purple then, I would put on the grits, the only thing he eat, and everything was quiet but for L.C. The cars ain't started yet for the morning, the people still asleep, and the pot clink just a second, like money, on the stove. The grits falling out the bag, marking the minutes like sand in a egg timer I seen at a white lady's house. One morning the light in the kitchen seem to turn pale so slow, and I couldn't hold nothing inside. I let the tears sink into the grits and disappear, not like when you catch them on your cheek or in a tissue and they stays wet and clear. Salt sinking into the grits, salt I pour on top, through my fingers. I never cry so he can see me. I heard him pushing hisself up on his elbows, heard the bed cracking exactly that, and he call, "Pashion?" the way he do. I stood there next to him holding the water glass, but he just looked at me. That weren't what he need. He lay back down, had his eyes open, shake two or three times like a cold bird. I know he trying to push that cough down in his chest so I won't get out the bed every night. I seen the window shade moving in the draft, seen his eyes look away from me. Soon enough I be cold and trying to keep warm. I won't be making no trail, whispering my feet across the floor like the widow upstairs, rubbing over my head back and forth trying to pass the night.

I stay in the bed now, keep my head in the hollow down his back. When we first marry, forty-nine years ago, I were sixteen. That winter, I use to watch L. C. put oil on his arms, his chest, reach up and try to get it on his back. He were always in a hurry to get to work, cause we been in the bed playing, and he couldn't reach nothing but the sides of his back, under the shoulders. Gray skin got left all ashy in the valley between the muscles. I use to pull the oil in from the sides and rub it down the center, where his backbone like a river. Now when I lay here, I keep a ear to that valley and wait, listen to the bubble in his chest like water running.

The walls get settle long after midnight, cracking and popping, and I can hear the rats running through they trails. I know I'm fixing to think the same things all night, every night, like there only a few certain sounds and seeings left in me. I wait for those few. I can look at the wall and see wood, not cinderblock. When we first move to California, after the mine closed, I spent all my time looking in the street, seeing the light shine off the cars and puddles. All I want to look at then was West Virginia and my porch shadow, when the moon full and the birches outside my door look silver thin like needles in with the black trunks of the other trees. I use to watch the sun going down behind the buildings here, put my face up to the screen while I was cooking, and sometimes when it was a breeze, I could smell the night coming like we were at home, clean like water and trees was close by. The wind stop, and then I smell the air coming back out the room behind me, warm from the greens on the stove, but like somebody else's air. L. C. knew. He came up behind me and said, "It get dark too fast here. It be light and then gone. No shadows."

We came cause L. C. cousin Rosa tell us Rio Seco warm, better for his lung. But the rent so high. We have to stay in a senior apartment, no house.

I look at the walls and see wood floors, the wood I split for the stove, the sides of the washtub I had my face in trying to get the black out of L. C. clothes. I smell the boards and trunks of trees when they get wet, smell the smoke.

Sometimes I think I can't lay here no more, I can't wait for them seeings and listen to these walls with they little feet scrabbling and hear the sound L. C. make in his chest all night. I want to get up and be far away from him, take down them shirts I hang to dry in the kitchen, put one round my back and sit up in the front window. I see the shadows of them shirts from where I lay, I see the way they hanging over the stove. They L. C. old flannel ones, the only thing he wear now. This morning I caught myself fixing to pull out a sleeve turn the wrong way; it was light-color in the sun, all the checks and stripes pale as nothing, so I reach in to get the cuff and then I realize that is the right side. The shirt too soft and thin, like the back of L. C. arms when I pull him over on his side so he can breathe.

But if I get up, if I leave, he can feel the bed shake, and he call out for me. This bed tell you anything. Long time ago, he were trying to get in this bed real quiet, been out late and knew I was fixing to get mad. He was easing into the sheets and a spring busted and shot up through the mattress. Scratched him on the behind like a cat, long and deep, and I laughed so hard. He still got that scar. I use to run my finger down the scab when it were healing, wait for that right minute to catch him there, just to hear him cuss and fuss.

I seen how he got most all his scars, because we was together so young. When I marry him, Mama say, "Pashion, he a baby, only twenty. He got nothing." She want me to wait for someone with more, a older man from town want a young wife. But I don't want no old man like she had. I never remember my father, only my mother walking all them years, fourteen years, like the widow upstairs. A house empty, no deep voices and nobody to hear her feet on the floor, only the dogs sleeping under the house.

It start to rain. I can hear the cars on the streets blocks and blocks away, moving like a fast touch of wind. And a train, so tiny calling that it could be a dog howling in somebody trees. It be so cold now, in winter, and my fingers curl up like I'm fixing to push the scrub pad round the sink or the floor with my knuckles, getting a stain off. My hands don't come straight. When I yawn, seem like my back relax and a big chill of air go in my mouth. Then I start shivering and can't stop till I stiff up my back again. It like the air inside me now, and it determine to stay cold. Mama use to say, "That why you cover the mouth when you yawn, so nothin bad fly inside." But my fingers too bent up, and if I put my hand close to my mouth, the nails touch my cheek hard like a rake.

I can see by the shadows in the kitchen it about five in the morning. It get darker for a while, the darkest cause the moon gone. I push my face closer to L. C. back, and I can feel the rib bone under my cheek, feel that rasp inside him come right out the skin. What kind of black they say in his lung? What color? Black like his eyebrows use to be? Like when his fingernail use to fall off, a purple black? He use to bang one up every week at work. Black inside the nail, inside the finger. His skin still smooth like a flower petal beside his eyes, I look every day, and the sleep stay dry as dust in his lashes sometimes in the mornings. In a while, cars start passing on the street, sending noise up to the window to mix with his breath, with all the feet that start to walking in the building, on the sidewalk, all shaking and humming like waiting in a church.

I think of when I were sixteen and my neck soft as powder. It still soft now, when I touch it, but the wrinkles so many L. C. finger couldn't run down the front like it use to, draw from my chin to my chestbone, not pulling hard. My neck darker now, muddy color. I hear the way he breathe wrong, it that time in the dawn when he do that, and I stop. It worse again, like rain, hitting the tin roof on the shed back in the woods, coming in waves and spattering. Forty-nine years and I lay in the bed thinking, long as I touch him, he still mine, and it keep me awake, listening. I keep a hand on his back and reach around with my other hand to feel the bottle. It stay under the mattress, tuck into a hole. They gave him pills at the clinic, to make him sleep. I take two out each time, and now I got eighteen, twenty, but I don't know if that enough to let me go when I want, when I choose. His breath stop raining in his chest, soon, dry and finish, but not yet, not while I touching him and listen. Next week, when I get more pills, when I know, then it my choosing, when it stop for good. I remember his arm across my chest long time ago, his lips round my ear and then he fall asleep in the middle of a kiss, he so tired. How many years I listen, he always sleep before me, and wake up to call my name.

off-season

ROSA / FEBRUARY

For six years I had been sitting on hard bleachers watching Donnie play basketball, watching him run until his chest and neck gleamed gold brown like smooth palm tree wrapping. All those years my butt bones got tired, and I slid down to rest them on the wooden boards where feet belong, propping up my thighs on the bench in front of me. Donnie always came up during practice or warm-ups and told me to close my legs because I looked like a boy. Now we were married and I was a wife, so I was supposed to sit normal and put my hands on my knees, knit, or read romance novels like the other team's wives opposite me, plump and pale, screaming politely when they thought they should.

I wanted desperately to slump down in comfort and figure out why these white boys from the suburbs were beating Donnie's team by eight, but I slid a little and couldn't arrange my legs over the bleacher seat because of the bruises. Donnie had decorated my thighs when he threw me around the apartment, put serious rainbow stuff there, first rosy, then purple, and now fading to gold and green. Team colors, Notre Dame.

Since the week before when he did it, I'd been sleeping in the front room on the mattress we called a couch. That morning, I woke up thinking I heard the shiver of the windowpane, the pause and roar of a winter Santa Ana wind at home in Rio Seco, on the Westside. The sun, shining warm on my eyelids, had fooled me into thinking that this was California, but then the wind came through the cracks around the window, icy and silent, and I realized that there were no palm fronds hurling themselves against each other, no eucalyptus leaves to whistle and hold the air. I pushed the shade and looked outside to see the glare of light on February snow, and then heard Donnie in the bedroom getting ready for the game. His size fourteens crashed to the floor after he took them from the closet shelf.

Past the metal railing in front of our second-story door, I could see the long, empty lot that led down to the park where people sold weed in the summer, when we first moved in. The snow was thin over the ground in some places, steel gray the color of trash cans. Donnie came into the kitchen and looked at me. I could tell by how quickly he turned away that he was scared to say anything. Good, I thought, maybe if he's chicken he won't do it again. He sat on the folding chair and reached down to jerk his shoelaces tight, the muscles in his arms pulling downward, fluid like silty, dark water. The two tiny marks where I had stabbed him were flat black now, healed over so they could pass for beauty marks. When he'd bent my arm backwards, I poked him with the closest thing I could reach, and two drops of blood like ruby stud earrings stood out on his bicep. He'd been using his hands, his best weapons, and I found mine, the pen I practiced writing sports stories with, the pen with a long, sharp nub.

I pulled on two pairs of sweats, so I could go along, when he came close to the front door. "I thought you wouldn't want to be with me," he said.

"Nobody else to be with," I said. "Only game on TV is Indiana and Northwestern. I ain't hardly staying here and freezing to watch them." I stopped at the door, near him, and smelled the sleep on his skin, the little bit of my perfume that was still in the sheets. He looked away, like he couldn't stand to not touch me, and I smiled. Maybe if he won today, I would feel the same longing I always had, for touching wet curls at his ears, for everyone watching when I did, when I tasted the salt on his skin. The familiar feel of all those eyes on him might make Donnie into himself again.

But these country boys from Middlefield were playing Danny Ainge ball, that scrambly kind full of flying elbows and guys who pretended to fall and then tried to low-bridge somebody. One dude was using his beer belly as a second man to guard James, the skinny forward who had asked Donnie to play in this tournament. We were in a junior-high gym outside Hartford, at the second round of the Middlefield YMCA Tournament.

Donnie's team was all black and Puerto Rican guys from the city, and when they walked in, everybody looked nervous and started whispering. They hadn't been playing together but a week, though, and I could tell by the way the other team warmed up that they went way back. I didn't want to watch a bunch of pink-skinned, raw-kneed guys on TV, but here they were. The point guard was one of those little ones who stomps his feet between the legs of whoever's dribbling, constantly trying to steal the ball, pushing his eyebrows up all cocky and excited. Donnie had gotten three jams in the first-round game, dunks that everybody had heard about, James said, and the Middlefield crowd loved it now when this guard rogued Donnie's ball and got a clean, practice drill layup. You could tell their kind: they hated big-city flashiness on the court, which they automatically associated with car theft, annoying rap music, and the loss of their in-dash stereos when they drove into Hartford. Good team ball was the American way, hustle was much better than black and cool, and they'd much rather see one of theirs fall out of bounds for a save than see Donnie do a one-handed slam. "You show that big guy, he's not so tough," somebody yelled from the Middlefield ladies to my right after the steal.

"He ain't about nothin, Donnie," I said loudly. It was habit. "Come on, box out." He wasn't supposed to be the big guy, at center; he was a power forward, and he should have been putting the ball on the floor the way he loved to, hiding in the corner now and then to shoot his old low-trajectory jumper, rebounding better than anyone else. I had watched a hundred times while he positioned himself surely, his hands slanting nervously up and down like fins to guide him in his own part of the water, his long arms fencing out the others behind him. He would sway for a second, his mouth hung in a triangle and eyes rolled upward, waiting for the ball to leap within reach, as it almost always did. It was like he knew instantly from the rotation of the shot where it would fly. But now he backed up in the key and swung his head around to look at the backboard, all wrong, late. Middlefield's center was old, with a hairy, concave chest and those ancient player smarts from pickup games. He could tell Donnie's familiarity and ease were gone when his back was to the basket, and I saw him smile again and again. He threw Donnie off with a pinch to the side and snatched the ball off the boards, passing it way downcourt to the cherry-picking little guard. They were up by five a few minutes before halftime.

"Don't let him get happy yet," I called out.

"Tell him, baby," Three said, from the row below me. Three was Donnie's oldest brother, Charles Morris King, III. "Get back downcourt, man."

"You shouldn't have kept him out so late, Three," I said. "Coming home at two, and he had a nine o'clock game."

"Shit, we was workin, Rosa."

"First time all week. This on-call stuff ain't getting it."

"It's better than bein at home workin on the truck with Pops. That make you old before your time." Three looked back at the court. "He gettin tore up. Donnie ain't about no center. Look at that gray boy doggin him."

I always had to smile when Three called people gray. My mother was white, my father light-skinned, and I came out sort of gray, especially in winter, when I didn't get much sun. Here in the cold, my hands looked see-through and smoky as cheap paper, and my eyes had wells of pencil-colored skin underneath.

When I was fourteen and Donnie had taken me for the first time to see Three, in back of the high school where Three and his cousin Snooter laughingly coerced change from small white students to buy malt liquor for lunch, I could tell by the way Donnie stood still and held his face carefully that he was worried about his favorite brother's estimation.

"So my brother here tell me your mama from some other country," Three had said, stroking his chin with two fingers. "You got some exotic foreign blood in you, huh?"

"She ain't no regular ghostie, cuz?" Snooter said, and the faces around him waited to laugh. I waited for somebody to say "half-breed," but I heard nothing. I wondered what "exotic" meant to Three.

"My mother's Swiss," I said, and Three's face stretched in surprise.

"Don-nay, man, don't you know Sweden is where they be makin all them porno flicks and thangs? They *free* over there! Oh, ho, ho," he laughed.

"Swiss people are from Switzerland," I said. "It's far away from Sweden."

"Yeah, baby, I was just jokin with you. Check her out, she blushin," Three said.

"You better be careful, man," Donnie said. "She got brains. And a mouth."

"Long as the brains don't outweigh the better parts, bruh," Three said. Each word was separate, like a pronouncement, and when he looked around, they laughed. Donnie's hand had been wet and cold in mine.

We watched him walk toward the drinking fountain now. "Didn't you give him no early morning lovin?" Three said, and I was angry when he didn't even bother to look at me. "He need some of that sweetness to keep his game sharp."

"Shit," I said. I was tired of Three being the only reason we'd moved to Hartford after Donnie quit college ball and ran out of money. He'd been hauling trash from construction sites with his Uncle Floyd, listening to Three talk about how the East Coast was live every time he called. All I'd been able to find was a secretary job, and Donnie the part-time guard. Winter didn't seem live to me. "He need some sharpness in his head."

"Y'all can't be fightin, now. You still eligible for the Newlywed Game and shit," Three said.

I looked at Donnie's back, bent over while he breathed. "It ain't a game," I said. They were beating up on him under the boards because he'd gotten so big. Donnie was 6-5, and the bulk he'd put on during college was still there. He was up to 220. Sometimes I couldn't believe I held him up when he lay on top of me, but in all our time together, it hadn't mattered how heavy or light he was, only whether I wanted him or not. When I put my arms around his neck and pulled him down the way I had all those years, the way I had when we first came to Hartford, his flat stomach fit over mine and my ribs had room to fall up and down when I pulled in my breath sharp with love. But now I couldn't breathe under him, felt only his chest crushing mine and his hipbones against my thighs.

He sat on the bottom bleacher while James argued with the other guys about strategy. Sweat dripped from his chin onto the floor, and his face was glossy and blank. The strategy before had been to get it to Donnie, and at center, he wasn't doing what he was supposed to do. I knew he was going to ignore them and go where he pleased after halftime.

"Man, what up?" Three said. "Why you lettin the old dude make you look bad and shit?"

"Shoot, he got it figured out so he don't have to run nowhere, just pick off the back and elbow silly under there," Donnie said. He waited, watching me. He was wondering if I had kept track.

"Ten points," I said. "Only seven boards." For years, I had named the number of rebounds I wanted, and I had to pay in kisses. "You're slow. Why don't you guys try a backdoor?"

"Shit. With who? Williams?" Donnie looked back at the court. Williams was the other forward. He'd been shooting bricks all morning, even missing two lay-ups.

The third quarter was all Middlefield boys, playing hustle ball, harassing James and kicking passes away, clunking up plays. There was no rhythm, no city ball; they didn't allow jumpers and trade-off that they couldn't have kept up with. Donnie got some tip-ins, but the team stayed five or six points down. I saw Donnie coming back up slower and slower, going outside the key and leaving the basket unprotected, trying to fade into the corner. His skin flushed red where it stretched over his collarbone.

At the start of the fourth quarter, Middlefield's center reached in to try another steal from Donnie as he whirled much too slowly in the key. He poked Donnie in the face. I knew what would happen, remembered how many times he'd said, "They can hit me anywhere they want, bow me and shit, but don't be messin with my eyes. I only got two." He popped the center in the mouth, chased him to the corner, his big shoulders rounded like a bear's with anger and concentration. I had never seen him fight. People pulled him away, and he shook them off, walked to the fountain. "Chill out, D, man," Three called, and I felt fear rising at the back of my scalp. When he walked back toward the stands, the center laughed and said something I couldn't hear, but I knew what it was, because Donnie went after him again. I closed my eyes. Donnie used to break up fights, not pursue them with legs stiff as a boxer. The Middlefield crowd was shouting, and after Donnie was ejected and sat on the bench, they stared at his back with disgust and pointed him out to the people coming in for the next game.

Thin icicles had attached the underside of our car to the street like web threads when we went outside. "I don't want to hear it," he said, and I waited while he tried to scrape the ice off the windshield. I looked at all the trees. Some had delicate bare branches standing straight up like the piece of elegant coral my mother had found somewhere and kept on the table at home. There were other trees like coaches' heads, with square-edged crew cuts, bristled and stiff. Everything was black, white, and gray here. I tried to watch the wind blow, but you couldn't see anything move here. Donnie walked back toward the gym to say something to James, and I saw that the stiff heaps of dirty snow covered anything light, anything that would move. At home, the wind would mean tumbleweeds piled so high outside my mother's door that we couldn't open it, and pink pepper berries, ferny leaves and bits of mesh from the palms, ribbons of eucalyptus bark all collected in banks by the sidewalks, in piles behind the cement barriers in the parking lots. And I was always in those parking lots during winter, during the season, at the city college gyms or the convention centers, watching practice, coming early with the team for the games, telling Donnie to watch out for the pick and roll the other team always ran, packing down his hair a little more where it was uneven near his ears. His hair grew faster there.

When we were back at the apartment, I drank bitter herb tea my mother had sent me, something she said was good for stomachaches. Donnie stomped around, hanging his wet clothes outside on the railing, turning on the TV. "Why you gotta drink that stuff?" he said. "It stinks up the kitchen. Why you can't drink something normal like soda?"

"Soda's bad for you," I said.

"Miss Body, the one always got a stomachache cause she so healthy."

"I got that because of you, fool."

"Now I gotta be a fool."

"You don't gotta be, you *wanna* be." That was what we had said into each other's ears in the dark before. I watched him lie on the bed. "You going to work tonight?"

"They said they don't have nothin for a couple of days."

"They never have anything for you any more. You and Three got all kind of time on your hands."

"You *been* asked me about fifty times, and I told you it's slow." The light from the TV, in the dark bedroom, jumped back and forth, and the glare made his face shift crazily.

I had found a Xerox copy of one of the incident reports the security guards were required to write for each job site. Donnie's illegible handwriting and secret-code spelling, which only I could unlock, had been circled and someone had written, "This is not acceptable." I knew, but I wanted him to admit it.

"Why don't you go find another job, then? Maybe you could chase some lizards out from somewhere." Donnie sucked his teeth and swung his head around, away from me. "Yeah, remember when you called me and said you found a job. Coach got it for you. 'I bounce the basketball in the gym, in case any lizards and snakes get inside, so I'll scare em away.' Really prepared you for the outside world, huh, baby?"

"Rosa, you getting on my third nerve. I'd look for another slave, okay? Let me get some rest."

"Yeah," I said, and then I stopped. I'd seen him back in Rio Seco when he quit school, carrying a small piece of paper in his wallet; he had copied his address from a bill, because when he filled out applications he couldn't spell Picasso, the street he lived on, or Rio Seco. I couldn't say it to him. In the kitchen, I picked through a bowl of pinto beans, looking for small stones that sometimes got into the bin. It seemed that every night we ate beans and rice, or *raui roesti,* the Swiss-fried potatoes and onions I had eaten daily as a child. From the kitchen window, I could see the back of the Puerto Rican restaurant across the alley. Hartford had been an escape, an adventure at first, the crowded streets, red leaves in piles, the good smell of the Puerto Rican food. But now the long tangle of icicles on the black waterpipes wasn't clear and sparkling; it was milky and old, no longer fascinating. When our car broke down, Donnie had to pay someone to fix it, because he couldn't lie on his back in the snow. We turned up the heat to 79° on my twentieth birthday, in December.

We had read the temperature in Los Angeles in the newspaper, and we wore shorts all morning and laughed. It wasn't funny when the bill came. We had no family but Three, no one to call when the pipes in the toilet froze, when somebody slashed our tires. We were suckers of the world.

Donnie switched the TV to his favorite cartoon, "Thundar the Barbarian." I had always been amazed and irritated that he and Three watched Saturday cartoons, staring and still like children.

"So we're going to have some intellectual stimulation now, since we worked out our muscles with early-morning boxing," I said, unable to stay out of the bedroom, to stop talking to him. I pulled clothes off the edge of the closet door that stuck out from under our mattress. We'd bought the bed from a hotel, and it sagged in the middle. We slid one of the closet doors underneath and sat on the shelf it made at the foot of the bed to watch TV, since there was nothing else in the room.

Donnie said, "At least Thundar got a woman who keeps her mouth shut. Maybe I should jump on into cartoon life, cause mine ain't about shit."

"You the one laying around here waiting for something to fly to you. You refuse to go back to school. You can't find another job. And you want to stay here forever because you chicken to go home and be a nobody. That's the only reason we're still here. One time you were a bighead star, everybody wanting to know what you thought about the Skyline game and what about your knee, is it better for tonight? Now you know you're gonna hear, 'Donnie King? He couldn't hang, man.' I can say it for you right here, any time. I'll be your friends *for* you and tell you all about yourself."

But he didn't put his hand over my mouth, which was how most of our fights began. He ignored me for Thundar. I pushed at his shoulder, and the flexible closet door bent a little under his weight. "You got nothing to say?" I prodded.

"You gon whup me with your tongue and then when I get mad

I'ma do something you don't like. I just want to say shut up now, okay?"

When we fought, he would get up and leave me wherever we had been rolling, on the floor, on the bed. Last month he had banged my head on the jutting corner of the closet door after I kicked him close to his family jewels. If I was in the front room, he would turn on the TV while I yelled at him to leave. He loved it. He'd watch something that allowed him to make noise, a show he could laugh loudly at, a sporting event where he could shout instructions. He knew his voice echoed off the cement walls. If I lay on the bed, throbbing in spots on my legs or arms where he had pinched me or bent something backwards, I knew he had scratch marks and blood too, but he would flap his house shoes loudly into the kitchen, banging around pots, making something to eat, taking up all the space. "This is my place, I ain't gotta go nowhere," he crowed. "You don't like it, you go." Outside there was snow and cold, and he laughed.

Thundar called upon his magical powers. He was getting ready to fight some evil, so I got up from the shelf to leave, but Donnie's arm reached out to push me onto the bed. His skin was filmed with dried sweat, and I thought of the salty taste I had wanted that morning; now his skin only rubbed dull against me. "I don't feel like messing with you," I said.

"You used to kiss me all over my face after Cal State Merceno games, and I was more sweaty then," he said. "I was soaked."

"You were somebody special then," I said, sliding out of his hands and going into the kitchen.

"I'm somebody different now, and I don't gotta ask for what I want," he said, following me and raking me onto the floor. He held both of my hands against my chest with one of his, and pulled my sweats and underwear off like he was changing a baby. "I'm somebody mad now," he said. I waited, watching his small smile, and then he laughed and dropped my legs onto the floor. "I don't want none right now," he said, and slammed the front door.

My water glass fell off the couch onto the tile. I lay on the icy linoleum; it was gritted with sand from the streets. I tried to sweep it out every day, but it crept back on our boots. I knew Donnie's breath would be smoking out of his nose like a dragon when he walked to Three's in the cold, and when I closed my eyes and felt the floor touching my backbone, I thought, he hadn't even been hard when he pushed against me. It wasn't about wanting. The cold floor and my skin were getting friendly, and the tiny rocks pricked my bare thighs. At home, in Rio Seco, my skin and Donnie's had seemed to meld together, on those hundred-degree days. Was the linoleum warming to my body, or was my skin cooled and hard? They were growing together, fusing, so I stood up, and like a tongue stuck to a rough ice cube, I left skin behind when I pulled away.

The dust joined itself together like webs along the walls and between the spidery legs of the card table and two folding chairs. I swept the webs toward the door and mixed them with the glass shards, glinting like dew in the dust.

The air outside was very still and frozen; I pushed the dust and shards close to the wall and stood at the chainlink railing. When I sniffed, the dampness in my nostrils clicked, turning icy, and I started to feel the crying, the heat in my jaws when I held it back. I lifted up my face, and remembered Donnie's father teasing him about me, laughing with his uncles. "Is the boy in love?" "She got his nose wide open." "Don't let it come a storm and he look up, cause he drown in a minute." Donnie had taken it, wouldn't move his arm from around me even when his cousins joined in.

The broom lay on its side where it had fallen, and when I narrowed my eyes, it looked like a palm frond; at home, after the wind, curled stiff palm fronds would litter the streets and yards, the high school. We had searched for places to lie down, places where the cops wouldn't find us, and after one of his games, Donnie led me back to the field near the street. I had said, "This ain't no place," and he smiled, draping the fronds over the chainlink fence, hooked by the curved bark end, until he'd made a shack in the darkest corner, away from the streetlight. When we lay on the grass, I saw the papers and trash clinging to the fence where the wind had blown them, hiding us.

The pile of clothes was damp against my hands. I touched them where they hung on the railing, the shorts and practice jersey from Cal State Merceno, the tube socks long as my arm. I breathed in again, felt the air. I went back inside and turned on the weather channel; it was fourteen degrees. I brought the plastic pitcher outside and poured cupfuls of water over the clothes, my hands red in the cold, and watched the cloth cling to the metal. I poured again, waited, poured, standing there for a long time as the water shimmered down the bumpy surface and my ears ached with cold.

I waited inside, by the window, where the light from the yellowed, dirty window shade made everything golden. Donnie's face was beautiful in that dulled brightness. When we walked home, and I'd forgotten my gloves, he sat on the couch and put my fingers into his mouth, one by one, and sucked gently until they were warm again. His face was pale gold from the winter, glowing, when I leaned toward him. His eyes were closed, and the black fans of his lashes, his straight eyebrows, the thin-feathered wings of his faint moustache were like the markings on a tiger, soft and precise.

The light would shine over the three slanting scars on his cheekbone, arranged around a small black mole like Arabic writing that I couldn't read, and I would slide against his side like a palm against the tongue that's licking the sugar, or salt, from it.

I took paper to write him a note.

July will be seven years since I kissed you, after you lost the
Doloreux game. You lost again. I am going home to the Westside.

When I went back outside, the clothes were frozen to the railing, coated with ice in a dimpled opaque pattern thick as shower glass.

tracks

TRENT / MARCH

As I'm heading down the driveway, I stop the bike because I can see the dripline at the willow tree. It's a problem spot, always too hot because the heat reflects off the white concrete, and I can't get the verbena I planted for ground cover to hide the skinny black hose. Irrigation has to be invisible, so you can't see the money you're spending. That's the point. You don't *need* to see it, or have it be seen, like my cousins with their gold jewelry and El Dog.

In the beginning, the yards I do look really funny, tubing everywhere, circles around trees like I lassoed these scrawny trunks and plants out in the middle of a brown desert, everything flattened by the bulldozers except where the banks cut in steep so we can all fit on the side of the hill.

Two years is the longest it takes to decorate right, let the yard mature, wait for the market to go up by itself. Southern California. Just live here, eat and sleep for long enough, and if you're in the right place, you make money. Do the house up, and you make more. Whenever she happened to see prospective buyers at the second house we sold, Brichée would tell them, "My husband and I love the house, we've just got it to where we want it. We're only moving because of my job."

That's not true—by then I'm tired as hell of the whole place, pouring the cement for the patio, building the deck, matching the colors inside.

The back tire crunches off the curb, and I coast down the street, check out the progress of the Spanish-style three houses down and the Cape Cod next to him. They're slow—still got cement bags piled up, none of their walkways poured yet. On the street, I have plenty of room to ride because no sidewalks are built here. The heat comes straight down my back; the city doesn't do trees here, not like in the old neighborhoods with the huge carobs and elms. It seems even wider here, with the popsicle-stick baby trees and no cars parked in front of the houses. I can fit my truck and Brichée's Honda in the three-car garage.

Brichée won't be home until damn near ten, and I haven't been riding in a long while. It's tax time, end of March, and only 5:30. After four years of this, I know the seasons for accountants. Not that she's ever home early, but tonight there's no question. At the end of our cul-de-sac, I whirl around the corner and see a woman standing at her mailbox, giving me a funny look. A who-the-hell special. Nobody knows me, even though we've been here for a year. I leave at dawn, before anyone except the commuters starting their way to L.A., so I can do most of my banks and offices when it's cool. Out in yards and parking lots all day, especially doing new sprinklers and irrigation, even winter can be too hot in Rio Seco. I usually get home around four, again before most everyone else, take my nap. Then I'm out in the back, trying to keep things under control, staining the deck, staking the trees. I have a half-acre lot, like everyone here, and the weeds are steady trying to kill me.

Riding out of Grayglen makes me dizzy sometimes, the curving short streets until you get to the main road leading down the hill to the city. Cars crank past me once I get to Gardenia. I can see the wooden signs by the side of the street, most of the arrows pointing over the hill the way the cars are going, the yellow lettering carved in: Grassridge, Rosewind, Rivercrest, Haven Hills, Grayglen. After the last, an arrow points at me, where I'm still waiting to pull out. The slope across the road is bare, with a slash down the middle where the rain made a rift, and pepper trees, wild tobacco bushes scattered near the place where the moisture gathers. I see illegals picking the prickly pear cactus, *nopales* in Spanish, I learned from the signs people put up below their houses telling the guys to stay away. The illegals ride ten-speeds down the hill every day, away from all the new tracts they're working.

That was where I started. I bought a three-bedroom in Woodbridge for $89,000 and sold it two years later for 105. In Stonehaven, I bought into the first phase for 126. Six months later, the second phase, on that land I had been watching from my back patio, where tumbleweeds kept flying over my fence, went for 149, and the third phase started at 162. I sold and came back to the better side of the slope for Grayglen.

I hear cricket buzzes near my ears when the wind flaps my lobes; Brichée's always teasing me about my big ears. Gardenia is steep. There isn't any smog for a change, and I can see most of Rio Seco spread out from here. That's the whole idea. The Westside, where my parents live, is past the long arroyo that stretches like spilled green paint in the brown fields. The last couple of days have hit 90°. I follow the strings of gray freeways, the cars close and even as beads on my mother's rosary. Brichée drives from L.A. every night, an hour and a half minimum. Two hours tonight, looks like. All these L.A. people are keeping my prices high, running out here for a cheap house, shaving and putting on makeup in their cars. I won't drive like that. One of the banks out in San Bernardino, about twenty miles away, offered me a contract seven years ago, and my father was cussing mad when I told him I wasn't going to take it. "Boy, I woulda killed for a couple of banks, the easy life. They ain't got but a scrap of lawn to cut, edge, a little trash. Shoot, I thought you had sense."

"This isn't just cutting grass," I told him. "I'm doing custom landscape, remember? This is a month of driving out there with all the materials, completely different."

"Is the money a different color? Goddamn. And you think you gon buy a house before you old as me?"

I turn at the four-way stop and cross over to Edgewild Estates, a section of custom-builts. All the streets are named after mountains: I drive down Rainier, Matterhorn, Everest. I did two of the houses here, but they didn't want anything too spectacular. Nice border gardens, and for one on Matterhorn I did a beautiful grape arbor in the back, but the front yards were ordinary. Better than most of these I'm passing, though. They look like Singletary's work, the usual boring petunias, marigolds, snapdragons in circle planters near the mailboxes. A couple of bougainvilleas along the cinderblock walls. I stop at my favorite, three weeping willows on a mound, and then head down the newest street, where they've just finished a house I saw months ago only framed. A total brick facade in front, three chimneys twisting and spiraling to a damn turret at the top. A castle. I've never seen anything close. I turn the bike around and come back for another look, stop to check out the patterns on the front walkway. Basket-weave bricks, beautiful with the rest. Three chimneys, and it's 90 in March. But yeah, that's it. I look across the street to see a woman in the bay window, staring hard at me. She glares straight at me, doing her best crime-watch frown. I laugh. You build bay windows, river-rock entries, brick facades so people will look, right? But from cars, circling around and around, or from the path where they're walking up to the front door for dinner. Not looking like me. I know I should wear the uniform, the damn biking shorts and maybe one of those stupid little caps like Tour de France, but I like to ride in my sweats. My ass looks like two canteloupes in those tight Lycra shorts. They aren't made for people of African descent. Shit, I keep wearing the sweats even though it's hot because Brichée's always complaining about how I'm going from brownskin to blueblood like my father too quick in the tender years of my life, in the sun.

Just to bother this woman, I get out my little pad of paper and write down the name of the brick contractor from the lawn sign. I always carry the pad and a pen. Since I moved to Grayglen, the cops have stopped me twice talking about, "Somebody reported suspicious activity, loitering, checking out houses."

I laughed real careful. "You want to see what I'm writing?" I showed them the pad, and then I read it, in case they didn't know some of the words. "Wisteria on gazebo, Japanese maple, agapanthus a good color combo." Yeah, right. I want to rob you, so I ride a bike past your house in the middle of the afternoon and write down how I'm going to break in. I see you looking at me, and I keep making notes about the accessibility of your windows and doors.

I turn to go back down the street—you can't ride through, like in Grayglen. You have to go back out the way you came: a closed community. She's still there. Hey, I watch people drive past my yard, slowing around the cul-de-sac to check out the way I painted my garage doors or how nice my roses look against the brick edging. Nobody plants big roses anymore.

Sometimes I can barely stop myself from running out the front door and yelling "Booga booga!" I say to Brichée, "That car will depart at some *high* speeds. There goes the neighborhood." She gets pissed when I talk like that. She's chatted with our neighbors—on the right, a stockbroker, on the left, another accountant. She doesn't run them off. But Brichée's light, bright, and just about right—she's Louisiana. I remember when she showed up at the city college, brothers were falling all over her and her sister Brandy.

Past Edgewild, there's nothing but orange groves. I pass a dry bank, and the colonies of red ants are tossing up mounds of coarse sand. I watch them carrying bits of palm bark, dry straw, big loads weaving back and forth along the asphalt. Even though they name these places half-nature and half-England, Hampton or Fox or Hunter, this is as close as you get to wilderness before the dozers grade it. I have to break out the Diazanon granules for months because the ants are the worst problem. They eat flowers and stems, where in my parents' neighborhood I only saw them eating regular ant food like sugar and soda. Up here, I find deep holes from ground squirrels; I hear coyotes at night.

I watch to see if the old beat-up house is still here in the next grove, past the canal. I was keeping an eye on it a few months ago. It's gone. I walk around the razed area, where the foundation and chimney are left, with lots of trash from partying rich kids. No For-Sale sign yet, but I look closer at the groves and see the milkweed, straight and perfect as military boys, marching up and down the irrigation furrows.

The old farmhouses spaced in the groves were sturdy, some of them three stories. One old man I met told me that was so the farmers could look out over the tops of the trees and watch for people stealing oranges. I kick the edges of the foundation; the walls are thick, wide, and every room would have touched the outside, had a window. The walls in my house are thin. When Brichée watches "Wiseguy" or "Miami Vice", I can hear the guns and screeching tires way upstairs in the bedroom I use for an office. I like sitting there, drawing plans, circles for each plant in the flower beds, curving paths and raised rectangular planters. I etch in the leaves sometimes.

When Brichée's in her office, down the hall from our bedroom, I hear her 10-key sounding like the mice that tapped inside the walls when I was small. Everything's thin in this new house. One night she was bitching about the parquet floor—she said another splinter got her, and she was tired of trying to keep the wood shined. "We should have picked tile," she said. "I'm going to get a maid. I see their cars down the street when I'm home late in the morning."

I told her no way, no maid. That was too close. "Don't get black on me," she said. "I'll do it if I want."

"What am I, the field nigger?" I yelled, and then I did something I remember my father doing when he wanted to prove his house was his. I punched the closest door. But when my father did it, the frame shook, and everyone was quiet. My whole damn door caved in, hollow as a wafer cookie. I bought a carved oak door after that—it matched the floor anyway, and it'll recoup the money I spent.

I sit down with my back to the chimney and watch the crows parade and fight in the field across from the grove. My father saw a house as old as this one had been, a small Victorian with all the gingerbread trim, when I was still at city college. He took me downtown to see it. "Take you a belt sander to some of that wood inside, stain it up," he said, standing on the porch, looking in the windows with me. The front room had a built-in china hutch. A mess, but it had potential. "Paint the trim with all them different colors. This the kind of veranda I always thought your mama would like," he said, and it was true; she spent hours outside on the little square cement steps at our house, shelling peas or pulling the husks off corn. "Can't fit but one more woman out there with her," my father would say while we were working on a lawn-mower, "and you know she need at least two to talk about me like a dog."

At the old house downtown, he stood next to me, close, and said, "You buy this, you won't be stuck on the Westside, but you won't be far away." I remember looking at the street, ragged at the edges, thinking it could go either way, restored or run-down. "What?" he said. "It's cheap. You want to own, right?"

I'd already thought of Woodbridge then, of location, but I was still saving up the down payment and starting the business. My father died a year after that, left me the down payment—two insurance policies that he'd been paying on for years, since he and my mother had first moved here from Jackson, Mississippi years before I was born. They'd lived in their house for thirty-one years, bought it for $9,000, paid it off. A $9,000 house in southern California. Everybody, my aunt, cousins, they've all been in the same houses for as long as I can remember. I knew exactly when their plum trees were ready to pick, when they'd call me to come stake the baby fig because the Santa Anas were blowing.

I bought in Woodbridge. I asked Mama to come live with me; I'm the only child. "You can't walk to nothin up there—it ain't no store, no church, nowhere. Uh-uh, baby, don't worry. Sister and them can come here." My aunt Sister and cousin Tarina came to stay with her, and they can all fit in the kitchen to talk at the same time, if not on the steps.

Mama comes to the newest house and laughs at the self-cleaning oven, the garbage disposal, the trash compactor. Brichée loves this house, with the most appliances we've had.

"What is this, self-cleaning?" Mama reads.

"Brichée spilled some barbecue sauce in there one night, and the next day she turned it onto self-clean, came back from work and it was just a little gray ashy spot," I said, pointing to the dial.

"She still have to wipe out the ashy stuff?" Tarina asked.

"Yeah, I guess."

"Why she don't just wipe the damn stuff up in the first place then?"

"Hush," Mama said. "Brichée got all these rinds and peelings in the sink, though. Why you don't put them on your compost heap, Trent? Ain't no need to be grinding them up."

"Mama, nobody keeps compost anymore. It just breeds bugs and disease."

"Shoot, you gon have bugs anyway. Everybody got bugs. Less you got a self-cleaning yard, too," she said, and Tarina cracked up, loving it. On Labor Day, Memorial Day, any of them, Brichée won't come down to Mama's yard for ribs and potato salad and peach cobbler. She says she has bills or accounts to do, but I know it's because Tarina and my cousins always start on her. Tarina looks out the etched-glass pane in the front door, checking out the street. "All y'all got the same kind of houses in this track?"

I know better than to correct her word. "Three models, but each one's slightly different, and that's why the landscaping's so important."

"Huh," she says, looking back at the living room. At Christmas, Tarina told everyone, "Brichée got it so clean and pale in there you don't wanta *walk*. And don't bring no babies, now." The house *was* light—Brichée did this one in cream carpet, cream walls, light-oak picture frames to match the mantel and banister. Pale mauve furniture. Even the living room fireplace was light marble—alabaster, I think she called it. She does the insides, looks at those funny curtains, balloons and valances she says, and I do the outsides.

I used to study the old-money houses my father cut, where the ladies gave teas in their rose arbors. Those gardens have subtle colors, silvery gray and blue salvia, huge cabbage-headed dahlias, bronze chrysanthemums. I read the *Architectural Digests,* the *Horticultures,* the high-class stuff. I looked at the hedges, the shapes, the blending colors, before I did mine.

No huge plum trees in the front, no figs or apricots, no beans and tomatoes growing up the side of a chainlink fence. No food in the front yard, because that meant you were raising something you needed. And nothing like morning glories, geraniums, common flowers.

I remembered the gardens at the very top of the hill, the estates that had been there for decades. I did mine English country, with old-fashioned borders and white wooden arches, the trellis for roses, and this time, a gazebo with purple clematis at the sides. Perennials, flowers no one else around here uses, columbine and delphinium and veronica. We always sell in the spring, when everything is blooming. Next year will be the same.

They go fast because it looks like Prince Charles or some earl lives there, as close as I can get it. We'll arrange with the realtor to show people during the day, as usual, when we're gone. If the lookers saw me, they'd bug.

I ride past the last grove, around the corner toward Gardenia again. The cars are still racing, I can hear ahead of me, and the sky lightens up near the edges of the hills, getting deeper above. This whole area will sell, I think, sell fast. I know Rio Seco, all of it, so I watch for my next move. You have to learn the boundaries, the newly-razed trees or cleared fields, the right hills. I tried to tell my cousin Snooter last year when he visited. He rode Brichée's bike, the one she never touches anyway, and I showed him the layout of our tract, told him about location and resale. He started laughing when I shifted gears. "Hey, I used to ride this bike for *keeps,* you forgot?" I told him. "I had to learn to do it right."

"Yeah, Trent, we used to see you *motorvating* home from school on that ten-speed, talking about that was your cruise, man." He pulled next to me. "Let me ax you something, cause you don't never stop. When we were kids, you use to just let go, you know, ride with no hands. When you do that, man, you know what you steering with? Your crotch. Remember?"

He was in my face then, and I couldn't laugh, but my crotch *is* sore now, on the way up the slope, and I have to smile. My legs, too. My father used to holler at me when I said I was tired of pushing the mower. "Go on, you better pass me and improve that shit. Cause if you lag behind, I'ma turn around and run yo ass over."

"You wouldn't tow me, Pops?"

"Shit, I didn't raise you to pull you."

I pump hard up Gardenia, scaring the last of the crows out of the empty field before Grayglen. They join the flock flying down toward the river, over the city. I used to see them every night about this time, when I was standing in my father's yard, and I'd watch them dive at each other when they got mad. Inside Grayglen, an illegal is still swiping circle patterns into the cement of an entry, and past him, I look up my street. All the garage doors are closed. Now I can hear the sprinklers coming on, the clicks of automatic timers starting them up; I pass the vibrating air conditioners, the buzzing pool filters that seem to float heavy in the air. I never put in pools—

they're a liability sometimes, not a sure asset. I think of a spa, but then I remember our house has a spa, in the master tub. We've never used it. The dark is coming down fast now, making all the hisses and humming seem louder, and by the time I get close to the end of our street, I see TVs flashing blue through the windows. In each of the yards and driveways I pass, no one is outside.

chitlins

LANIER / AUGUST

Lanier got off work right at six, not waiting around to talk with Robert and the younger guys coming on shift. He pulled the small Ford truck out of the lot quickly; the cab was already hot, the windshield full of dry light and bright floating dust. The dawn didn't take but a minute to make a day in August, he thought, no messing around with haze and low clouds to burn off in a few hours. Serious hundred-degree days, and he wanted to get out to the place and fill the wallows with water.

Nearly all the other cars were going the opposite direction on the freeway, fenders flashing in the low sun. They were heading into L.A., had an hour to go, and he was already cruising down the slope into Rio Seco, taking the offramp just past the old railroad bridge to the Westside. He drove parallel to the tracks for a few minutes, putting his head out the window when he came to the citrus packing house, looking for the too-small, unsaleable oranges and grapefruit that Perez sometimes left in a pile for him. The dirt was bare, hard-packed by the feet that stood and rubbed there during lunch. All the Mexican workers peeling and licking at oranges; he saw them if he woke up early and went to talk to Perez.

The '49 Chevy dump truck was in the alley behind his house. He checked to see if Red Man's Apache was there, too, the one he parked behind Lanier's because his own yard was full of cars, motorcycles, and junk. The two-ton was half-full, flatbed covered with splintered wood, chunks of plaster and wallboard, concrete. Red Man must have cleaned out another old building for one of the contractors. The dogs heard Lanier now and threw themselves against the bent fences all up and down the alley, did it every morning at 6:20 knowing it was him. From the sandy path, he could see into the backyards, long and narrow, through the chainlink or barbwire braced with cardboard and scrap wood. The old sisters across the way, on Picasso Street, had put in corn again this year, when they'd sworn it was too much trouble and they were going to buy it at the store. Their tomatoes flopped, too hot already, against the wire cages.

Unlocking the shed that opened onto the alley, he heard Lee Myrtle's ducks murmur and shift on the other side of the wood. Every morning, he had to load the shovels onto the Chevy and then put them back into the shed at night, or the gangs that ran the alley would take them, take anything: chicken wire, trash cans, hoses, hoes. On the wooden slats that closed in the flatbed, he'd had to paint a black rectangle to cover LOS DEMENTES DE WESTSIDE SECO.

Through his fence, he could see the back porch, where the light was on. When he was younger, Lee Myrtle would sleep during the day, while he did, but now she woke up as he came home. He turned before he saw her, because he wanted to hurry.

"Lanier," she called just when he'd gotten up into the seat. "Ain't you gon eat?"

"I got a load to get," he shouted, firing up the engine, listening close when it popped and stopped. The truck was huge and scarred as a rhinoceros he'd seen on TV, and in the rearview mirror he saw the shreds of lettuce and carrot tops hanging from the gates, dangling and jumping with the bumps in the dirt.

The fish market was only a few blocks away, next to Top Cat Liquor. When Lanier started to pull around the back, he could smell the clams and oysters from the street. They were piled by the wall, some scattered on the asphalt close to the open door, and after he'd scraped the spilled ones into the boxes, he leaned into the doorway to holler. "Hey, Jim, ain't you got no shrimp? You know they love some shrimp, them big ones you be lettin go when they get green. Don't be stingy, now."

"Shut up, Lanier," Jim said. "Too many of them Louisiana niggers makin gumbo or whatever they want to cook with that big shrimp. Go on."

The L&L Market had left a heap of smashed watermelons and a mound of empty smiles, cut rinds that rocked back and forth on the ground when they fell off the truck. Lanier was sweating, his work shirt wet all down the back, and he pulled himself away from the seat now and then to let the wind touch there. People always shook their heads at him, said, "Man, you just get off a nine-hour shift and want to shovel up all that stanky stuff? You ain't got *no* sense. I'd be in the *bed,* no questions axed."

"This my cocktail time, fool," he would say. "You don't come home from work and get in the bed, you gon sit there with your beer. Red Man gon sit there with his twelve-pack." They all laughed. Red Man said, "Well, shit, what you drinkin for relaxation, then? Hog slop? You's a crazy nigger."

The truck blew dust along the frontage road, and now he was driving along with the traffic still going to L.A., but he was higher up on the bank. When he shifted gears to turn down the curving dirt road, the cab shook and roared; he saw four of the pigs out again, waiting for him, pushing through yesterday's boxes and a pile of cardboard. The sow with the broken hind leg stood alone, a shadow near the pepper tree.

He didn't want to kill her yet. She wasn't nearly the fattest, and no one would want meat for months. He'd just done a sow, one that hadn't had a litter for two years, for somebody's Fourth of July.

This one kept her distance, not letting him near to examine the leg; she was wild as ever, running jerky when he tried to get near. Big, about two-hundred-fifty pounds, her hair thin as brown summer grass, and she seemed happy to be separate from the others, fed by herself. He dropped a heap of rinds near the straw mound where she usually hid from the sun.

The others kicked up puffs and trails of dust, running for the food he threw over the fences: first the babies and females, in the pen to the east with the tin-roofed shelters, then the males and yearlings in the large, free-range section. They ran in close to the wood that squared around the rocky ground and baby tumbleweeds, still blue green now and the only plants left anywhere in the heat.

The males screamed and fought over the clams, and the new piglets, dog-sized, snuffled into the watermelon meat, almost buried in the fruit, then shoved out slimy-pink by their impatient mothers. Lanier sat under the ancient pepper tree, branches hanging limp and dusty as a sick rooster's tail feathers. Across from him, the killing shack was empty and silent. He fed the pigs corn and water there for a few weeks before they were shot and pulled to the cement slab. The smaller pepper tree's limbs stretched over the slab, dangling the chains that lifted the meat.

He would wait until the pigs were finished with the first frantic crunchings, listening to them click the clamshells together, before he checked the fence. New holes had been pushed out somewhere, because the twin piglets ran across the dirt road to the hillside. Lanier threw a rock behind them. Black faces, black butts, with a white stripe wide as a sash circling their middles. He hadn't seen two so perfectly matched, running so closely together, for a long time. They darted into the fence and Lanier stood up to follow them, find the opening, but the heat waved in the dust, and he sat back against the tree. Another wooden pallet would have to be stood on its side and pounded into the dirt between the rotted gray posts that were on the land when he bought it. The plywood and scrap he jammed into the gaps always came loose, but he fixed only the largest holes. The pigs never went anywhere, never strayed far from the food. They nosed outside, rooted in the scatterings of junk Red Man dumped, the bedsteads and fenders and cookstoves he had found and insisted he'd need later, and if they found no leftover tatters of cabbage or a clamshell that still smelled, they walked back inside and lay under the shelters or slid into the deep furrows they'd worn in the earth, the pits he filled with water. When he closed his eyes, he heard Mississippi, heard himself fifteen and trying to hide from the plow and his father's field; he was fifty-four now, but when he leaned his head against the pepper tree, the hair at the back of his neck was still thick enough to cushion against the rough bark, and the police helicopter, probably swooping over the Westside as usual, was just a hummingbird. The sounds of sirens and the rushing cars from the freeway weren't loud enough to cut through the pigs' hollering and threatening each other over the oysters.

When he woke up, at about two, he went out to the front porch for a few minutes to clear his head. The fan turned back and forth behind him in the kitchen, where Lee Myrtle sat writing a letter to her sister. Lanier heard the deep hum from down the street, mixing with the fan, and then the vibrations separated into drumbeats, quick, echoing, metal-sharp; they pounded in his head for a moment, a blacksmith hammering mule shoes back in Grenada. He shook his hand, which he'd slept on, felt the tingles in his palm and then his ears. "Damn sideshow. Why I always gotta listen to what they do?" he said. The customized Toyota pickup, speakers in the covered bed, pulled into the yard next door and parked diagonally across the dirt.

"One or another of em was in and out all night," Lee Myrtle said, not raising her head. "They been up there hollerin for the girl, bout she owe them."

The driver sat, unmoving, and his doors vibrated with music. Lanier touched the side of the house, went into the backyard to check the melons and tomatoes. Two ducks ran from the pounding drums, past Lanier when he stood next to the peach and plum trees.

The girl next door was out now, in her robe, talking to the boy in the passenger seat. She must don't sleep till I do, Lanier thought, cause she wake up about the same time. Lee Myrtle had said the stereo was loud until long after she gave up and went into the extra room to sleep, and the girl's three children ran the streets after dark. Rencie, that was her name. The house had belonged to her Auntie Viola, a widow who'd never remarried. Viola was from Jackson, moved in only a few years after Lanier and Lee Myrtle. Picasso Street was all Mississippi then—Biloxi, Mayersville, Grenada—only Red Man and Lonzo from Oklahoma.

This Rencie was from L.A. He'd heard her talking to another girl one day, while they sat on folding chairs in her yard. "I can't believe Mama sent me to take care of this country-ass house. This a backward place, Rio Seco."

Huh, Lanier thought. *This* country? Best not send you to Grenada.

"Shoot, yo cousin told me the court was tired a seein you. He said you had to get out the county."

"I only had to get outta Compton. She didn't have to send me all the way out here and shit."

She never even spit on the greens tree that her aunt had planted ten years ago, along the chainlink fence. It yellowed and shrank away from the wire, and the apricots on the side-yard tree near Lanier's morning glory fell and turned see-through brown, fruit flies misting everywhere.

"Ain't you gon pick em?" he asked her once, walking over to where she sat against the wall, watching the street. It was May then.

"It's too many. Keta the only one like em." She had two girls, Naketa and Fatima, and a boy, Teddy.

"You know your Aint Viola put up twenty-one jars of preserves offa that tree last year."

"Shit, it's too hot to be in the kitchen. I buy me some preserves. And they givin em away at the government program, with that cheese. Grape jelly."

"That stuff just thick-up Kool Aid," Lanier said. "It ain't no good for your kids."

"They eat it. They ain't dead. Why you so nosy? Ain't you got cows or pigs or somethin to feed? Somebody told me you the original Old MacDonald."

"Just some hogs. People want fresh meat now and then, stead a that Burger King." He looked at the empty bags near her chair.

She half-closed her eyes. Her arms were thin, glistening iridescent in the folds at her elbow. "You must want to get in the kitchen *for* me, huh? I ain't all up in your face. My kids stay on my side of the fence. Why you don't do the same?"

Now she said loudly to the boy, "Come on. I swear." He shook his head, patted the pinstriping on the door. Rencie glanced at Lanier and turned back toward her house. "It's plenty other niggas in the world," she yelled at the boy, and the driver sped off the yard, leaving only faint marks in the packed-hard dirt. When the drums were gone again, Lanier could hear her kids further down the street. Even her cat lived on grasshoppers, came to Lanier's yard to drink from the puddles around the peach tree.

He was waiting for Floyd. Lee Myrtle said Floyd had come by the night before to borrow ten dollars.

The aqua truck pulled up after four. Roscoe was with Floyd, who waved the money when he got close to the porch. "Shoot, almost had to send one a them boys home with heat stroke. Lee Myrtle got ice tea?"

"Who said I want you on my porch? Take your stanky grass-smellin truck down the street where it belong," Lanier said, going into the house for the sun tea.

Roscoe sat on the steps, his baseball cap on his knee. "Been out to your place, Lanier," he called. "Took a load of extra pallets about a hour ago. Seen two white men out there, pokin around."

"Don't tell me I'ma have to get Tique out there again, put him in the trailer with a shotgun," Lanier said.

"Remember when that dude from Del Rosa tried to sneak up there, what was it, two years ago? How many he get?" Floyd asked.

"He got four till I moved Tique in the trailer. Boy ain't got no sense, but he do got ears," Lanier said.

"Naw, listen," Roscoe interrupted. "These cats was from downtown, man. Ties, white shirts, county car. They was checkin fences and shit, lookin for you."

"Wasn't they bulldozin that land on the other side of you, up on the ridge, Lanier?" Floyd asked. "Raisin all kinda dust." He looked past the house from where he stood on the grass. "Uh oh, I see another cloud of dust. Red Man headin down the alley to what he call a garage."

After the grinding gears had stopped, Red Man came through the side yard. "You gon do a hog for me next month? We got that family reunion down at the park. Ain't but once every five years, and all them people from Tulsa and L.A. some greedy eaters. Give em some to take home."

"Goddamn, don't you even speak?" Floyd shouted. "Could say hello and shit." He pointed down the long street, to where the end was hidden in the smog. "Ain't you never gon clean up yo yard? Don't you know I *live* near here?" He turned to Roscoe and Lanier. "Fool done brought home another truck, one a them king cabs."

"Hell," Roscoe said. "Your property value ain't shit anyway. *You* live there, and look at you."

"Man, you think you safe with that shit? Don't you know they was down there at my end of Picasso last week, talking about a beautification project? Call theyselves about to build some big cement flower boxes all along the bank where it go up to that new development, where Green Hollows use to be."

"You a lie."

"Serious, now, they was walking all up and down in front of my yard, pointin and starin. Told me and Maitrue next door that in New York City, people did some study bout flowers and window boxes."

He imitated a woman's voice. "People were so much more willing to spend time on upkeep when they had flowers, Mr. King." Floyd put his hands behind his back. "Then she want to go and pull on my greens tree. 'Now rather than allowing weeds to front yo fence, why not try flowers?' she said. I told her, 'Man, that's my dinner you tuggin on! That's one a Red Man's greens trees, been there ten years' "

"Bout as long as his Cadillac been in the side yard," Roscoe said, and Lanier laughed, but he thought about the city men and the holes in the fences.

They came again the next week, while he stood in the truckbed. He had brownish heads of iceberg lettuce, soggy, dimple-skinned grapefruit, and more watermelon rinds. The men picked their way around the straw heap, and he could tell they didn't see the sow's twitching ears.

"Mr. Chatham," the taller one said, after shaking Lanier's hand. "Your lot here is worth much more than you paid for it originally, I'm sure. When did you acquire the property, what is it, just over an acre?"

"Long time ago," Lanier said, watching the other one who shook his head slowly near the fences.

"Was it around 1969?"

If he know, why he askin? Lanier thought.

"Have the, uh, hogs been here all that time?"

"No. Twelve years."

"Well, I'm sure you know the situation. People are moving out to Rio Seco for affordable housing, people from L.A., and on a piece of acreage like this, ten houses could be built. That means your land here is going to bring a remarkable profit, I'm telling you. Is this farm running at much of a profit? How many hogs do you have?"

"I don't know, last count," Lanier said, and the man's head dipped like a bird drinking. "About a hundred, probably. It ain't about profit."

"Huh," he said. "Well, as you probably know, the city has owned the land abutting yours, here to the west, for years. We'd like to purchase yours in order to offer a parcel that would extend from the edge of the hillside there to the frontage road." Lanier swung around to look at the steep ridge where the baby piglets tried to climb every year and rolled back down, their bellies sliding over the squirrel holes. He turned to the west, where the bulldozing was done.

"That yours, too?" he asked the man.

"That parcel's already been sold. The developer has people lined up for the lots there, and he wants this adjacent parcel, too."

Parcels. This ain't about no parcel post. The shorter man was behind him now. "How do you keep track of them all? It looks like you've got several holes, and they're well used."

"They don't run far," Lanier said. "Always hungry." He stared away from the two men, at the straw heap that looked like it was breathing, shuddering.

The water pump was out on the Ford. Lanier pulled it under the spreading carob tree at the edge of the street so he could work in the shade. The heat was all day, all night, now, like Mississippi. His wrists and shoulders seemed to buzz warm after he got off work, and he couldn't sleep in the sweat that coated him when he lay down.

Naketa watched Lee Myrtle pick peaches for a cobbler; she leaned against the fence, staring at the shaky leaves, the june bugs that whirred out angrily.

"Here, baby, take a coupla these. I got too many. My kids ain't comin out for the weekend," Lee Myrtle said.

Naketa edged around the fence. "You got kids?"

"Two daughters and two grandbabies. They live in L.A."

"My birthday is next week. I'ma be eight." Lee Myrtle laughed from inside the branches, Lanier heard. Naketa stood under her now. "Can I have some plums?"

Lee Myrtle filled the lines of Naketa's arms where they pressed against her belly in a cradle, and then Naketa walked across the yard, backward-slanted as Chuck Berry to balance the fruit against her chest.

"Go on and give them to your mama, Keta," Lee Myrtle called. Lanier saw the girl's head turn quickly to the open door of her house, where the sounds of laughter came from the television, and then she scuttled past, to the far side of the yard. She rolled the plums carefully onto a piece of cardboard by the dying rosebush and crouched, eating the fruit so fast the juice dripped from her elbows into the dust.

He washed his face with cold water inside, and Lee Myrtle followed him into the back room. "You know, Maitrue's daughter told me Keta's mama on that stuff they put in the pipe and smoke. She said they be sellin it at that pink house, down the way off Tenth. I swear, Lanier, a pipe. My mama smoke a pipe back in Grenada, remember? I like to died every time people seen her, so country."

"What they puttin in the pipe?"

"Maitrue's girl talkin about some rock cocaine, somethin crazy."

Lanier brushed her shoulder on the way outside. "Goin out there to check the fences."

"That's all you ever worry about now—them fences."

He stopped for a moment. "That girl, Rencie, she think *this* is country."

On Sunday, he drove past the place and down the road to where the new model houses were being framed. The land was cut in flat squares up the ridge, like descending rice farms he'd seen pictures of somewhere.

"He said they was waitin in line?" Floyd said a few hours later, when they brought the beer and dominoes. He squinted at the crow screaming from a telephone pole.

"Man, you done told us a hundred times, all last month," Red Man said, righting a barber chair that had tipped over. "What you fittin to do?"

"Shoot, they slow," Floyd said. "I knew L.A. was a nutcase back in 1965. Didn't want my boys in all that, niggas shootin each other for a quarter."

Roscoe stood and threw a peach pit at the crow. "Westside was the only place we *could* buy. Now look, Carnell and Retha's boy, what's his name? Trent. Yeah, he bought into that fancy tract, the other side of the hill."

"Grayglen," Red Man said. "I had a couple of yards up there."

"Trent probably the darkest thing even *drive* up there. Even they maids is all Mexican now," Floyd said.

Lanier thought. "Lee Myrtle used to work up there, in the older part. The Culvers. Ten dollars a week."

"What you mumblin and grumblin about, Lanier?" Floyd said. "Start countin your money. Give it to me—I'll count it."

"I ain't sellin," Lanier said. The snuffle-talk from the pens drifted through the slats into the quiet.

"You a fool," Floyd said. "You gon *get* you some cash."

"You ain't makin no money off these hogs," Red Man said. "I seen you pay for them damn pig pellets, if it wasn't nobody givin you trash to feed em. And you always talkin about that corn cost money, when somebody finally poke you into killin one a these suckers."

"Meat taste fishy as seaweed he don't give em that corn," Floyd said. "Shit, he gon get enough money to buy *lobster* and who need pig?"

"Shut up, man," Roscoe shouted. "Play."

The city men came again, came to the porch of his house. "You really need to decide, Mr. Chatham. The developer is anxious to get started."

Like it ain't no question, Lanier thought, but what bothered him more was taking the food morning and evening and not knowing whether they'd been at the place while he was asleep, touching the fenceposts, kicking at the pallets, laughing at the piglets with sashes widening around fat bellies. He couldn't even put Tique out in the tiny trailer; Tique would love to shoot anyone. He couldn't guard anything from the two men, and Lanier bet they breathed in the smell from the wallows and still frowned, many times as they'd stood there.

In November, Red Man woke him early one morning, wobbling sheets of paper near Lanier's face. "They done put notices on the trucks, both of em," he shouted.

"Don't be hollerin," Lee Myrtle said, standing behind him.

The papers said that the trucks were public nuisances, that property owners in the neighborhood had complained about their being parked in the alley. The owners had thirty days to move the vehicles.

"And ain't put nothin on your Cadillac been in the street for a month now?" Lee Myrtle said. "Huh."

"Don't start," Red Man shouted, and Lanier grabbed the papers from him.

"Catch yourself," Lanier said, angry. "That's my wife. Go on home."

His wrists ached from work, felt wider and wider, like the bones had tiny jacks inside pushing them apart. He went to the back, saw the dust still hanging ankle-high where Red Man had driven down the alley. He could hear Rencie's music all the way back here, now that the too-early morning pulled away from his ears and eyes.

The Mexican market on Seventh Street had been happy to give him spoiled loads now, too, because the city had closed the dump. He drove from there to the L&L, shovelled up the cabbage, carrot tops, cheese without thinking. But when he drove along the freeway, he remembered the dump, how far away it had seemed when he moved to Rio Seco. A few years ago, a new tract had been built across the arroyo from the landfill, and the houses were big, with bay windows, garages the size of his yard. The new people had complained about the smell when the wind blew from the east. Now it was twelve miles out to the county sanitation, and ten bucks a pop, Red Man told him, so the market had gotten word to him.

"They gon change the zoning on you," Floyd said every day. "Ain't nothin you can do."

"Shit, change the zoning for *us* we don't watch out," Roscoe frowned. "Build all around the Westside and have them people complain about the smell of barbecue. They rewrite that zoning faster than you can holler 'Got him by the toe.'"

Lanier drove faster, the engine roaring so loud he could feel it in his hair. Make yo Mississippi ass feel at home, Roscoe had laughed. Lanier remembered driving out from L.A. with Lee Myrtle, seeing the miles of tumbleweeds pillowing over the fields. It had been November then, too, and they were round as his daughters' Afros, thick at the centers.

When he touched the fences, listening to the scrape of the pigs' feet and the thuds of their bellies hitting each other, he pulled out the notices, balled them up, threw them into one of the greenish wallows where they floated light as popcorn on the water. One of the younger males ran frantically for them, splashing in to eat them quickly.

"You see the signs?" Floyd asked. "What they callin it?"

Lanier was silent. The three model homes had lawns now, instant sod, wrought-iron fences all around the yards. "Morning Ridge," he said.

"Shit," Red Man laughed. "Been Rattlesnake Mountain down to this side since we got here."

"You can't sell no rattlesnakes," Roscoe said. "You have to name it right."

"I call it Traffic Ridge," Red Man said. "Get up in the morning and face the traffic to L.A." The dominoes clicked in his hand, and he slammed down the big six. "Go to the bone yard, Floyd. You ain't got none a that," he shouted.

Floyd took three pieces from the scattering at the edge of the table and added them to his hand. "Lanier, feed this dog of yours. You and your strays. This one so hungry he trying to eat the dirt off my pants cuff."

The chain hanging from the pepper tree laid a shadow over the table. "You pull out that Cadillac engine yesterday?" Lanier asked. "I still don't believe it."

"I still don't believe you gon make me move all my stuff off this place," Red Man said. "My boys gon be moanin and groanin if they have to help me."

"You want the city to move it for you?" Floyd said. "Keep throwin away them notices, they do it. Only charge you thousands of dollars." He slammed a domino on the table. "Which is what Conklin here could have tomorrow, dollars. Fore they take it away."

"Ain't nobody takin nothin away," Red Man said.

"Talkin bout a eyesore and a health hazard? Shit," Floyd shouted. "He better get him what he can *now!*"

Every time he saw them, it was the same, and he heard their voices behind the machines at work, alongside the cars from the freeway, and in the crunching of dried out tortillas the pigs ate. He stood up, thighs bumping the table and making wide cracks between the lines of dominoes. "And if I fix all the fences? If y'all come out tomorrow and move all Red Man's leavings . . . " He paused, felt the tickle of an ant crawl up his ankle. "If I act like the place ain't even mine? They ain't gon want it? I don't want y'all out here. Don't come. It ain't your land, it ain't your meat. Go sit on the Westside and jaw till hell freeze over."

Just before New Year's, when the wind blew the pepper tree branches against his face like stockings hanging from the shower curtain, he and Lonzo, who always butchered the pigs, did two of the largest males. Feet, frosty-white tripe, chitlins and hog maws. Only two this time—Lanier took the meat around to the people who'd ordered it, and gave some to the Streeters out in San Bernardino who didn't have the money this year. It was quiet at his house the day after New Year's, when his daughters had gone back to L.A. already because they didn't have any time off work. Lee Myrtle held a plate of shiny chitlins, grayish from the long cooking and then pink with Tabasco sauce. She called out to Rencie, who stood in her yard looking down the street for her kids.

"Come on and slide some a this down your throat. Bring a shine of good luck to your forehead," she shouted. Lanier looked up from the table, saw Rencie laugh. Rencie came closer to the fence, and her legs were thinner, narrow as new mulberry branches, pearly-ashed. While she grew smaller, her eyes seemed to expand, rounder and shiny, moving faster than her mouth or her hands.

"Huh! I might as well be in Oklahoma with my daddy's uncles. Always talkin bout luck and gimme a pigfoot and a bottle of beer. Play them old-timey songs." She turned back to the street for a moment. "Beer ain't gon give me no luck or nothin else. And ain't no pig's foot got enough meat on it for me." Her voice trailed off, and she went back to the front of the yard, looked down the darkening street again. Closing the grimy door, covered with the children's dark handprints, she looked at Lanier where he stood in the kitchen screen, and then the TV light, tinged pale blue as winter sky cleared by the wind, leaped into the sheets covering her windows.

He lay in bed for three days, not going to work, his wrists aching. Someone had brought Lee Myrtle chocolate candy, and the smell filled the room, murky-sweet as the time one of Red Man's sons had dumped a truckload of carob pods and the pigs had crushed them underfoot to chew out the sharp, sugary powder. Red Man's junk was still there; Lanier had been slowly moving it out to the edge of the land. He closed his eyes, heard their voices, the cars and pigs and shouting, and then he got up, threw the phone across the room at the candy. The dial tone hummed when he picked it up; he called Lonzo again, picked up his .22 and got into the big Chevy.

At Floyd's house, he was still for a second, then felt his heart beat so loud it hurt his skin, the way it did when he woke up from deep day sleep because someone was shouting at Rencie's or the telephone rang. He waited for the pounding to stop, but it felt harder, harder.

The pigs weren't used to anyone but Lanier moving around inside the pens and the men moved as a group: Lonzo, Red Man and Floyd and Roscoe, even Floyd's brother Charles. Lanier and Lonzo cut out the largest male first, the huge black hog, and when Lanier shot him in the head, the other pigs called and screamed but it was almost practiced, like they hollered when he fed them. Then when he and the men shot again and again in the males' pen, the females and younger ones raised their screeching immediately, high and long, like cars that waited at a red light and then accelerated, bursting forward together.

They carried the slabs of back meat and ribs, the tripe and feet, all night and all the next day, driving; blood stiffened in the hair around his ears, in his knuckles, dried in the webbing of his thumbs. Lonzo drank two pints of Yukon Jack, screwed his grindstone onto the edge of the table where they'd played dominoes. The sisters on Picasso said, "You didn't clean out them pigs with corn, and this smell fishy, full a that garbage," but he left meat with them, with Maitrue and Frank Brown, Floyd's wife, and there was still more. Viola was dead, Tates gone, too, and some of the older people were in homes now. No room in those senior citizens' apartments for meat, small as the studio rooms were. Neither of Lanier's daughters, none of Red Man's or Floyd's kids knew how to cure the meat or salt it, cook it either, unless it was already cut up and pancake thin, dry as old sponge under plastic in the store. Like the girl next door, Lanier thought, his fingers refusing to bend under the coat of blood; she'd looked at those apricots like they were strange, something she'd never seen.

Floyd loved being right. He said carefully, "The zoning, man, they was gon get you." Lanier looked at the sun rising just over the freeway. He drove toward the Westside with another load in the back of the Ford. Lee Myrtle was wrapping, tying, marking words on the sides, he knew. When he pulled onto Picasso Street, he saw that the door to his house was open, and then he saw Rencie's door open, too.

She sat near the jamb, in the still-dark living room, only the light tumbling from the TV so the bare walls seemed to close in and then recede. Lanier realized after a minute that the pounding rhythm wasn't coming from the screen, but from the huge radio set beside it on the floor, and when he looked carefully at her face, her eyes weren't focused on the flashing faces at all, but on the bar of red light that pulsed on and off at the radio's face. He listened, watched, and it reached out a long line when the drums hit hard, weakened in their absence.

"What you want, old man?" she said suddenly. "I thought you was somebody else, bringin me . . . What you bring me? You don't know what . . ."

Lanier molded the rough brown paper Lee Myrtle had split from countless grocery sacks, made it tight around the meat, and placed it gently in her lap.

los angeles stories

buddah

"Look at this little Buddha-head dude, man," one of them said. He pushed closer. "He got them Chinese eyes."

"He got a big old head, too, man. I think we should make him say somethin. He don't respect us," another voice said from behind him. Buddah kept his lips pressed warm together and felt the voices slide forward, tighter, taking away the air. He couldn't breathe, and woke from the dream with the dry heat pressing through the walls; hot air seemed to waft into the room as if a giant mouth were hovering around it. A tickle of sweat curled around the skin behind his ear. He lay still, listening for the snores of Rodriguez and Sotelo, the two boys who shared his room. But their beds were empty, he saw, and fear pulled at his ribs. Did Gaines and T. C. make them guys leave so they could jump me? he thought, and when he turned his head and felt the rough pillowcase against his neck he remembered that Sotelo and Rodriguez had gone home to L.A. on a week pass.

It was his seventh day. I can't go on home-pass till I been in this place for a month, he said to himself. They gon talk me to death, bout behavior and pattern of your life, and them Crips gon try and dog me every time I turn around. He opened the door and looked out at the bare land, the stiff yellow grass like dog fur in patches, that surrounded St. Jude's School for Boys. Now everybody on they home-pass, and ain't nobody left but me and them guys that messed up or

167

don't got nowhere to go, he thought. The gray-green weeds close to the fence shivered in the wind. Every day he thought of the miles of desert and boulders he had seen when the social worker drove him in from L.A. "Your program is six months," the man had said.

No one else was awake yet; none of the other boys were roaming the walks in front of the buildings, hanging over the balconies, waiting for an overheated car to pull in off the highway. If a woman ever got out to look for help, they would swarm like dust toward her. Buddah listened to the wind. Must be lettin us sleep cause nobody goin home. He looked down the railing to the other end of the building to see if Jesse, the counselor for the thirteen-to-fifteen-year-olds, was awake, but his door was still closed. A long row of doorknobs glinted in the sun. Third door Gaines and T.C. Sotelo said they ain't got no home-pass. They gon be on me all the time, talkin bout am I gon buy Gaines some pants with my state money. Am I gon give up the ducats.

He thought of the dream, the shapes pressing forward, and he touched the trunk on the floor by his bed. That circle of voices was how he had gotten his name, months ago. A delegation of Bounty Hunters stood around him when he neared the project. "Fuckin Buddha-head, can't even see out them eyes, they so slanty." He'd been waiting for it, and had gifts ready for them: a car stereo, sunglasses from the Korean store, and himself. "I can pull for you," he whispered to them.

At St. Jude's, he had covered the scarred top of his trunk with a sheet of white paper, the way the others had, and written his name in curved letters:

BUDDAH
SOUL GARDENS BOUNTY HUNTER'S

He thought the name might protect him here, but it had been a mistake. He wanted to be left alone, to collect his things invisibly, not to speak. That first night, when they were asked, Sotelo and

Rodriguez read the trunk and told the other boys, "New baby? He's red, man." Bounty Hunters wore red bandannas, called each other "Blood." Crips were blue-raggers, and shouted "Cuzz" before they shot someone.

But there were only two other red rags at St. Jude's, and they were in the oldest group. In Buddah's group there were two Crips. Gaines and T.C. Harris had flashed their hands at him, their fingers and thumbs contorted in the signals Buddah had always run from. Gaines fanned his fingers out over his biceps and said, "Oh, yeah."

Now it ain't nobody in the room but me, six more days. Buddah looked at the low, wide windows and imagined the shapes he would see at night, blocking the light from the parking lot when they walked past the curtains; he saw the room as dark and gold-toned as if it were night now, and the crack of light that would cut in as they opened the door.

He let the lock clink against the metal edging of the trunk. It contained everything he had at St. Jude's: the jeans, white T-shirts and cheap canvas shoes Jesse took him to buy with part of the state money. "You got to lock your shit up all the time if you want to keep it," Jesse had said, and Buddah laughed through his nose. Locks ain't about nothin. Shit. They tellin *me* bout locks.

Buddah opened Sotelo's nightstand and saw only paper covered with drawings of heavy-eyed girls. He bent and looked under Sotelo's bed; he'd seen him drop something behind the head one night. This was the first time he'd been alone, able to look. He saw a blunt shape against the wall, lying in the folds of green bedspread. It was a short length of pipe, dull heavy iron. Shit, everybody must got one a these, he thought. He bent to Rodriguez's side and heard Jesse's voice, heard him banging on doors with the flat of his hand, calling, "Get up, hardheads, we got places to go."

Montoya's clipped words came from the doorway next to Buddah's. "Hey, man, Jesse, you wake up so early? You miss me already, man?"

"Yeah, Montoya, I couldn't wait," Jesse said. "Get ready for breakfast."

Buddah slipped to his trunk quickly and dropped the pipe behind it. He heard it land, muffled, on the edge of his bedspread, and then Jesse swung open the door, saying, "Five minutes, Smith. How you like this heat?"

Buddah looked at Jesse's long feet on the hump of the doorway. Ain't here to be likin it.

"Still can't speak, huh?" Jesse said. "Maybe you'll talk at the beach if we cool you off." He turned and Buddah saw the flash of a bird diving to the parking lot for potato-chip crumbs.

They waited for Jesse near the long white van. Montoya, his hair combed smooth and feather-stiff, walked his boxer's walk in baggy *cholo* khakis. Carroll, a white boy, leaned against the van, arms folded under the "Highway to Hell" that crossed his T-shirt. Buddah stood apart from them, in the shade of a squat palm tree, preparing to be invisible. His arms were folded too, and he pushed down on his feet, feeling the long muscles in his thighs tighten. The ghostly bushes past the fence turned in the wind.

Won't nobody see me. Them Crips be busy talkin shit to Jesse, and I ain't gotta worry bout nobody else. I'ma get me somethin at the beach. It'll be somethin there.

The sound of electric drums, sharp as gunfire, came from the balcony. Buddah waited until they approached. T.C. wore new razor-creased Levis and a snow-white T-shirt, a blue cap set high and slanted on his sunglasses. He carried the radio, a box of cassettes and a can of soda, singing loudly, "It shoulda been *blue*" over the words of the woman who sang, "It shoulda been you."

Gaines followed him, pointing at Buddah when T.C. sang "blue."

"If we was at home, nigga, it be a .357 to the membrane," he whispered to Buddah, taking the pointing finger and running it around his ear.

Buddah pulled in the sides of his cheeks, soft and slippery when he bit them with his back teeth. Yeah, but I wouldn't be wearin no red rag, cause I ain't no Bounty Hunter. I'm a independent. Red, blue, ain't about shit to me. He was careful not to let his lips move; he had to be conscious of it, because when he spoke to himself, he would feel his lips touching each other sometimes and falling away as soft and slight as tiny bubbles popping. Probably look like I'm fixin to cry, he thought.

No bandannas were allowed at St. Jude's, no careless hand signals, nothing to spark gang fights. Gaines looked carefully for Jesse, and smiled close to Buddah's face. "The red rag is stained with the blood of disrespectful Hunters, slob. You gon respect us." He got one a them devil peaks, Buddah thought, like Mama say when people hair all in a point on they forehead. Mama say them some evil people with peaks. He glanced away, at T.C., who was uninterested, popping his fingers and singing.

You don't never stop talkin. You always runnin your mouth, that way everybody look at you, know where you are. He saw Jesse appear from the office, and Gaines moved away. Not like me. I'm bad cause you don't see me.

It was easy because he was so small and quiet; he walked into the stores imagining that everything in his face blended together, skin, lips, eyes all the same color. He wasn't hungry with hard rings around his stomach, like when he didn't eat anything for a long time, but he wanted something else in his mouth, a solid taste like he had chosen whatever he wanted. When they still lived in a house, when he was ten, his mother left pots of red beans on the stove when she went to work in the afternoon. Sometimes she left greens and a pan of cornbread, or three pieces of chicken, one each for him, Danita and Donnie.

He used to walk with her to the bus stop, saying nothing, watching her skin begin to shine from the heat, like molasses, with a liquid red sheen underneath the color. Her mouth moved all the time, to smile, to tell him to hurry and get back to the house and damn it, don't be hangin out in the street. Say somethin, David! All right, now. Lock the door.

He always waited until five o'clock had passed and then left the house, saying sternly to his younger brother and sister, "Y'all watch TV. Don't move. I be back."

He stepped over the jagged hole in the wooden porch and walked past children riding bicycles, thin knees angling like iron pipes. The store was five blocks away, a small grocery store with a Korean man behind the register. Women crowded the store then, shopping before they went home from work. They walked around the stacks of cans blocking the aisle, picked over the bright, shiny vegetables and fruit.

Fingering the quarter in his pocket, he brushed past the women near the bread and potato chips. He bent next to one woman, watching, and slid bags of potato chips into the pit of his dark blue windbreaker; they rested silent and light against his stomach. For Danita. He imagined his eyes were like ball bearings, greased, so that he didn't move enough of anything else to rustle. Zingers for himself. At the counter loaded with candy, he knelt to look at the bottom row and beside his knee, pushed a Butterfinger up the sleeve of his jacket. He paid for Donnie's pack of gum, watching the Korean man's eyes, comparing them to his own, holding his plasticlike jacket very still. I got somethin, he thought, looking at the man's hands. I got your stuff.

Walking home quickly, he always touched the food with the same pride. The store was different. He had slipped in and out, and something was changed, missing.

"Oh, man, look who comin, Loco Lopez," T.C. said. "He done lost his home-pass cause they busted him with that paint thinner. My man was *high.*"

"*Qué pasa?*" Lopez said to Montoya.

"Shut up, T. C.," Jesse said. "Let's go. Only reason I'm takin you to the beach is cause it's so damn hot out here I can't think."

"I got shotgun," T. C. said.

Jesse looked at him hard and said, "Who are you, ghetto child goes to the beach? Where's your lawn chair and picnic basket?"

T. C. opened the van's front door and said, "I left the caviar at my crib, homes. Too Cool only taking the essentials. And I *been* to the beach, O.K.? Me and my set went to Venice, and it was jammin, all them bikinis and shit."

"Yeah, well, don't expect to pick up any girls at this beach, not dressed like that," Jesse said. He looked at them. Buddah watched Gaines sit alone in the long seat behind T. C. Montoya and Lopez sat together in the back seat; Carroll and Buddah sat far from each other in the middle of the van.

"Anybody gets out of my sight, we go back," Jesse started, turning onto the highway. "Anybody talks shit, like you guys did at the skating rink last week, T. C., we're gone, right back to the Jude's." Jesse paused to look in the rearview mirror. "I'm takin you guys to Laguna. It's not the closest, but it's small, so I can keep an eye on you."

The back of Gaines's neck glittered with sweat. Buddah felt the hot wind from the window scour his face; he watched T. C. rest his hand on the radio and pop his shoulders so they rippled. Buddah felt a tremor in his chest, a settling of his spine, and he touched the window.

The low purplish mountains that rimmed the desert were wrinkled in strange, thin folds and trenches, like his grandmother's neck. He saw her, sitting in her tiny yard in Long Beach the way she'd been the only time he'd ever visited her. She was silent like him, her body rocking slightly all the time, watching her greens and peas grow against the chainlink fence. The velvety skin near her hairline was still tight, and her eyes were slanted upward like his. The mountains came closer as the van began to leave the desert, and soon they were smoother, covered with burnt-gold grass and stunted trees. Buddah was thinking that he hadn't seen a beach in Long Beach when the music began to beat through the van. T.C. drew circles with his hands in the air, and Jesse reached over and turned the radio off. "Man, you ain't got *no* soul," T.C. complained.

"I'm gonna tell you guys, no blasting the box when we get there," Jesse began again. "And something else. Montoya, Lopez, Smith, I don't want you guys even *looking* at anybody's stuff. Montoya, you see what happened to your buddy Jimenez when he took that jacket at the skating rink. Two months added to his program."

"So, man, I been a good boy," Montoya said, and Lopez laughed.

"That's why your mother said she didn't want you home this time, right?" Jesse said. "Last home-pass you took twenty dollars from her purse."

Now he gon start all this talk about behavior and why do you steal, Buddah thought. But Jesse said, "Smith," and looked into the mirror again. "You been doin pretty good, but this is your first off-ground, so don't blow it." Buddah felt them all look at him, and he turned his face to the window, angry, tasting the inside of his cheeks again. Bunk you, man. Don't be tellin me shit. A wine-colored Thunderbird pulled past the van. The faces inside were green behind their windows, staring at the name painted on the van door, at the boys. What y'all lookin at? He felt the glass against his lips. You lookin at me, and I had your T-Bird. Woulda been set.

They had moved to the seventh building of the Solano Gardens housing project, an island run by Bounty Hunters in an ocean of Crips, just after his eleventh birthday. At the welter of railroad tracks behind the junior high, he walked rapidly, seeing the blue bandannas, the watching faces.

But he lived in Soul Gardens; the Bounty Hunters owned him. He had to be occasionally valuable to them, because no one could step outside the project alone, without a protective cadre of red rags. He watched them gather in the courtyard and then walked slightly behind. They left him alone until they needed something.

The dent-puller, long and thin, pierced into car locks easily and pulled the entire silver circles out for him. The cars were like houses, each with its own smell and a push of air that he felt against his face for an instant when he bent to pull the stereo, someone else's smell that he let escape. He learned to start the car if Ellis told him to, and the feel of each steering wheel under his fingers for a moment made his stomach jump. Soft, leather-bound he'd felt once, but cold and ridged usually.

They hadn't gotten caught when they stripped or stole cars in the neighborhood, but Ellis decided he wanted a T-Bird. At the house he finally chose in Downey, where the 7-11 they passed had only white faces inside, a wine-red Thunderbird was parked. Ellis looked at Buddah with a strange smile on his face. Buddah had been waiting for this, too. "Ain't doin no house," Buddah said, and Ellis pushed him. "You know they got a VCR. You better be *down*," Ellis said.

Buddah loved the cars, their metallic shine like crystal sugar on the fruit candy that was his mother's favorite. Some of them even smelled sweet. But the house, even when he stood under the eaves moving the lock, smelled heavy and wrong, and when the door opened and the foreign air rushed at him, he heard the screaming of the alarm and then running.

The ocean glinted like an endless stretch of blue flake on a hood. Buddah had never seen so much water, so many white people. Jesse said, "What you guys think, huh?"

"None a these women got booty," T.C. said. "No ass to hold onto."

Jesse drove down a street that curved toward the water. Clean, shining cars lined both sides: Mercedes, BMWs, station wagons, a Porsche. Buddah looked at the cars, at the chalky clean sidewalks and smooth grass. Jesse circled twice before he found a parking space, and then he said, "Damn, we don't have quarters. We're gonna have to walk to a store to get some, cause if I pull out we won't find another space."

They trailed behind him like fish, swerving and shifting. "Where we goin, man?" Lopez asked. "I don't see no 7-11 or nothin."

Up close, the cars looked even better, a gleaming line unbroken by a parking space as far as they walked, the perfect doors and weak round locks. Ellis would tell me to pull the Mercedes, Buddah thought, and just then Gaines said, "Mercedes, the ladies, when I get one they gon be crazy." Buddah slowed; he'd been thinking about telling Ellis where the cars were, but when he heard Gaines's voice, the same one that had been whispering to him every day for a week, he thought, shit, I don't even know where we are. Ain't tellin Ellis shit when he ax me where I been. Think everything for him.

They walked through an art show that lined the sidewalk, and had to go single file to get past. Buddah watched T.C. rock his shoulders in step to the beat inside his head, passing closely by people to brush them with air, making them move and look at him. Jesse pulled them inside a restaurant lobby and went to get change. "I ain't seen *no* brothers, man," Gaines said to T.C.

"I'm tellin you," T.C. said. "We gon be specks like on a sheet."

At the start of the steep asphalt trail down to the crescent-shaped beach, a large sign read:

Glenn E. Vedder Ecological Reserve
PLEASE DO NOT REMOVE
Shells, Rocks, Plants, Marine Life, or Game Fish
so that others may see and enjoy them
TAKE OUT ONLY THAT WHICH YOU BROUGHT IN

Jesse stopped and read the sign silently for a moment; T.C. said, "Man, it ain't school time," when he read it out loud. After Jesse finished, T.C. said, "Thank you, Mr. Man. How people supposed to know you went to the beach if you don't got no souvenir?"

"You suppose to come back with a suntan, man," Lopez said. "Big problem for you, huh?"

"Man, I'll kick your ass," T.C. said, and Jesse pushed him away.

Buddah stared at the shifting colors, felt the sand against his palm when he sat down. Green plants cascaded from the cliffs behind them, and the bathing suits and water were in motion. He saw a sea gull overhead, hovering. It was clean, thick white, like his T-shirts after his mother bleached them. The gull glided, circled, dipping slightly to turn; it never moved its hard, sharp wings, just bore down on the crowd of people and suddenly pulled up to place its feet on a rock ten feet away. He look just like T.C., Buddah thought. Think he bad, showin off.

T.C. had been watching, too. "That's how we is in the set, man, be swoopin, just like that bird, ain't never move false," he said. "We see what we want and we on it, cool." Buddah looked at Gaines. His shoulders were hunched uncomfortably, like loaves of bread against his neck, and he stared out at the water. "What we suppose to do?" he said to Jesse. "Just sit here?"

"I didn't say you guys couldn't move, I just said you can't disappear," Jesse answered. "Do whatever you want. Look at the scenery. Don't drown." No one moved. "Can any of you swim?"

Carroll said, "I used to know. I went to a lake one time." They looked at him. "A goddamn lake ain't no ocean," Gaines said. He looked back at the water.

"Just go touch it," Jesse said. "It won't kill you." He took off his shoes, and his long feet were ashy gray and rough. Walking toward the water, he said, "Come on, I'll save you if you trip and get your hair wet."

Somebody else gotta move first, Buddah thought. Not me. We specks for sure, like them rocks. T.C. turned up his radio; he and Gaines watched girls walk by and stare. Carroll, Montoya and Lopez had gone to the water's edge, where they stood near Jesse. Buddah saw Jesse gesturing to boats far out on the ocean.

"Forget this shit, man, I ain't sittin with no slob red-ragger," T.C. said. "Ain't shit to do here." He stood over Buddah. Gaines was watching the waves; he seemed to have forgotten Buddah.

You ain't bad now, Too Cool. Nobody payin good attention to you like you want. You just a speck. T.C. picked up the radio and pushed Gaines's foot. "Dude down there sellin sodas, homes. Come on, man, fore I have to fuck this red boy up." Buddah waited. Gaines looked at him and said, "When you givin me my money, punk? I ain't playin." He stood up. It ain't your money. Buddah got up and walked forward slightly, waiting until he heard the music leave.

He looked at the tangle of wet black rocks on the left end of the beach, about twenty yards away, the spray flying from behind them. He felt eyes on him, from the blankets and towels. Now I'm botherin you, cause I ain't movin, I ain't swimmin or nothin. How you know I ain't come to this beach all the time and it's boring?

Three kids made a sand castle, looking up at him now and then. It was plain and round, and the walls sagged because the sand was too wet, too close to the waves. See, I woulda had that castle sharp. Have me some shells line up on the outside, have a whole fence made outta shells. Jesse and the others walked back to the blankets. "Where's Gaines and T.C.?" Jesse said. Buddah lifted his chin toward the soda seller. "Don't get too happy about bein here, man," Jesse said impatiently. "You could be sweatin back at the Jude's."

"I'm goin over here," Buddah said.

Jesse raised his eyebrows. "He says. Don't go past the rocks."

When he made it to the first rock, it was dry and grayish; he ran his hand over the hard warmth. Tiny broken shells were jammed inside the rock's holes. Buddah walked toward the wet, glistening black closer to the ocean. He stood on the edge of the wet sand, feeling his feet sink, and saw the smallest waves, the tiny push of water just at the edge, after the wave had washed up on the beach and before the water pulled back. The dying waves lined the sand with circlets of bright white. He walked forward and smeared the lines with his shoe.

The tall square rock in front of him had a smooth side, from which a fat pale boy climbed down. Buddah stopped, turning away from the boy's staring face. When he had passed, Buddah walked to the wet part and sat on one of the low, flat rocks. From far away, it had looked deep black, but he saw that it was only slightly wet. Green feathery plants hung near the bottom, and he was surprised at the shells and animals clinging to the top. The shells clamped down tightly when he touched them. Lockin up, like you a house. But I could get you if you didn't stay inside.

I could get some a these shells, like them big pretty ones. I go out on them rocks and people only see black, not me. The rocks led to a long formation—a pier, almost, out into the water. Buddah pulled himself up the face of the first rock; at the top, white foam spilled over the end. Small pools of water, still as plastic, were everywhere around him as he walked, picking his way past clumps of seaweed, until he found a dry spot to sit on.

I'm gone. Can't nobody see nothin. He felt his skin warm to the rock. Snails and long insects that looked like roaches dotted the rock. Buddah saw a small snail near his hand; its shell was dull and dry, ashy like Jesse's feet. He touched it with his finger and it didn't move or tighten down like the round shells. He must be dyin, too dry. Must of got left here when the water dried up from one a his holes. A pool of water nearby was empty. He pulled at the snail lightly, wincing at the sucking resistance. Let go. You know you can't be out here all dry. It's some water for you right here. He turned the shell up to look at it; the rim was pink, and a blank, hard eye covered the snail inside. You can open up, let me check you out. But you probably ugly like any other snail.

He dropped the shell into the shallow pool and it was suddenly vivid under the water—the pale dull purple darkened to green, and brighter markings showed in a spiral pattern. The snail came out after a second and rocked its shell. Buddah pulled it from the water. You done lived dry that long. I'ma take you back, get some salt from the kitchen, make you some good water like you need. He waited for the snail to right itself in his palm, but it stayed inside. Cool, stay locked till we get back. Gently, he pushed the shell into his jeans pocket.

The darkness of the rocks made him secure. He turned around slowly, squinting until he could see Jesse and the others. They were drinking sodas. Carroll stood with his feet in the water, arms folded, watching the boats.

Buddah walked farther down the rocks. He sat again near the largest pool of water; whole and broken shells and round, smooth stones waited on the bottom, their colors clear and glossy like red beans soaking in a bowl.

"Slob, man, you been out there playin with yourself?" Gaines said when Buddah approached.

"Shut up, Gaines. That's why we gotta go, cause you guys get bored and talk too much shit," Jesse said. He turned to Buddah. "I was hoping you would see us packin up, Smith."

Jesse started up the beach, talking to Carroll. T.C. and Gaines waited to walk behind Buddah. He felt the shells in his pockets, hard weight against his thighs like money. "You lettin us get behind you, slob, so watch out," Gaines whispered. "You all alone."

Buddah let his head fall back a little so that he looked up the sandy trail. I got something from here. Y'all could be lyin bout bein here, but not me. He felt himself out on the rock, in the spray, listening to the power of the waves, and Gaines's and T.C.'s voices were like bird cries, far away. "Why you look at the water? You can't hide in no water. I'm tired of waitin for my money, pussy."

Buddah fingered the sharpest of the shells and smiled with his head turned toward the cliff.

It was almost ten o'clock, lights out. The noises circled around the courtyard and flew up to his room; through the window screen, Buddah could hear the older boys in the next building shouting something to their counselor and Gaines and T.C. talking out on the balcony, the radio still playing from their doorway. Jesse would come by in a few minutes and make sure they all went into their rooms. Buddah listened in the dark.

"Inside, guys. If you didn't run your mouths so much today, I was thinking of takin you to the Stallone flick next weekend."

"What flick?" T.C. said.

"First Blood," Jesse answered.

"Shit, man, why you gotta say that word in my *presence* and shit," T.C. said. Buddah imagined his head jerking violently. *"First Cuzz,* I told you. You disrespectin me."

"You see, T.C.? I'm so tired of that shit. It ain't the real world. You got table clean-up all week."

"Man, Jesse, you the one don't know. You could die for that shit."

"Inside, punks."

Jesse stopped at Montoya's door, and then Buddah heard the feet slide to his. Jesse was wearing house shoes; he'd be going to bed now, and the night man would watch St. Jude's.

Light flashed in the doorway. Buddah sat motionless, but Jesse didn't leave. He walked to the trunk suddenly, where the white paper was brightly lit. He see the pipe, Buddah thought, and pushed hard with his feet on the floor. "Bounty Hunters, shit," Jesse said. "What bounty did you get? Nothin valuable to you, just shit to sell and all this red-rag crap. Soon as you start talkin, you'll probably bore me with all that shit, too." He waited, and then closed the door.

Uh uh, cause I ain't workin no job for the blue, like T.C. and them. But now Jesse got them mad, and they probably come. Buddah got the shells out, arranging them in lines, in fences. He leaned forward and touched the cool pipe on the floor. I could wait and wait, and then what? He went to the sink, where the snail was in the soap dish, and pushed at the tightly-closed shell. You waitin, too, for me to leave you alone. But you could wait forever.

The night man's hard shoes cracked the grit on the balcony when he opened the doors every hour in the beginning. Buddah knew he would quit checking after he heard no noise; he would sit in the room downstairs and watch TV. Buddah waited until the moonlight shifted in the window. He sat, still listening, until the brightest part had gone over the roof. He took off his shirt and opened his door.

His bare feet pressed into the sharp sand. He imagined himself on the black rocks, invisible as he pressed close to the stucco wall. T. C. and Gaines were breathing hard and long, he could hear through their screen. The doorknob turned easily, since it was turned so many times every day and night. Buddah stood in the close air by the wall and listened to them breathe. He had stood by his mother every time, hearing her throat vibrate, before he went out to meet Ellis and the rest of them. Buddah moved away from the wall. The cassettes were on top of T. C.'s trunk, in neat stacks. Buddah lifted off the top four from the closest stack and held them tightly together so they wouldn't click. He pulled the door slowly, straight toward him, and turned the knob. On the balcony, he stood for a moment, looking down the dark tunnel of the overhanging roof to the edge of the stairway and then the flat land past the fence that was exposed, lit silver as flashbulbs by the moonlight coming from behind the buildings, from behind his back.

the box

The bench at the bus stop was covered with black spray paint. PB'S, it said, the squared letters making spidery, jointed patterns on all the buildings and walls in the neighborhood, even on the elephant-skinned trunk of the palm tree Shawan leaned against while she waited for the bus. When she had gone out into the yard this morning, she thought, her sisters had been scared. Nygia and Tanya held her shoulders, but she shook herself sharply and frowned. "Quit, y'all, I'm goin outside and tell them sorry-ass punks get out my yard. Mmm-hmm, in my robe and all." She walked out onto the step quietly, letting the wrought-iron screen door click into the lock.

Five of the Playboys stood on the sidewalk, leaning against the chainlink fence that surrounded the Johnsons' square of yellow grass. Shawan knew that they were watching the apartment house across the empty lot, waiting for the old man in the downstairs apartment to leave. He had a new TV, delivered in a box that anyone could have seen. Shawan stared at the boys, their arms draped over the fence casually, but the backs of their necks tight and wary. She had seen the short one run his palm, fingers spread, over the slight bulge made by a gun in his jacket. "Shawan, they packin, you know it," Nygia said through the screen.

"So. What y'all doin in front of my house?" she said loudly from the step. They all turned, heads swiveling like those submarines in the cartoons, she thought, and the short one said, "None a your damn business, bitch." He was maybe sixteen, three years younger than Shawan.

"I don't want you doin it in my daddy's front yard," she said. "And don't give me no trouble cause you think I ain't about nobody." She thought of V-Roy. These were young ones, who had probably forgotten V-Roy already.

"Nathan Thomas my uncle, and he be over here in two minutes if I call him. You know who I mean," she said, nodding her head at the only boy she recognized, with shiny-curled hair and a sliver of pink on his lip that looked to her like a tongue always poking out. They stood, hands in pockets, their eyes filled with hate and their elbows stiff as hangers; she kept her arms folded over her robe, afraid to move even backwards. The pink-lipped boy spat into the cool morning dirt and cocked his head toward the avenue. Nathan had been in the 102nd Street Crips years ago, and Shawan had known that they would recognize his name and his arsenal of weapons, even though he did nothing now. The Playboys moved slowly, pushing off the fence with their backs, keeping hands crushed to their thighs. "I'ma get that bitch," the short one said. Shawan was shaking, but she pressed each thumb hard against a rib and became calm. Nygia scratched the screen mesh and said, "Uncle Nathan still got his rep."

Now she was late. The deejay said it was 5:42, "Wake up with Willie G. Time," and Shawan usually caught the 5:30 bus. In the early morning cold, the avenue was nearly deserted. Them boys might be hidin out somewhere, she thought, waitin to jump me. Let em go head on. I'm tired of they mess, running the street like they own it. If they gon try and snatch my box out my hands, they better use the piece. Just kill me, cause I'll kill you.

Willie started a new song, the congas beginning the beat, and then the rest of the drums and bass pounding the rhythm. Shawan turned the knob on top of the radio all the way to "Bass." She loved the deep reverberations, the snap of the bass and its power under the surface of guitars and organ and, underscoring all, the cupped-palm handclaps. Church in the funk. She never turned the knob to "Treble" because it made the radio sound tinny, like white music.

Shawan leaned out over the curb. The bus was still several stops away. Drumming her fingers on the side of her thigh with one hand, she held the radio close to her body with the other, and the bass thumped in her chest. The ornate black grill covering Sims' Liquor became soft and pretty as lace when she looked at it with unfocused eyes.

With the hiss of opening doors, she had to turn the music off. Holding the box in her lap, staring at the black mesh and silver knobs, she felt the screaming of the brakes and engine pound her with noise. She needed the music, the box, each moment to calm her. When she opened her eyes every morning, she heard menacing silence, empty air without rhythm, for only an instant. She would reach out and turn the radio on, watching her own fingers grasp the lever. It never disturbed Nygia, sleeping next to her, and Shawan sometimes lay in bed for two or three songs, looking at the walls and the thin curtains. Some mornings, just after she woke up, things seemed sharp and unusually defined. She could see each thread and the square, regular weave of the curtains with the sun piercing them, and the hole in the plaster just below the window looked as if it was filled with tiny chalk beads.

With the bass sliding and changing in her ears, the steady clapping which made her imagine a line of people swaying, heads thrown back, she could think clearly and her thoughts slid along lightly on the sounds. Often at work she would tell her supervisor she was going to the restroom, and then she would stand in the tiled break room and listen to one complete song echoing from the walls.

They were putting the calls through rapidly, scattering voices all over the building. "We in the groove now," Mary T. said to Shawan. The calls finally slowed at lunchtime, and the switchboard operators sat back; Shawan felt the hollowness of her head with the earphones pressed in tightly.

Leonard was singing Diana Ross's song "Muscles" when no calls came through on his headset. "I want muscles, all over his body, from his head down to his toes," he sang in his falsetto, moving his shoulders delicately.

"You better stop dreamin, baby," Mary T. said. Leonard was six-four and weighed two-hundred-forty pounds. He shape like a tear, Shawan thought, the way somebody draw a tear, not like it really look if it's on a face. After it leave your eye and go down your cheek.

His head was small, with a bald spot at the crown, and his hips were square. He had to turn sideways to pass through the narrow spaces between desks. His desk was covered with pictures of Diana Ross, cut and pasted over carefully with pictures of him so that they stood close together, the way Mary T. said the National Enquirer had famous people secretly married when they hadn't even met. Taped to the backs of the operators' chairs were Xerox copies he had made, announcing "Diana Ross and Leonard 'Mr. Entertainment' Jackson appearing now at the Roxy." Shawan had brought him Diana's picture, from *Ebony*. He wanted to be just like her, he said, but he'd have to settle for singing like her.

"Girl, what you think of the new song by Aretha?" Leonard asked Shawan. He turned to Mary T. and Cherie and said, "Note, I'm askin our resident music expert, y'all."

"Mmm hmm," Cherie said, hummed, in her high voice; it was the way she emphasized everything Leonard said. When the supervisor, Mrs. Badgett, left for a doctor's appointment or to run an errand, Cherie and Leonard would leave their seats, turn on Shawan's radio and do the new dances, looking over their shoulders at the office door. Shawan could measure the two years she had worked in the building by the first dances Cherie had done—the Smurf and the White Girl, long ago. Shawan never danced. She stayed in her seat and moved, not wanting anyone to see her from all angles, vulnerable.

Mary T. said, "Yeah, Shawan, what you think of Aretha's bad self? Is it the new jam?" Shawan dipped her shoulders and said, "It got potential." She snapped her fingers, and a call came through to her ears. When she had finished with the voice, she drummed softly on the table.

"She be doin all kind of stuff with her voice," Leonard said. "I personally have a different style. Mr. Entertainment, y'all!" He rocked his narrow shoulders. "But I still rather have a little butt like Diana's," he smiled. They all laughed, and Leonard's hand went up to the tiny patch of grayish hairs over his ear.

This was when she missed V-Roy the most, on a Friday afternoon, coming home from work. He would have been there at her house, waiting in his blue car with gray primer like camouflage. They'd be gone, riding for hours. V-Roy cruised, cool and slow, and Shawan deejayed, switching radio stations to keep only their favorite songs playing. They didn't stay in the neighborhood. V-Roy drove out to the beach, and along the coast past the airport. Sometimes on late summer evenings when the sun was just dropping they drove to Hollywood and watched the people. Or they went all the way down Sunset, starting from downtown, watching the neighborhoods change colors—Chinatown to Mexican to any-color Hollywood, to huge gates and houses and hedges, rich white neighborhoods near the hills and then blue, the ocean.

"Let me get a gangster lean," V-Roy would say, "so we can cruise right." He kept his lower body directly behind the steering wheel, shifted his shoulders toward the middle of the seat, curving his waist as gracefully as one of the samurai swords he wanted. "Say, baby," he teased, close to Shawan, looking out through the center of the windshield. "Do I got it now?"

She nodded, laughing at his exaggerated cool, his half-shut eyes. V-Roy had been her best friend since high school. He lived one street over, and when they walked together and people teased them, Shawan always said, "Nuh-uh, don't be thinkin that. He's my partner. We don't mess with each other." He wasn't in the Playboys, but his older brother Antoine had been, and V-Roy hung out with Rollo, who had been in for three years.

He was going to teach Shawan to drive someday. She was in no hurry. She liked him to drive so she could take care of the music, lean her head on the smooth vinyl seat, and watch people walk slantwise. Mrs. Badgett at work, with fine red veins in her nose like broken windshield glass, couldn't believe Shawan didn't drive. "Everyone drives," she said. "It's just impossible to get around in L.A. if you don't."

"Don't have a car," Shawan said. Her bus had been late, and Mrs. Badgett was disapproving. "I've seen a car key around your neck," she said to Shawan. Shawan pulled out the key V-Roy had made for her one day. "It belong to a friend," she said, her voice hard. After Mrs. Badgett left, Mary T. said, "White people think everybody born with a car under they ass."

"I heard that," Shawan said. "I'ma get me one someday, though. Watch me."

V-Roy had taken her downtown to buy the radio. It was her present to herself for her nineteenth birthday. They went to one of the Mexican-run stores where the radios crowded the windows and blared out onto the sidewalk.

"Girls don't never be sportin boxes like that," V-Roy had said, pointing to a black suitcase-sized radio. "Rollo got one a them."

"I know what he got. I could carry it if I wanted to," Shawan said sharply, walking into the store.

"Girls don't be jammin that much, period," V-Roy continued, smiling, waiting for her reaction. "That's for dudes."

"You gon quit with the 'girls' stuff?" Shawan said. "I ain't every girl, and I do what I please." She stared at the radios lining the wall.

"You know I'm just botherin you," he said, leaning on the counter. The way his legs crossed over each other as he stood made long, smooth folds in the silky material of his sweatsuit, Shawan remembered. His small teeth showed when he stuck his tongue in the corner of his mouth, the way he did when he smiled. She bought the silver radio because it was different from all the black ones, and it had a clear, strong sound. It was the size of a large shoebox.

V-Roy died three months later. He was sitting on a picnic table at Ninetieth Street Elementary School, with Rollo, just after the sun had set. Lemoyne Street Crips shot Rollo twice in the leg, and V-Roy in the head, once.

Shawan watched Nygia's stomach in their bedroom when Nygia undressed, imagining it hard and round and soon shiny as the domelike bald spot on Leonard's head. Nygia was three months pregnant and had quit her after-school job at McDonald's. "I'ma need some money to go to the store tomorrow," she said to Shawan. "Daddy ain't got paid yet."

Shawan went slowly to what had been her car money, hidden in a hairdress can. She had saved $420, with the smell of gasoline seeming to come from the bills, but now since Nygia wasn't working and needed so many things, the tight roll of money was spindly, thin as a cigarette.

She lay on the bed, listening as Nygia left with her boyfriend and Daddy rustled into his uniform. He left for work at 9:00 p.m., to guard a building only four blocks from hers downtown. Tanya would sleep, and the house would be silent but for the music. The shadows of the iron bars across the windows lay over her chest. Look like I'm on a barbecue grill, she thought. The moon must be bright.

It was full, she saw when she stood on the step, and it moved fast across the sky. The street was bright and silvery, the cars glinting. She could see stars through the telephone wires. The radio played a slow saxophone and a caressing voice, and she changed the station until she heard the staccato beat of a Whodini rap, fast as a scary person's heart.

She walked down the street, toward the Ninetieth Street school, past the benches where V-Roy was shot. His blood, what she had been sure was the dark stain of his blood, was indistinguishable from the spilled wine and black circles of ground ash left by other people since. She watched two boys play basketball. The moonlight glared white on the cement wall behind them, where Shawan had been playing with Tanya's tennis racket several weeks ago. A teenage boy on a ten-speed had ridden up and tried to take the racket. He grabbed it from behind, jerking her arm up like a chicken wing, but she turned and swung her other fist into his chest. She ran forward to kick at the bicycle tire, and he fell. She kicked him, let him flail the racket at her like she was the thief, and trapped the netting against her thigh with the heel of her hand.

She remembered how she had told Leonard and Mary T. at work, and how they had laughed. "Ain't nobody takin nothin away from Shawan," Mary T. said, and Leonard pinched her biceps. "She like it when somebody try and dog her," he said. "Don't you?"

She turned up the music and walked away from the school. A lowrider cruised by very slowly, a car she didn't recognize, the same song on her radio pouring out through the car's open windows. The loud, uneven throbbing of the engine sounded like drums. She didn't look at the car, but kept her eyes straight ahead. Could be the dudes shot V-Roy, she thought. She saw the sharp flashes of gray-blue light from TV screens as she turned her head toward the houses, and the car's taillights drew away from her, the strong threads of song from the car and the box separating imperceptibly.

Walking in step to the beat, she dipped at the knees; this was V-Roy's street. She moved her eyes over the yards and looked into the alley next to his house. Three large trash bins, pale with white graffiti, stood against the fence, and Shawan walked past them cautiously, tensing. Come on, she thought. Where you at? She fingered her necklace, the key, the way she always did when she walked; boys would run up behind people and snatch hard so that the clasps broke.

The blue Dart was parked far back against the fence; she couldn't see who was in the yard, but she heard Antoine's voice and laughter. "Let's book, cuz. It's time to go," he said, and Shawan saw him then, his blue bandanna tied around his head and knotted in the front. He stared at her. "What you need, now?" he called.

"Nothin from you," Shawan said. She didn't move.

Antoine got into V-Roy's car, and two boys followed. He turned the headlights on; they lit up the radio, made it shine. "Get outta the way," he yelled over the noise of the car. She walked past the driveway.

She was almost back to the house, her eyes blurred with staring at the sidewalk and seeing the gray primer of V-Roy's car, the one crazy hair that poked out from his eyebrow when she looked at the side of his face, and someone said, "Hey, girl, what you doin walkin around? You trying to get jumped?"

It was Marcus, whose aunt, Mrs. Batiste, lived next door. He had come to L.A. the month before, from Virginia, when the Navy transferred him to Long Beach. He opened the door of his car, a big Buick, and walked into the yard. "Why you walking? Ain't you got sense?"

"I got legs. I can walk," Shawan said, looking at his knees.

"Why you want to stay here and you could be with me, at a club?"

Shawan said, "Not if you act like last time." She lifted her chin and bit a tiny piece of her inside lip. He had taken her to his apartment and put his hands all over her. Like he own me already, and I don't have no say, she thought. He want all the say, not like V-Roy. Marcus looked at her with admiration, but it was mixed with admiration of himself, for picking her. He had run his hands over her buttocks, said he liked how she walked like a boy.

"You want to go drivin, right now?" he said. Shawan looked down the street. The sidewalks, the cars, were brighter than in the day.

The seats were plush, light blue like the car. They drove down the avenue; the deep yellow light from a bar was a triangle of color in a block of dark doorways. Shawan reached down to turn on the radio, but Marcus pushed her hand away and put in a cassette of love songs. "Why you don't sit over here?" he said, touching the seat beside him. His eyes were green, his skin the same gold brown as hers. Nygia and Tanya said he was fine. Shawan thought, he look good but he know it. He think too much when he smile.

"Cause I don't feel like it," she said. Facing out the window, she leaned her head back and saw herself in the glass when they passed streetlights.

"Where you want to go? Anywhere you say."

"Not to your apartment," she said. Her face faded and reappeared. "Just drive." They headed toward the ocean. She had gone to the beach once after V-Roy died. She took two buses, to Santa Monica, but the bus wasn't right. You couldn't cruise and listen to the music unless you had headphones like the boy several seats away from her. Every so often he sang out in a piercing voice, teasing her because they were songs she knew were playing on her station, and she was holding her silent radio.

Flames shot up into the sky outside the window, and Shawan sat up. "Natural gas," Marcus said. The fire released itself from a needle-thin white tower, reaching higher suddenly and then shrinking back until the flames were sucked into the opening, again and again.

He drove past the harbor, talking about the ship he worked on. Shawan watched his leg when he pressed the brake; the muscle was short and thick. He saw her. "Why you stay away from me so much? I ain't hurtin you," he said. "I want you to be my lady." She saw his tongue when he said "lady," just touching the underside of his teeth.

"I ain't nobody's 'mine'," Shawan said, looking past his face to the window. "Don't nobody own me."

She reached down and pulled out the cassette, listening to the deejay's familiar voice fill the car. Her voice could be smooth and beautiful as his when she wanted. V-Roy had recorded a cassette with her favorite songs, and she talked between each, using her low, sweet work voice, the one she had learned on the phones. V-Roy played her tape in his car whenever they went driving. He wrote "The Master Jam" on the case. Every time Shawan answered a call at work she practiced, making her voice sure and strong, not breathy. Mary T. and Cherie laughed at how quickly she could change, how assured she made herself sound. "My deejay voice," Shawan said. Leonard smiled and sang, "Last night a deejay saved my life from a broken heart."

Marcus stopped the car on the side of the highway. He turned to her and said, "Why you scared of me?"

Shawan felt anger rise in her chest. "I *been* told you I ain't scared," she said folding her arms. He turned the radio down, and his hand on the knob made her more irritated. "Why you do that?" she said.

"Cause I'm trying to get serious with you. When you gon let me do what I want? We could get married, I ain't playin with you."

"I don't want to get married. Why don't you teach me to drive?" Shawan said. He leaned forward and touched her breast, brushing his finger against the arm she kept over herself.

"Let me teach you something else," he said, pushing his chin forward. His hand stayed on her shirt, and Shawan felt the anger rise into her throat. She thought, Why it always what *you* want to do? She closed her hand around his wrist. She held it and squeezed as hard as she could, but he twisted his arm and fastened his hands around hers; his mouth was tight. Shawan looked at his hands. They were red, ruddier than hers. Hers were gold in the light from the streetlamp.

"Girl, you should see what old Spiros up to now," Mary T. said to Cherie, crumpling her paper bag from lunch. "He messin everybody up, evil man." Mary T. and Mrs. Badgett took lunch together now, because Mrs. Badgett had brought her tiny television to the break room so she could watch "All My Children."

"He kidnapped that girl, Shawan," Mary T. said. She slid into her seat next to Shawan. Leonard said, "You went and got hooked on them shows," laughing at her excitement. "Mmm hmm," Cherie said. "She know everybody's business."

"I know as much about Spiros and Brooke and them as Shawan know about deejays," Mary T. said, smiling, brushing against Shawan.

She didn't smile. "Don't nobody care about them white people," she said, looking away. "Don't even put them with the music."

Leonard clicked his tongue. "Ain't no need to go off on her like that, Miss Shawan," he said impatiently. "You been nasty all week."

"So. She the one want to live in ice-cream land, I ain't gotta go with her," Shawan said. She couldn't stop the words, or smooth her voice. It was thick and rough. Mary T. looked at her with lips drawn in at one corner.

"And who are you?" Mary T. said. "You somebody more than me?"

Shawan said nothing. She had always waited for Mary T. and Cherie to admire her voice, to ask her about music, when she came to work; now she felt herself wanting to shout at them for no reason. "I'm sorry," she said, looking at the gray metal desk. "But them people life ain't about nothin."

"They got some brothers and sisters on now," Mary T. said. Leonard came to stand behind Shawan's chair, and he touched the back of her neck. "Not no real ones," he said gently. "You want me to sing?"

"No. Diana's songs is all old," Shawan said coldly. She went into the break room, but while the drums and hands clapping bounced back at her, she cried instead of swaying.

She liked to see their suits, the elegant tailoring, how the coats made a sharp line from shoulder to hand as if nothing could soften it. Marcus had a suit like that, she thought, walking toward the bus stop. Two men who looked like bankers in her building approached, flicking their eyes over the radio quickly and then glancing away in disgust. "Everywhere you go," one of them said, and Shawan smiled, curling her arm tighter around the metal.

The only open seat was in the middle of the bus, just ahead of the rear door. Her foot was partly in the aisle, flat on the rubber floor, to steady her body when the bus lurched and swayed. An old man sat by the window, leaning his head against the yellowed glass. She stared at his clenched hands; they were black between the wrist and knuckles, ashy gray between the fingers and on the joints.

The bus stopped often in the downtown traffic, and soon the crowds of people waiting impatiently at the crosswalks and the crush of bodies standing in the aisles of the bus surrounded her. Nearly empty buses with signs flashing for Santa Monica and Westwood passed like mirrors. She made her eyes blurry and dreamed until she felt the drag of stops much less frequently and knew they had left downtown and entered the long avenues of South-Central L.A. Her calf muscles relaxed, and she put one hand on her knee.

A young man stood up in the back of the bus and pulled a gun out of his jacket. Shawan had moved her head to the clear space by the door, and she saw him walk to the crowd's end and turn his back. "Everybody shut up," he said, not loudly. He faced the people in the rear of the bus, holding a shopping bag with brown-string handles, and the people near him began to drop their wallets and watches and rings into the bag. He held it with one hand, his wrist curving up and the bag falling open in front of the people he pushed it near. With the other hand he held the gun close to his waist, so that only the people he watched could see it.

He stood at the other side of the rear door for a moment, waiting as the long crush of people moved forward to leave by the front door. Shawan turned her head forward. Everybody always get off here, she thought. He gon get off, too. He moved just past the rear door and turned quickly, keeping his back to the driver and the passengers in the front. He looked down at Shawan and brought the bag close, pushing against her when the bus began to move. She took off her watch, and he still stared, the gun pointing downward. The watch cracked against something hard at the bottom of the bag. She saw the man look out the window at the streets, at the old man next to her. He was asleep, his mouth open. He wore no watch. The man with the gun looked at Shawan's radio, between her clenched legs. She slipped her hands up the sides and under the handle, curling her fingers around the smoothness. I ain't givin it up. The bag quivered, and he said, "The box, man," thrusting his head forward slightly, the way Marcus did when he talked. She sat still, staring at a point just past him and to the left, feeling the line of his body waver as the bus slowed. His knee pushed sharply into hers, and she made herself look up at his neck, round and dry, gray as a palm trunk, and then at his eyes. She didn't blink, only let her eyes shift out of focus so his eyebrows became one thick mustache over the trembling single eye she saw.

He yelled, "Open the door, man," as the bus stopped, and then he leaped out onto the street. No one moved. As the doors clamped together, in the moment before the gears shifted and roared, Shawan heard the gun fire. The bullet pierced the window behind the door, over the heads of the women in the long seat, and went out the other window. People curled their backs instinctively, putting their heads down. Shawan crossed her arms over the radio and leaned her head back against the metal frame of the seat. He had been shooting at her, she knew. She felt the cold iron on the nape of her neck, watched the buildings slide by, faster and faster.

When she stepped down at her stop, she turned on the music. Her heart felt out of rhythm, and her hands slipped with sweat against the metal handle. You chicken now? she thought. Too late to be chicken, too late to be gettin scary. She looked toward her house and turned to walk down the next street. She listened for the Playboys, for any voices, when she neared V-Roy's house. It was quiet, and the car had been backed into the yard. It looked far away, dark and indistinct in the gray light of evening. Shawan undid her necklace and pulled off the key. She opened the car door, touching the primer's roughness, and looked toward the house. When she turned the key in the ignition, the radio came on loudly.

I'ma just sit here and listen, she thought, but then the car smelled like weed and beer, not like V-Roy, and she saw the back door of the house open. Antoine looked outside. Shawan moved the gear shift the way she'd watched V-Roy move it; the car seemed to spin forward out of the driveway.

She stopped at the corner, watching the crowd of buses and cars on the avenue. Everything seemed too slow, just as it had on the bus when the man stared at her, and Shawan looked at the radio on the car seat beside her. She turned quickly onto the avenue, forcing another car to stop, and the radio fell forward. She remembered driving one night with V-Roy, watching two boys run from the sidewalk to smash the windows of the car ahead of them; they took the woman's purse and ran. There were no boys in the doorways now, but she pushed down on the gas pedal, and the car sped toward the light. Think I'm ignorant, huh? Me and V-Roy never stupid like that. Wait till the light red, then gon stop and show me your piece, say give up the ride or give up your life. Antoine's boys. No, baby. She saw the yellow, then red, and only pushed harder. The bus driver saw her coming. He stopped in the intersection and honked as she flew over the rut in the street. Shawan looked up, higher than the street, and tried to see where she was, which way she should drive to go to the ocean, but she couldn't see, couldn't remember. Another red flash appeared in front of her, and when she sped up again, she hit the front of the car heading across her path. The steering wheel pushed hard at her ribs and collarbone, and then she sat back against the seat. She tried to breathe and couldn't. She locked the door and turned on her radio, which had fallen to the floor; she turned it up high, changed the car radio to the same station, and filled the car with music while people slapped the windows with the palms of their hands.

author's note

Aquaboogie was first published seventeen years ago, and I still remember with vivid clarity how I felt when I got the news that the manuscript had won the Milkweed National Fiction Prize. I had a six-month-old baby and our car had just died, and I propped her on the kitchen counter in a carrier and had her hold the check, if random grasping could be thought of as holding.

My husband and I bought a car with the money. We had two more daughters, and then we divorced. But I still see him nearly every day, as well as all of our family and friends. I still live in the same house, and from the back window I can see the hospital where we were all born—us, our siblings, our kids. My children are nearly grown now, and they like to joke about how pathetic it is to see me gazing out that window, to think that I haven't gotten very far at all from my beginnings.

But I have, and yet I have never wanted to leave this landscape and these people behind. Everything I've written since *Aquaboogie* has been connected to it somehow. The character of Big Ma, in "Cellophane and Feathers," became Marietta, the soul of *I Been in Sorrow's Kitchen and Licked Out All the Pots.* Darnell, whose girlfriend Brenda was pregnant in "Safe Hooptie," was the hero of *Blacker Than a Thousand Midnights,* and he has shown up in *The Gettin Place* and played an important part in *Highwire Moon.* Roscoe, Esther, and other characters are in the novel I'm working on right now, which is a sequel to *A Million Nightingales.*

Not many writers stay. I know this. Sometimes this place is a hard place to live. So many people we've known have died too young, or have lost their way. Seventeen years ago, I wrote that this is a large city, and it is larger now, one of the fastest growing places in America. We were "country" back then, and are less so now. But I have chickens, as do my neighbors, and my brother used to bring avocados and oranges, and my friends bring plums and tangerines, and we all live that way even now. Back then I wrote that this is a talking place, and it still is. I write alone, but at family reunions and gatherings there are usually hundreds of people telling me stories, and I always listen to the legends of our pasts and presents—slavery and broken-down cars and wildfires and cocaine, parties and dancing and love and betrayal. I always will. I said that I wanted some stories to be on paper, rather than floating in the air with our barbecue smoke and laughter and shouts, and so these stories remain on paper, and in someone's hands.

Before they were published in 1990, I worked on these stories for years, often writing longhand in our car while my husband was fixing it in the gravel driveway. I would be sitting in the driver's seat, holding my notebook, while he said, "Rev the engine now," or "Step on the brake." The exhaust colored my words, I thought back then. That driveway is now cement, and our three daughters shoot basketball there, often with their father. But I write in the car all the time, more so than at my computer, because I'm driving kids around these same neighborhoods, to practice or to visit someone. I write my stories longhand, in a series of notebooks, just as I always have, and I realize that maybe as a southern Californian it's not the exhaust that shades my sentences, but the promise of movement and the air in the open window while my father-in-law waves at me and a cousin calls out, "Hey, girl, did you bring your rice? I got a place for it right here. And I've got something to tell you right now."

Riverside, California   March 2007

the milkweed national fiction prize

Milkweed Editions awards the Milkweed National Fiction Prize to works of high literary quality that embody humane values and contribute to cultural understanding. For more information about the Milkweed National Fiction Prize or to order past winners, visit our Web site (www.milkweed.org) or contact Milkweed Editions at (800) 520-6455.

Visigoth Gary Amdahl (2006)

Crossing Bully Creek
Margaret Erhart (2005)

Ordinary Wolves
Seth Kantner (2004)

Roofwalker Susan Power (2002)

Hell's Bottom, Colorado
Laura Pritchett (2001)

Falling Dark Tim Tharp (1999)

Tivolem
Victor Rangel-Ribeiro (1998)

The Tree of Red Stars
Tessa Bridal (1997)

The Empress of One
Faith Sullivan (1996)

Confidence of the Heart
David Schweidel (1995)

Montana 1948
Larry Watson (1993)

Larabi's Ox
Tony Ardizzone (1992)

Aquaboogie
Susan Straight (1990)

Blue Taxis Eileen Drew (1989)

Ganado Red Susan Lowell (1988)

milkweed editions

Founded in 1979, Milkweed Editions is one of the largest independent, nonprofit literary publishers in the United States. Milkweed publishes with the intention of making a humane impact on society, in the belief that good writing can transform the human heart and spirit. Within this mission, Milkweed publishes in four areas: fiction, nonfiction, poetry, and children's literature for middle-grade readers.

join us

Milkweed depends on the generosity of foundations and individuals like you, in addition to the sales of its books. In an increasingly consolidated and bottom-line-driven publishing world, your support allows us to select and publish books on the basis of their literary quality and the depth of their message. Please visit our Web site (www.milkweed.org) or contact us at (800) 520-6455 to learn more about our donor program.